Fi[illegible]e

CW01624063

Alisa
Happy reading

127 Publishing

Chapter 1

Christos

As I DRIVE INTO the street, a large removal van pulls away from the house, and abandoning the car on the drive, I hurry into my home. My footsteps echo through the hall to the living room, and I stand, my fingers linked behind my head, as I survey the empty room. My wife Ana has taken me at my word and emptied the house. All that remains of our life together is a wedding photograph on the mantel, and the hideous painting an aunt gave us as an anniversary present.

Upstairs, my holdall, which had been sitting on the bed ready for me to pick up, now sits in the middle of an empty bedroom. Boxes of my clothes and personal stuff line one wall. It seems I might as well move to Bristol today. There is nothing keeping me here now. Nothing at all.

Downstairs, I take the photograph, drop it into the bin, and place the last box on the step. Turning back, I slam the door so hard the brass knocker jumps up and rattles back into place. There's no one there to hear it now.

Lifting the box, I force it into the rear of the car with all my other worldly goods, and ignoring the For Sale sign, I pull off the drive for the final time. I don't look back. Even a glance in the rearview mirror is impossible, with the remnants of my life shoved into bin liners and boxes blocking the view.

Bristol, here I come.

Three Weeks Ago

The familiar whooshing sound makes me smile as I hit the send button on the latest completion. I lean back in my chair and lift my coffee mug, toasting my success. Another deal successfully closed. More Brownie points. Fingers crossed. I've applied for a new job, but at the very least want to keep the one I have.

My boss and mentor, Bradley Thomas, is retiring. His wife has been ill, his daughters and grandchildren live all around the UK, and he wants to spend more quality time with them. Family is everything to Brad, and I'm lucky enough to have him treat me like the son he never had.

But all good things must end, and he's selling this business to an American group, Gemini. Their ethos is the same as ours, but they're Americans and everything is bigger, brighter, louder. Including the job titles and salaries. I've almost forgotten the number of interviews, assessments and hoops I've had to jump through over the last few months, and it's not over yet. But I am cautiously hopeful. It means moving back to Bristol. Which, being honest, I'm looking forward to, but Ana, my wife? Not so much. I'd put money on her hoping I don't get the job. Still, I've got a year to persuade her.

My phone rings, and my smile gets a little bigger. It's Brad. Perfect timing. He's going to love this. I snatch up the receiver.

"Brad. Great timing! Guess what I just closed?" I ask, knowing he'll guess easily, given the smugness in my voice.

"You just completed the Spanish contract, is my guess. Well done, I knew you'd get it. Have you checked your emails?" he asks. He sounds distracted.

"My emails? Not for the last couple of hours. I've been completing this deal. I have to say, Brad, I thought you'd be a little more chuffed. Is everything okay?"

I try to sound concerned, but I'm miffed. I was expecting, at the very least, the offer of a celebratory drink. This is a big deal and should help Brad secure the Gemini sale. He confided last week that he thought, after the initial burst of chaos, Gemini were dragging their heels a little. If Brad is getting jumpy, perhaps that's why he sounds distracted.

"Yes. I...just check your emails, Chris. I'm on my way down."

Brad hangs up. I can't ever remember him doing that before. Shit. What could have happened?

My chest tightens, and I loosen the top button of my shirt as I click into my inbox. My eyes scan the unopened list. The email he wants me to read jumps out at me. *Re: Executive Director Bristol UK.*

Shit, shit, shit. I bet I didn't get the job. That's why Brad is so distracted. He didn't want to be the one to tell me.

Clasping my fingers behind my head, I lean back and try to be positive. It's only my pride that's hurt. I tell myself. No one died, and it isn't like I'm out of work. I'm sure I'll still be going back to Bristol just in a lesser role. Won't I?

"Shit!" I curse again and sit upright. Am I out of work? Is that why Brad sounds odd? I know they will close this office eventually, but are they getting rid of me, too? Was there no other position they thought me worthy of?

I open the email. My eyes scan the opening paragraph, skimming the words as my heart thunders in my chest. I can't be out of work. With a mortgage that feels like the size of the national debt, and don't get me started on the credit card bill, I need this job. Any job. Ana likes nice things. I've spoken to her, rowed with her, and accepted all her promises to rein in the spending, but we're on a never-ending loop. I need this promotion, but failing that, I really need this job.

Yes!

I've only bloody got it. Wow. Christos Baros: Executive Director. I tap out a drum roll on my desk with my fingers before I scroll to the crucial details.

There it is. Job title. Executive Director UK. Start date first of May. Salary almost doubled. Commission absolutely bloody stonking. I stop reading and punch both fists into the air. I already know about the generous benefits. Closing my eyes, my head falls back, and I grin. Finally. I'm on my way. Gemini are serious players, so who knows where I'll end up? Currently Sales Director in York, next May, I'll be Executive Director in Bristol, in two years who knows...New York...My eyes open when someone clasps my shoulder.

"Congratulations, Chris. You deserve this, I'm proud of you." Brad smiles at me. "You're going to have to move quickly. They want you down there to start the ball rolling, but if anyone can pull this off, you can."

Jumping to my feet, I pump his hand up and down. "Thanks, Brad, I won't let you down. Have they signed, then? How soon do you reckon it will go through?"

"It's done. As of two hours ago." Brad raises his eyebrows.

"What? Congratulations! I didn't realise it was so close."

"Neither did I. Apparently there was no point in dragging it out. Their due diligence is complete, and the key appointments made." He winks at me. "Although it's taken so long to get to this point, I thought we still had months to go. To be honest, it feels weird to know it's done,." Brad grimaces. "I'm ready for retirement, I think, but...still, it's done. Signed, sealed, and the money is in the bank."

"Already? So what happens now? You won't lock up and walk off into the sunshine today, will you?" My heart sinks a little. Brad is a good bloke. He cares about people. If it weren't for him, I'd probably never have made it past being the manager of the estate agents where I'd worked when we first met. My stomach churns as I question if I'll be able to do it without him.

"I'll still be around for a little while. For the next few weeks I'll be swamped by a load of accountants as I hand everything over, as well as communicating with our existing investors and clients, before you take the reins." He grins at me. "Then there are the fund transfers, you know, all the exciting stuff. Take that daft look off your face. You won't have time to miss me, because you'll be house hunting in Bristol whilst launching the Gemini UK office. It's going to be tough, and you know, lad, I might not be your boss anymore, but I'll be at the end of the phone if you think I can help."

I swallow back my nerves, wanting the blind excitement back. "Thanks, Brad, I might hold you to that. I know Gemini's expectations, but by the time they're ready for me, I'll be ready for them."

"I'm sure you will. Look, now you've closed the Spanish deal, take next week off to set things in motion and don't forget to find some accommodation. You'll need to rent for a while. Living out of a hotel soon loses its charm. It might be a while before you get time for another holiday."

"I know, it takes a while to sell in the current market. But not a year. Being pessimistic isn't like you. I don't think I need to panic about a roof over my head just yet." I slap him on the shoulder. "Might finish early today though if you don't need me here, *Operation Convince Ana* needs to begin in earnest."

Bradley's brow furrowed. "You didn't read the email fully, did you? And I didn't know Ana was still doubtful."

"I did read it, and Ana will be fine. Why are you looking at me like that?" I can hear the doubt crawl into my words.

"You didn't. You didn't read it properly, and you're supposed to be the one who checks all the dots and crosses are in place."

I sit back at my desk and read the email.

Dear Christos.

Congratulations! I'm delighted to confirm your position as Executive Director Bristol UK. The pertinent details are below, and a formal contract will arrive shortly. Should you have any queries, please contact Bernice in our New York office.

You'll be delighted to hear that Gemini Solutions has closed on the premises in Bristol, and as a result, we'll bring the opening of Bristol UK forward by a full year. You will be expected to work closely with the project manager, George Feebry, in bringing this together. I appreciate this is unexpected, but we know you're up to the challenge and will dedicate yourself to our success. These are indeed exciting times.

Bradley will fill you in on the details about York closure.

I'm tied up in Hong Kong for a few weeks but will be in the UK for the launch in July. Wouldn't miss it for the world.

But for now...

I stop reading.

"Bloody hell! That's only three months away," I gasp.

"You mean weeks. May starts in three weeks."

"They want me in Bristol for the first of May! I, um..."

My brain misfires and I snap my mouth shut. Ana is going to go apeshit. She was already reluctant, and now the twelve months I thought I'd have to convince her has been reduced to only a few weeks. I'll have to up my game. But with what? I force a smile.

"Like you say, a hotel will be fine for now. Jesus, they don't mess about, do they?"

"They don't. Their investors want to move fast. This place will be shut down within the month. Not sure how many staff will relocate at such short notice, but I'll get something sorted for them. I've no doubt you're going to lose a few more of them, so there's a risk that you might find your biggest problem is recruitment. Still, these are exciting times for you, Chris. I'm almost sorry I'm not coming along for the ride."

Despite his upbeat words, I can see the sadness in his eyes. This company is his baby. He built it from the ground upwards, and although he was already considering retirement when Gemini made their offer, he, like me, thought he had longer to adjust.

His smile returns. "I hope Ana doesn't give you too much grief and that she can get away with you quickly. You'll need her support. It's going to be tough until you have things settled. Do you know, when I started this business all I wanted was a better life. I didn't want to be rolling in money or rip anyone off, I just wanted to earn a decent living, help other people take care of their money and have a safe future. Competitors used to scoff. When I attended conventions and conferences, where everyone had a new way of squeezing a little extra out of their clients, they couldn't believe I was happy with my declared percentage. They laughed even louder when we started investing in eco companies to help give the kids a better future. They won't be laughing now. It's the only reason Gemini made the offer. Who knew being honest would make me this rich?" Brad clamped his hand on my shoulder. "Never forget your principles, Chris. I'm hoping Gemini are as straight as they appear to be, but if you think the wrong path is being taken, make a noise. Being honest and having a clear conscience helps you sleep at night. You might not be able to change things but always have your say. You'll have a family of your own one day, and you'll want the world to be a better place."

"Bloody hell, Brad, don't put that on my shoulders, or I really won't sleep at night." I smile at him. "That said, I'll do my best. Do you want me to speak to the team with you?"

"No, those that come won't be down until the end of June. They'll need a few days to think about things, and I'll keep you posted. You get yourself off home to Ana." Brad flapped his hand towards the door.

My stomach turned to lead at the thought. "I've got the weekend. I'd like to help, not to mention I've got all these emails that need to be dealt with."

"Nothing that can't wait. I'll tell everyone you're excited, and that they can phone you if they need your assurances. Three weeks, Chris, time is of the essence."

Shaking his hand again, I pull him into a hug. No words of thanks would ever repay this man. "You're one of a kind, Brad Thomas. See you next week."

I should be walking on air, singing happy triumphant songs, but the closer I get to home, the more I want to turn around and go back to the office. I've been doing that too often the last year, avoiding facing Ana. Would she be home? She certainly won't be expecting me. What will I do if she refuses to come? That is a possibility. The thought lightens my mood, and I thump the steering wheel. That wasn't right. This isn't Ana's fault. Our issues aren't Ana's fault. Not really. They aren't mine either, although I should have stood up to my father, or waited another year. He died eleven months after the wedding. We'd have both been free to do what we pleased then. But I didn't. I married Ana just like he wanted. Like her father wanted. We agreed we'd give it our best shot. Have we done that?

It was good in the beginning, finding our feet together, and agreeing which parental instructions we'd ignore. Ana was barely eighteen. We were babies. We'd always been friends, so getting used to being intimate took a few weeks, but that soon sorted itself out. Turns out we were naturals. But that was almost ten years ago now. The excitement, novelty, call it what you will, has fizzled out. We're still friends, but rarely lovers. Am I happy? Not really. Am I miserable? Not really. I do what's expected of me, work hard, try to provide Ana with what she wants, and make the best of it. Just like my mother told me she had.

Mama. My shoulders slump. I'll have to tell her soon, too. Another lead balloon moment waiting for me. It's going to be a shock because I've never even mentioned the possibility of me leaving, and no doubt she'll ask me how she'll get to see the non-existent grandchildren. Ana conceiving is a long shot. You need to have sex for that to happen, and it's been months.

Ana's car is on the drive. Steeling myself, I pull my shoulders back and let myself in. Ana's in the kitchen on the phone, so I remove my tie and jacket, and drape them over the chair in the hall while she ends the call.

"I've got to go, Christos is home. I don't know. I will....I will...Yes, I said so. 'Bye." Flustered, she hangs up, dropping her phone onto the breakfast bar. "You're early."

It sounds like an accusation, but I manage a smile. "I am. I need to speak to you, so I skipped out early." Maintaining my smile, I walk to the fridge.

"Oh. You can do that when you need to, can you? I hadn't realised that. But it's just as well. I need to speak to you, too."

I wait for her to continue, assuming she'll tell me what she had to say first. But she doesn't speak, and after a few seconds, one hand goes to her hip, while the other points at me.

"Well? I thought you wanted to speak to me?"

Her tone is unusually harsh, and I bristle. "And I you. You had the floor. I assumed you'd tell me what you wanted first. Beer or wine? Let's sit down." I open the fridge and pull out a beer, turning back as a stool scrapes the floor.

"Nothing for me. I might need to drive. I'm sitting." Ana gestures to the stool she's pulled out. "And I'm listening."

"You're going out?" She can't look me in the eye, and I cock my head, trying to work out what she needs to speak to me about. "And now I'm intrigued. I meant let's sit somewhere more comfortable because I have some good news." I decide to start off upbeat. No apologies, just the positives. "But now I'm curious. Where might you be driving to?"

After a beat, she lifts her chin to look at me. Her beautiful eyes fill with tears, and she shakes head. "I...I..." her chin drops back to her chest. I go to her, and stepping between her knees, I pull her into my arms, stroking her back as she sobs into my chest.

I might not love her, not in the way a husband should, but I am her husband, her friend, and I still care. It still hurts to see her upset.

"What is it, Ana? Come on, this isn't like you, you're usually spitting fire. Oh no. It's not your dad, is it?" Ana's father has been ill recently. I thought he was on the mend. He might be an overbearing, cantankerous, old man, much like my own was, but he was still her dad. "Ana, speak to me. Is it your dad?"

"No," she sobs.

"Is it you? Are you ill?" I squeeze her tighter. I can't go to Bristol if she's ill. I shake the uncharitable thought away and kiss the top of her head. "Tell me, please. Are you ill?"

She mumbles another "No."

"I'm out of guesses, and getting worried, tell me." Placing my hands on her shoulders, I push her back a little, lifting her chin with my finger. "Ana, it's me, Chris, or Christos, if you're pissed off with me. We've been friends since we were in nappies. There's nothing you can't tell me. You even told me when you got your first period. You hadn't even told your mum."

Ana snorts a laugh and blinks rapidly. Her tears subside, but she offers no explanation.

"What is it?" Pulling out another stool, I sit beside her, our knees touching. "Do you want a drink now? Because you're going nowhere until you tell me." I place my hands on her thighs and give them a squeeze. "Tell me. Whatever it is, I promise not to be shocked, angry, or laugh. I'll just nod sagely and offer the best advice I can. Deal?"

Ana nods but remains silent. I squeeze again, making her jump. A smile twitches at the corners of her mouth, and her eyes flash a warning.

"Ana, don't make me tickle you." My own eyebrows rise at this. It's been years since we messed about like that.

Ana groans and clasps her hands in her lap, then studies them as though she's only just found them. "I'm leaving you." It's little more than a whisper.

I'd promised not to laugh, but I do. "Don't mess about. Tell me what's wrong. Why won't you look at me?"

"I did. I'm leaving you, Chris. And I can't look at you, because that will make you sad and angry, but it's not you. It's not me either. It's us." She glances at me for a second before returning her attention to her lap.

I allow the words to settle as I finally open my beer. I take a swig. What the fuck? I can't deal with this. Not now. Not today.

"No, you're not," I tell her calmly.

Her head jerks up and her shoulders rise in a shrug. "Yes, Chris, I am. We both knew this would be the outcome, eventually. We even joked about how long we would last. And, now with your new job on the cards, a new life for you, and—"

The new job! The new family-friendly company with an exec director whose wife has left him. No way. "You are fucking not!" My hands are back on her knees, and I keep squeezing until she looks at me.

Ana gives a little giggle as she raises her head. "You see, you are angry. But really, Chris, how are you going to stop me?"

I open my mouth to tell her, but snap it shut again. How? Certainly not with an offer of a move to Bristol.

"I might tie you to the bed. What would you do then?"

Her eyes flare for a moment, and I lean in and kiss her. She returns my kiss, her hands leave her lap, and she pulls me forward. I slide off the stool and stand back between her legs. Bloody hell, is this where we went wrong? Is that all I had to do? I'd have done that willingly.

Ana groans and grasping her thighs, I pull her forward, and she grinds against my erection. I gasp as all thoughts of my promotion, Bristol and Ana leaving, fly from my mind.

"It's been too long, Ana." My hands cup her full breasts and tweak her nipples, earning another groan. "Am I taking you upstairs? Because right at this moment, the breakfast bar is looking likely. I could rip off these jeans, put your legs over my shoulders and—"

Ana groans, pulls her lips from mine, and pushes me away. Her face is flushed, her breathing a little erratic and taking my face in her hands, her eyes fill again as she rests her forehead against mine.

"We can't, because I can't. There's someone else. I'm sorry."

I should feel angry, shout and create, but I don't. Instead, I step back and wiggle my hips, trying to make myself more comfortable. "Wow. I wasn't expecting that. Is it serious?" I ask, my voice low, and nod again as she whispers she thinks so. "I don't suppose you'd like to give the being tied to the bed thing a go? You know, as a last hurrah. A sexy goodbye."

She huffs out a laugh. "Right at this moment, there's nothing I'd like more. I'm going to miss you. You're such a good man." She reaches up and places a finger on my lips to silence my response. "But it wouldn't be right.

It wouldn't be fair. You'll always be my best friend, Chris. I will always love you. But...well, you know."

And just like that, bar the shouting, the divorce and the divvying up of joint funds, my marriage ends.

My beautiful Anglo-Cypriot wife goes upstairs and collects two enormous suitcases she'd already packed. I carry them to her car, and wave goodbye as I watch her drive out of my life. I find out later that she drove into the arms of Yorgos Costi, the manager of her father's restaurant, but that's an aside. I'm free. Almost. Free to move back to Bristol. Free to build the life I wanted. Perhaps this was for the best.

Only things are never that simple, are they? I've got a huge mortgage, very little equity, and there's a stamp duty rise in the offing, making the large four-bedroom detached house Ana had craved an unattractive prospect to purchasers, and a millstone around my neck. After paying the mortgage, there's little left of my current salary. Ana's job paid for most of the smaller running costs. But now she won't be doing that. Will she? I'll have to ask.

I call her the next day.

"I hear you, Chris, but I have my own expenses now. It's a beautiful house, it won't take long to sell. Just reduce what you are paying to the bank monthly, because once it's sold you can pay it all back. I want nothing from you. No money, none of your shares or investments or anything. This was my fault. I won't even take any furniture. Except perhaps the sofa and chairs, I'll take them, unless, of course, you want them."

"Ana, you can strip it bare for all I care. I don't want any of it, but I can't have debt. I can't have a poor credit rating. It's unacceptable in my line of work, you know that." I thump my desk in frustration. She refuses to understand.

"Christos, you're the money man know-it-all. You'll sort it out. Now I must go. I'll get someone to pick up the furniture. That'll be one less headache for you."

Present Day

I'm at the hotel, and I found a helpful porter who helped me lug my worldly goods up to my room. This, for the time being, is my home. I've eaten and showered and with nothing better to do, I phone my mother.

"Christos, you've gone. Gone without telling me. Me, the mother who suffered for three days to bring you into this world. Me, the mother who you shared all your secrets with. Now, you leave your home without telling me, and you ignore my calls. I have to hear this from others."

"Mama, I wasn't ignoring you, I was busy. I was—"

"You were busy leaving me without so much as a goodbye. Busy getting on with your single life, abandoning your mother, leaving your wife to do what she will. The shame of it. What have you got to say for yourself?" She had spat out the word wife and I can imagine her gentle fingers rubbing her forehead.

"I'm staying in a hotel, Mama. I have not left without a goodbye because—"

"Because you have left. Your home is empty. Stella told me. Your wife is living with another man. Stella told me that too. I always knew that Yorgos was no good. And what about Yani's wedding next week? How will I show my face? Thank god your father is not here to share this shame."

"You have a beautiful face, Mama. You will lift your head high and say look at me, I am beautiful. Come on, Mama, Ana and I are not the first couple in history to get divorced. We would never have had to if it wasn't for Papa and Ana's dad. You know that. You were the one who told me how to cope, how to be. And I tried. We tried. It didn't work out. You were lucky, me and Ana weren't. It's just how it turned out. Now—"

I hear her snort before she interrupts. "It wasn't you who ran off with a lover, was it? It wasn't you who brought this shame to my door. How hard did she try? But, Christos, it was you who ran off into the night, not her."

"I didn't run off. And it wasn't night. This was always going to happen. I'm just doing it on my own. And I'm excited about it. I'll find someone to love, someone to produce grandchildren with. As soon as I have my own place, you can come and see me." I throw in the grandchildren, as my mother is convinced our lack of children must have been Ana's fault. "Now, I'll call you again to—"

"So. This is it. My grandchildren will live on the other side of the world."

I hear the rustling as she pulls another tissue from the box. It takes another half an hour, but eventually I can hang up. I flop back on the bed and close my eyes. Work will be hard enough, but daily calls to my mother will be far, far, worse.

Chapter 2

Cassie

I GRAB JOEL'S HAND, and we lift them into the air before taking our final bow. The applause keeps coming as the rest of the cast do the same. There are a few whoops and whistles, but no one will be demanding a rerun. Still, it's been fun while it lasted.

"I need a drink," I tell Joel as the curtain falls, and we head for the dressing rooms.

"Of course, that goes without saying. There's always drink at the after do. We have to go."

Joel was my leading man in this production, and always my best friend. He's every girl's dream. Tall, handsome, broad-shouldered, abs you could play a tune on, and don't get me started on what he looks like in a pair of tights. Joel has a lot to be proud of. Although that comes with its dangers. A few years ago, he gained a stalker who had taken too much of a shine to him when he looked at her while singing a romantic number. Resulting in me having to pretend to be his girlfriend for quite a few weeks. It put my street cred through the roof, or so I like to think. But that would never happen in real life because Joel is gay.

"Oh, do we have to? Everyone will be drunk in minutes, and I don't want to speak to Teddy or Gemma ever again." Most of the cast were great fun, but those two could burst bubbles with a glance.

"Stop moaning. We have to go, but we won't stay long. Put your glad rags on, and we'll disappear after we've done our bit," Joel soothes.

"We'd better," I warn.

We go to the after party, swap air kisses, and drink too many of the watery cocktails. But to be fair, it isn't that bad and we manage to avoid being dragged to some seedy nightclub when someone decides the party should go on elsewhere. It's a little before eleven, and we wonder what to do next.

"Now let's get a proper drink, I need to speak to you," I tell him, linking my arm in his.

"You do? Should I be worried?" Joel asks.

"We need to brainstorm. My next job doesn't start until July. Even Jan at the temp agency isn't coming up with anything, boring or otherwise, not even filing, and I need to earn some money. Now."

Joel points at the hotel we're passing. "I bet the bar is still open." He looks me up and down. "Mind you, in that dress, they might think you're there looking for business. Might be worth a try, though."

"Oi!"

I whack Joel's arm with one hand and stretch the hemline of my dress down with the other. I don't own many dresses, and I'd acquired this one from the wardrobe of a previous job. Is it tacky to admit I like it? It's short, black, stretchy and clingy, with a low back, high neck and long sleeves. Common? I don't think so. I like it, although, yes, it's short. Barely covers my knickers. The one thing I do dislike about it is that it also demands heels, and I'm more of a trainers and socks sort of girl, but beggars and choosers. Joel always looks immaculate and gorgeous. Even tatty jeans and an old T-shirt look good on Joel, but tonight his choice of attire is soft leather loafers, a pair of navy chinos and a white button-down shirt.

"I'll have to do. Anyway, if I don't take these shoes off soon, you'll be carrying me."

Laughing, he grabs my hand and drags me into the hotel. The guy at reception doesn't even glance up as we come in. Joel pulls open the door to the bar before heading to the gents.

"Grab a table. First round on me," he calls as I step into the bar and head for the nearest table. Sighing, I slip off my shoes and try to wiggle life back into my toes.

It's quiet in here, nice. Lots of wood and soft leather, with gentle music playing in the background, which suits me just fine. I've had enough noise for one day. I smile as Joel returns and heads for the bar.

"Surprise me," I call as he raises a questioning eyebrow and jerks his thumb towards the bar. I check my phone. Only one message from Steve, who tells me he's had confirmation that he'll be away for a month, so finding a person to share our house will be down to me. Sliding my phone back into my bag, I shiver, wishing I'd brought my coat or a wrap with me. It has been warm for a few weeks, but surely they didn't need the air con on now? This is England. Any type of weather only lasts a week at most.

"I'm freezing," I tell Joel as he returns with the drinks.

Joel looks at my chest. "Yes, I can see that. I'd have somewhere to hang my coat if I had one."

Laughing, I clasp a hand over each breast. "Excuse me, my nipples are my business." Realising I'd probably been too loud, I glance around, an apology ready for anyone I might have offended. I'm in the clear until my eyes meet those of a man at the bar. He holds my gaze for a moment before looking away.

Joel sniggers. "And close the mouth. Yes, he's hot. Mediterranean heritage, I reckon." Joel places a finger under my chin, pretending to shut my mouth.

"Bloody hell." This time, I keep my voice to a whisper. "Am I staring?"

"You are. But you're not interested."

"I most certainly am. Do you know how long it's been?" I demand, throwing a hand into the air.

"Eighteen months, three weeks and two days," Joel informs me. "And I promise you, you're not interested."

"Really? You know how long? How do you remember that?" I knew it was about a year and a half, but the weeks and days, never. What I do know is that I'm desperately in need of what Joel would call a good seeing to, but not desperate enough to have counted the days since it last happened. Not yet, anyway.

"Of course I don't. I was making it up. You're still looking." Joel places a hand on my knee and gives it a pinch.

The unexpected jolt that it sends through my body makes me yelp and bounce up off the chair. The hottie at the bar looks over and I wave an apology. "Sorry. He can't keep his hands to himself," I explain.

Why didn't I ignore him? I'll tell you why. The hottie laughs, and I swoon as a dimple appears through the stubble on his cheek, and I swear his perfect white teeth glint like they do on toothpaste adverts.

"I don't blame him." Hottie winks and turns back to his drink. Did he just blush? I grin. He likes me, but I shake my head to clear the naughty thoughts that are starting to take root.

I return my attention to Joel. "Adverts. Make sure I come back to that. But first, and far more importantly, why am I not interested? Did you see that dimple?" My shoulders droop and I slump back in my chair. "He's gay, isn't he?"

"Would he still be sitting alone if he was? No. He'd be sitting here with us, and I'd be bribing you to book an Uber. Get a grip." Joel runs his fingers through his hair and winks at me. "He'd never be able to resist."

"Then what? Oh, don't worry, he's going."

We watch the man walk towards the exit. Not as tall as Joel, but certainly as well built. We watch until the door closes behind him.

"And he's gone, taking his muscular rear end with him. So, back to adverts. You wanted me to remind you." Joel sips his drink. "That barman makes a mean mojito. We're going to have to have another one, even though I might need to take out another loan," he jokes.

"Yes, TV adverts. My agency doesn't seem to get many, and I know I said I didn't want to go down that route, and end up being embarrassed by Graham Norton, but I'm going to have to risk it. I'm absolutely broke. Jerry moved out last week, so I've now got to cough up half of his rent until we find someone new. Would it be wrong to sign on with another agent just to get ad work?"

"Yes, because you'd be breaking your contract. You can't afford to do that, especially with no guarantees. And I have work for you, it pays well. One little audition, which we can do at yours, and I know you have the right smoky tone for them to say yes. It's just a bloody audiobook, Cass. Voice acting. See, the word acting is still involved."

"No. I refuse. I'm not doing voice porn. Next idea?"

"It's not porn, it's erotica. But if you're adamant, you could always reach out to your dad," Joel suggests.

"It's more likely I'd start a nuclear war, which is pretty much the same thing. I've managed without him so far and I won't beg and grovel for help just because I'm broke. I'm an independent girl with pride. No, non, nein, never."

"Then I'm out of ideas. End of that discussion, if you are going to keep this unnecessary feud up, and refuse to take work that pays well, I'm not discussing it. Another drink?"

"How much were they?" I ask, pouting. Joel thinks he knows all about me and my family. But he wasn't there when my mother begged my dad to come home. He wasn't there when she dropped to her knees and wept when he hung up on her. I was. I had to deal with the mess he left behind. Just because Mum's now dead, it doesn't make his abandonment of her, of us, any less painful.

"Fifteen," Joel announces, and lost in thoughts of my parents, I wonder what he's talking about.

"Fifteen what? Do you mean fifteen pounds? Nooo. Fifteen quid! For a drink with a bit of mint in it? No, thank you. Oh god, I'm so broke and so depressed. Shall we go?"

"I can't. I'm meeting Sam later when he finishes work. He'll pick me up from here. I'll splash out and get us another."

"Not for me. I'm too depressed, and you've got a date." I pull out my phone and book a taxi. "Twenty minutes. I'll sip slowly," I tell Joel, as I fix my lips around the straw. My nose wrinkles as cold water hits the back of my throat. "It's only melted ice now. I can't even get drunk properly."

Settling back to wait for my taxi, sipping cold water through a wilting straw, we discuss Joel's next role and the play running at the Old Vic until my phone pings announcing the imminent arrival of my taxi. Slipping my feet back into my shoes, I sigh. "I'll call you tomorrow. Have fun later."

I pull the strap of my bag over my shoulder, raise my chin, thrust out my chest, and grit my teeth as I prepare to move my feet.

"No kiss goodbye? You look like you're ready to go to war." Joel holds out his arms.

"I am. With my feet." Leaning over without moving them an inch, I peck him on the lips. "Wish me luck."

"Channel your inner model. Sashay, darling. Strut. Big steps mean fewer steps."

Joel laughs as I wink at him and stride off, hips swaying, towards the door. I catch a movement behind the glass panel, and the door swings open to reveal Mr Hottie. I throw him my best smile and incline my head in thanks, wondering if I could slow my momentum and return to a normal gait, hence lengthening our exchange, and do you know, for just a flickering of a second, I pull it off. But pride, they say, comes before a fall, and fall I do. The shoulder strap of my bag hooks itself onto the door handle, and rather than proceeding to the foyer, I'm yanked unceremoniously backwards. My shoes then refuse to cooperate with my ankles, and I lurch from one side to the other trying to regain my balance, before my shoes give up the fight, and lay themselves side up on the floor, and as a consequence, me on my arse.

Did I mention my short, short, dress? The clingy one? Yes, that one. That one has now decided it would rather be a T-shirt. So here I sit, my dress slash T-shirt around my waist, in my skimpy black knickers, on a cold marble floor, legs akimbo and staring at Mr Hottie.

There's a glint of something in his eyes. Passion or amusement? I'm betting on the latter. Either way, he's getting an eyeful, so I clamp my knees together and fling out my hand.

"You know staring is rude, don't you?" I've decided, as a way of righting this humiliating situation, that attack is the best form of defence. "A gentleman would offer to help me up."

Hottie leans forward, takes my hand, and doesn't even grunt as he pulls me to my feet, his free hand hitting my bare hip to steady me. Did he just flick my knicker elastic? He leans in close.

"I never said I was a gentleman. But apologies. I think it was the shock. It's not every day I have a beautiful woman throwing herself at my feet and presenting me with a conundrum," he whispers in my ear.

His breath is hot against my neck. His hand feels positively volcanic against my skin, and he smells earthy. A woodsy, musky with a hint of lemon type of heaven. A gasp escapes my lips as I shudder. His eyes twinkle as he smiles, and the dimple reappears.

"Shall I do the honours?" He looks down at my feet, and I follow his gaze and shake my head.

"No, thank you. I think I'll carry my shoes."

His chuckle is deep and throaty, and I tingle where tingles have no right to be in this situation. "I wasn't talking about the shoes, although I agree with you on that. But I think..." Releasing my hand and my hip, he takes hold of the fabric bunched around my waist and my eyes widen, "This might be better if you're venturing any further. I'm not sure, but I don't think anyone noticed. Bob will have heart failure if you go into the foyer like this."

He gives a tug on my dress, and his fingers brush against my skin as he pulls it back into position. Goosebumps appear like a nettle rash. My brain is in overdrive willing my body not to betray me, and I know not to look at him, as that dimple would taunt me. I stare straight ahead. He takes a step back, and I immediately miss his closeness. I breathe in deeply, trying for one more hit of his musky aroma.

Brain to Cass, brain to Cass. Say something! Oh god, I'm losing the plot. What was he saying?

"Who's Bob?" I ask, holding back the groan.

Yes, there's the chuckle and the tingles are back.

"The night porter." Hottie tips his head to one side and my eyes flick to the bald guy behind the reception desk.

I nod solemnly. "I see." Jesus, now I sound like Miss Marple on the set of an *Agatha Christie* inspecting clues. Sneaking a glimpse at Hottie, I see I was right. That damn dimple is back. "Thank you for your help, better late than never. I should go. Now. Right now."

Hottie barks out a laugh before performing a sweeping bow. "The pleasure was all mine. But please don't leave on my account," he says as his eyes find mine again.

A girl could drown in those eyes. Deep brown and soulful, and the lashes. I'd pay a fortune for those. But I haven't got a life jacket, and despite Joel's words to the contrary, this girl is very interested, but there must be a reason why I shouldn't be. So I should trust in Joel's judgement and get out of here before I do something silly. I smile my brightest smile.

"You've already attacked me with a door, ogled my distress and manhandled my person, I really think I should escape. I also have a taxi waiting."

As if on cue, a dishevelled man with long hair and a weary expression steps into the foyer.

"Here, guv. Taxi for Cash?" he calls towards Bob at reception. "They around?"

Bob's eyes dart to me. He was watching. He did notice, and he must have been listening.

"I'm coming," I call and look at Hottie, who snorts. "'Bye," I snap. My humiliation is complete.

Hottie grabs my arm, and I jump as static arcs between us. "Just one thing you should know." He seems to breathe the words, and now I'm stuck with the hot breath and the smell of him again. "I've never heard it called a distress before, and if I ever manhandled you, you really wouldn't be able to walk. 'Night, Cash."

He hands me my bag. I snap it shut, and picking up my shoes, I hurry off to the taxi.

I weigh up Hottie on the short ride home.

Pros: Hot. Well built. Twinkly eyes. Long lashes. Hot. Good dresser of both me and him. Hot. Smells divine. Has a cute dimple. Hot. Has eyes and lashes.

Cons: I'll never see him again. My distress is safe. Unfortunate but true. What a depressing thought. At this rate, I'll need new batteries.

Chapter 3

Christos

NINETEEN DAYS I'VE BEEN in Bristol. Nineteen days of loving the job and feeling grateful for being so tired I don't care that I haven't got a social life. The only downer for me at the moment is, as predicted, I've not even had a viewing on the house in York. Ana refuses to talk to me about it, and my mother is demanding I come home and claim Ana back. To top it off, I can't find anywhere here decent enough to rent at a price I can afford. Prices in Bristol are almost as bad as London. If it weren't for the mortgage in York, I'd be fine. But even with the pay rise, we're talking thousands of pounds for the type of property I wouldn't invite my boss to. I need to find something in keeping with my new job. A two up, two down terrace won't cut it, but at the moment that's all I can afford.

Buttoning my shirt, I head for the bar. It's Friday night, I'm going to drown my sorrows. Who knows, now I can play the field again, there might even be some female company around. That's if I can remember what to do.

I glance round the bar and am disappointed. Three couples talking quietly. I'm in for a wild night. I climb onto a barstool and sigh.

"Evening, Jake. Brandy, please. Metaxa. Make it a large one."

"Coming right up. If you don't mind me saying, you look like you need it." Dropping ice into a tumbler, Jake holds it to the optic and puts several measures in.

"You're right there. Trying to find something to rent. I have to relocate with the job but can't buy until I've sold. Not having much luck and I'm running out of time."

"I hear you. Me and my mate got a joint mortgage because it was cheaper than renting. Don't know what will happen to the other when one of us gets loved up and wants to move on. I try not to think about it. On the room?"

"Yes. Please. Two ten. Does it ever get busy in here?" I glance around again, hoping someone sneaked in while I was distracted.

"Not really. Not unless there's a conference on, which there will be next week. We're fully booked. But generally it's just nightcaps before bed, and, of course, the odd guest trying to drown their sorrows." He glances at my drink. "Never works, and in here it's not even fun trying."

I raise my glass. "I'll give it a go. You know which room to roll me into."

Jake laughs. "I'll do my best. Just got to grab a crate of mixers. Give me a shout if anyone comes in." He disappears through the door behind the bar.

I nod and pull my phone from my pocket, resuming my search for somewhere to rent. A little while later, Jake is back, and he gives a low whistle, so I follow the direction of his gaze and hope my mouth doesn't drop open. Wow! The evening just got better. Much better.

A girl with a mop of blonde hair teeters in through the door. She's wearing a black dress which looks like it's painted onto her very shapely body, and as she moves, I swear to God her nipples grow as I watch. Her legs are long, slightly tanned and naked, and for a moment, given the lack of a bra, I wonder if she has anything on at all under that dress. I'm sure she does, but it doesn't stop my interest stirring in my boxers. I shift on the stool to make myself more comfortable, and I'm about to tell Jake to ask her what she'd like to drink when her smile appears. Dear God, she is gorgeous. I'm in love. Okay, lust, but my lust fizzles out when I see the bloke the smile is for. Tall, dark, and I suppose, handsome. And by the look of it, not a stranger at the gym. Nor am I, but it's not me she's smiling at. I turn back to face Jake as she tells tall, dark and handsome to surprise her. I think it's fair to say I'd like to surprise her.

Her man orders two mojitos. Bit of a girly drink, in my opinion, but each to their own. As he walks back with the drinks, I catch Jake's eye and order another brandy as I empty the first one. I nearly spit it out as she shouts out something about her nipples. Unable to resist, I swivel round to look, and there she is clasping those pert, full breasts with a grin on her face. Bloody hell, I can't take my eyes off her. She catches me looking, has a quick exchange with tall, dark and handsome, before telling me he can't keep his hands to himself. Who can blame him? Before I can stop them, my thoughts leave my lips.

"Who can blame him?" I call and then wink at her like the idiot I am. Jake laughs behind me.

Shit. Now I'm convinced I'm blushing like a bloody teenager. I wave a fist at a grinning Jake and return to my scrolling.

A message flashes up. It's from Mark Bowman. Mark is the top man in Gemini, and I mean the top, top man. There's no one above him. I've spoken to him once, months ago, for a couple of minutes via a video link. It must be important.

Christos, if you're free during the next thirty minutes, call me. Mark.

I catch Jake's eye and tell him I'll be back. There's no one in the foyer, so I hit dial and draw in a breath.

"Christos. That was quick. Thanks for calling so late. I hope I'm not interrupting anything."

"Hi, Mr Bowman. Nothing exciting. I was scrolling for a property to rent on my phone. Speaking to you is preferable. How can I help?" I realise my palms are sweaty, and I wipe them against my jeans, swapping the phone from one hand to the other.

"It's Mark, please, and to rent? I thought you were buying something."

"I will eventually, but it's been a while since I've lived here. Hotels are only good for a limited time. Renting is quicker while I sell the house in York and look for the right place in an area I like."

"Ah, Sensible. I'd almost forgotten you're a Bristolian. Me too."

"Really? You don't sound Bristolian."

Mark laughs. "Nor do you. I haven't lived there for many years. I'm settled in New York now, I think, but never say never. It's one of the things that interested me in you. You were up against some keen competition."

This irritates me. I work hard and deliver top results year in and year out. My clients love me, and I know I nailed more than one assessment, so to hear I might have got the job because I'd previously lived in Bristol pisses me off a little.

"And there was I thinking it was my skill, expertise and sparkling personality." Did I snap? I think I did. I need to dial this back. "Whatever the reason, I'm glad to be here."

"Hey, hey. Don't get upset. What I should have said is when you came to the top of the pile and I was told you were from Bristol and were positive about returning, I made sure I looked at everything we had on you. I also have skill and expertise, and where possible appoint the best candidate for the job. It was neck and neck at one stage, but you won. Congratulations."

It doesn't sound like he means it, so I change the subject back to location.

"Ah, so that's why you chose Bristol for your UK operation. I did wonder why not London. Can I ask what tipped the scales for me?" So much for changing the subject. The irritation is disappearing, but I'm only human, and I need a pat on the back as much as the next man.

"Honestly? And please don't take offence again, because I was only calling to see how it was going not to discuss your attributes. But, as you've asked, it was because you're settled. Married. Our business is built on family values and building a future for families. Greg is a player. Can't see him ever settling down. If anyone went looking into his past, there's plenty of it to find. We both know that shouldn't affect how you do the job, but appearances are king, and minor scandals to be avoided. But back to why I called. How is it going?"

Shit. Shit. Shit! I'm married, but only just. And not for long if I have my way. What would they do if they knew Ana had left me and was shacking up with her lover over the restaurant?

Hang on, he asked me a question. I close my eyes and rerun his last words.

"Sorry about that. I had to move for someone." I lie to cover my silence. "Things are going okay. I'm speaking to our investors and clients daily. Only a few more to do. I don't think we'll have any jumpers. The property is taking shape slowly. George is a good man, but it's like treading treacle some days. Keep your fingers crossed that we'll be ready for a July launch." Although I deliver the words confidently, I'm mentally crossing my fingers and toes. I'll be lucky if it's ready for Christmas the way things are going.

"Well, that's good to hear. I was going to ask if we should delay it. I heard there have been issues getting the materials there. You are sure, aren't you? We can't get this wrong."

"Give me another couple of days. Let me speak to George once we're into next week, and I'll get back to you."

"Please do. I don't want it to be a cockup, Christos. That would be...I've got to go. Keep me in the picture."

He hangs up and my shoulders slump. I just put my head in a noose. Now I really need a drink. I walk back towards the bar and a flash of that dress catches my attention. It's on the move.

The girl gets to her feet. She's not as tall as...oh, there you go. She's put her shoes on, and barely pecks tall, dark and handsome on his pouty lips.

My blood pressure rises again as she heads out of the bar. Those hips can swing. I'm not sure what to focus on, what with her breasts bouncing about, too. I don't know why she's walking like that, but it pushes all my buttons. Darting forward, I pull open the door. She inclines her head with a flash of that smile. Then the smile falls away and her mouth makes a perfect O as she comes to an abrupt halt, her shoulders jerking backwards, and her breasts jostling for position. She lurches about and I instinctively widen my arms, ready to catch her as she disappears from my eyeline. I miss.

I shake the poorly timed thoughts about her mouth from my mind and look down at her. Bloody hell! Those thoughts are back with a vengeance. I'm going to need another shower tonight. The door to the bar has closed and I shoot a quick glance at tall, dark and handsome through the glass. It looks like he's having a disagreeable telephone conversation, so I return to the more attractive view.

There's not much to the sliver of fabric down there, and as I'm trying to decide if she's shaved, waxed, or has a Brazilian, she shuts off the view, flings out an arm, and tells me I'm rude and not a gentleman. She's not wrong. Not at the moment.

I take her hand. It's tiny and my fingers swamp it. I rub my thumb across her skin. Soft except for the tiny scar that runs down between her ring and baby finger. Hauling her to her feet, I can't help but reach out and place a hand on her hip. It's not strictly necessary, as I don't think she'll fall now the shoes have gone, but I need to touch her. I was right. Her skin is deliciously silky here too, and before I can stop myself, I slip a finger into the top of her knickers. Common sense prevails, and realising how wrong that is, I quickly remove it. The elastic snaps back into place. I'm getting too hot under the collar now. I need to keep her eyes on my face. If she looks any lower, she'll know just how rude I want to be. As I tell her that, she gives a gasp and shudders. My mind is in overdrive. I need to get her covered up before I do something that really shouldn't happen in a public place. I tell her this, and I laugh as she tells me she'll carry her shoes. Taking hold of her dress, I drag it back down into position, allowing my fingers to graze her body on either side. I see her shudder as I do. She's feeling this too.

"Don't leave on my account," I whisper, and I'm back to mentally crossing digits again. Before I can back this up, her taxi driver appears, and she leaves me. Nothing but the smell of her strawberry shampoo, and my inability to walk comfortably, as a reminder of her presence. I adjust myself discreetly and head back to the bar, hoping Jake doesn't want an early finish.

As I pull the door, something flutters about at my feet. I pick it up and grin. It's her business card. Her name isn't Cash, it's Cassie. She's an actor and entertainer. Well, she can entertain me anytime she likes, and now I have her phone number. Sliding the card into my back pocket, I'm still smiling as I head to the bar to resume my search.

Tall, dark and handsome approaches with their empty glasses as I place my order and return to my scrolling.

"Are you leaving, or can I get you another one?" Jake asks him.

"No, I'm off. My date let me down. Think that's the last time. My lonely, empty bed beckons." There's a pause before he says, "Sorry, I can't help noticing, but are you looking for somewhere to rent?"

He's speaking to me.

I nod. Not sure I want to get into conversation with him. I'm going to call her, and he won't like that.

"I am. Unsuccessfully. I need something classy to go with a new job but can't afford anything but very mediocre at best." His face lights up, and I think maybe I do want to speak to him. "Do you know somewhere cheap and classy?"

"As it happens, and depending on what you call cheap, I might. Do you mind sharing?" His phone comes out of his pocket, and he scrolls through to a website I've not considered, finds what he's looking for and passes me his phone.

My smile reappears. It's only perfect if one ignores the sharer element. It's been a long time since I've shared with strangers. Lifting my phone, I jot down the details and pass his back.

"Thanks, I'll give it some thought. Not sure if I'm a little too old to share."

"You're welcome. And by the way, thanks for helping Cassie. I was on the phone and could see she was in good hands. You're a true gentleman, sir."

My eyebrows rise. "That's not what she called me."

He shrugs as he nods understanding. "Don't take it personally. She's always rude to someone she's got the hots for at first. It's like her own baptism of fire. Have fun." He taps his finger on his forehead and leaves.

Cassie Henderson, actor and entertainer, has the hots for me! Why didn't I know that ten minutes ago? Did she tell him that and dump him? Perhaps they're not a couple? I should have asked, but what would I have done if he'd said they were? Because I still want to call her. I finish my drink and head for my room.

Chapter 4

Cassie

I RUB MY EYES and force them open. Who the hell is calling me at this time of night? I glance at the clock. Okay, it's morning, but only just. Snatching up the phone, I snap a greeting, making sure whoever it is knows I'm less than impressed.

"Is that you, Cassie?" a female voice asks, clearly not expecting me to be so grumpy.

I'd check to see who it is. But I don't have the energy to force my eyes open.

"This is she." My chin lifts and my lips purse as I give her a taste of my Dame Maggie Smith.

"Oh, thank goodness. It's Jan. We have some work for you. Glen said you were desperate."

It's the agency. I sit upright, eyes still closed. I am desperate, but Glen shouldn't be sharing that, not even with Jan. Nobody wants an actor who nobody wants. Okay, it's early. I know what I mean. I remain with Dame Maggie. "Did he? He might have been incorrect. What job and when? I'll check my diary if it's suitable."

"Glen said you had nothing on. Hang on, I'll check." Jan rustles some papers.

Dame Maggie goes out of the window. "Just tell me about the bloody job, Jan."

"It's for today. A day's work for two hundred pounds."

Sounds reasonable. That will cover my phone bill and a month's shopping if I stick to pasta for dinner. "What is it? Please don't tell me a kid's party and some buffoon is going to saw me in half."

There's a brief silence. "There might be kids, although they're not planned or guaranteed, but no saws will come anywhere near you. Are you out of bed yet, Cassie? This gig starts at twelve and you need to be trained, health and safety, etcetera."

"You still haven't told me what it is." I'm considering bringing Maggie back into play.

"A promotion. Our client is raising awareness about the necessity of bees. They have hives and mini gardens on the roofs in town, and want donations and...yes, awareness."

"So I'm handing out leaflets with a smile."

"Not quite."

"What does that mean?"

Jan's intake of breath is audible. "Well, you'll be handing out leaflets, but a smile is not strictly necessary."

"Explain." Dame Maggie is back.

"You'll be in costume," Jan says quickly.

"What sort of costume? Am I to be a beekeeper with one of those net things over my head?"

"Not quite," Jan says and draws in another breath. I know where this is going, so I remain silent. "A bee," she whispers.

"I beg your pardon. I didn't catch that." Dame Maggie asks.

"A bee. One of those endangered species, without which our planet will die." Jan clicks her fingers. "Gone."

"Fuck off, Jan. I love you, but I'm going back to bed." Dame Maggie has left the building.

"No, no, no, don't hang up. I've not finished," Jan pleads, and as I need a pee, I walk with Jan to the bathroom and take a seat. "Are you still there?" she asks.

"I am. You said there was more. The answer won't change, but do, please, carry on."

"Glen thought you might say that, so he says he'll give you an extra fifty quid if you'll do it for us. We are also desperate."

"Make it one hundred and you're on."

"Done," Jan shouts gleefully, and I realise that was probably the fee all along. I really need to stop taking calls when I'm half awake. "Well done, Cassie."

I pull the flush and hit the button to start the shower.

"Were you on the toilet while you were speaking to me?" Jan demands.

"I was. As you correctly pointed out, I was desperate. Email me the details, and I'll call you if there's a problem."

I climb into the shower and wash the sleep from my eyes and the smell of sex with Hottie from my body. He might not have been with me physically, but that's who I was thinking about. How times change. Now all I can think of is if there will be complimentary honey I can nab whilst I'm there.

Two hours later, I'm sitting in the back of a trailer cum training room cum changing room being told how to interact with the public and being asked to read the leaflet again so I can get answers to questions I think I might be asked but don't know the answer to.

There will be three of us bees, and bee number one, Tarquin, and I'm not making this up, is keen. He has lots of questions. I glance at my watch. Only five and a half hours to go. If Tarquin keeps going, my time in the hideous costume opposite will be reduced, so I smile encouragement.

"Okay." Our instructor, Felicity, call me Flick, claps her hands to halt Tarquin as he raises his finger yet again. "We need to get going. Pop your costumes on and I'll lead you around to base camp. Take it from one with experience, the sun is shining, so it's going to be a little warm in there, you'll only need your undies on. On that note, there's bottled water in a cooler outside. Take a couple of bottles and store them in the pouch in your tummies." Flick gets to her feet and heaves bee number one from the floor. "Tarquin, let's start with you. Leave your clothes in the changing room. They'll be perfectly safe. I'll lock up behind us. Valuables can go in your tummy with the water."

Tarquin takes his costume. He's bouncing on the balls of his feet with excitement. I'll bet good money he won't be in five hours fifteen minutes.

"Climb in through the side, straps over shoulders, and zip up from inside. I'll have your gloves waiting."

Ten minutes later, I waddle out of the changing room and join the other bees. Flick produces some long, black silky gloves. Audrey Hepburn would have loved them. As I watch Flick distribute them, I'm wondering two things. The first is how will I know the time once my watch is covered up, and will Flick notice if I acquire the gloves? One of my few dresses is a silver, sleeveless, sequined number, which they would accessorise perfectly.

I have three dresses. The black backless one that likes to double as a T-shirt. The silver sleeveless one, that needs some long black gloves, and a twee Laura Ashley print smock thing. Not sure how I came by the last one. But I can wear it without underwear. A fact I discovered when...it doesn't matter. I just did. A girl can have too many dresses that require shoes but never have too many accessories.

I accept my new accessory. "Thanks. You know these costumes stink like someone has thrown up in the bowels of hell, don't you?" I say as I slide on the first one, so creating my little bee arm. "And as you were keen on the health and safety stuff, not only can I not breathe properly, I can barely see. Will someone be there to stop these little bees from getting squashed after we wander blindly into the traffic?"

"I sponged them down as best I could and thought the Febreze would do the trick. And why would you wander off? TARQUIN! You'll fall." Flick slaps the final glove into my hand and rushes to grab one of his legs before he attempts to climb down the steps of the trailer unaided. I roll my eyes and check the time before the glove goes on. Five hours to go.

Two hours to go, and I'm hot. Unbearably hot. My hair is sticking to my head, and I'm counting how many seconds it will take the droplet clinging to the end of my nose to drop off and add to the wonderful aroma of my stripy prison. Me and bee number two are lounging against the wall behind the cart holding honey produced by Bristol bees, and our supply of leaflets. Interest in what we were doing dwindled over half an hour ago, but there goes Tarquin. Another full lap on the strip of pavement. I swallow, my throat is dry, and my tongue feels too big for my mouth, because I stupidly forgot to collect the water, my pouch, and now my mouth is dry. I nudge bee number two.

"Because I'm stupid, I forgot my water. May I have a mouthful of yours, please? I think I'm dehydrating."

"All gone. Perhaps Bill will have some on the cart. Grab one for me if he has, please."

Bill the beekeeper is a cheery chap and looks downcast when he can't fulfil my request. He removes a thick leather glove and pushes the net screen away from his face. "Dehydrated? That's not good. No point in us telling the public to put a little saucer of water out for the bees if we can't keep ourselves alive. I'll call Felicity. I mean Flick. She never used to be a Flick, you know. No idea where that came from." His call is unsuccessful, so he leaves a message. "I know. We'll move to a new location. There's a cafe around the corner. They'll give us some water, I'm sure. Come on, little bees. This way."

I squint through the gauze and heave my bulbous body to the right and back again. I can't see a corner anywhere. This road seems to go on for miles. But Bill is confident, so I fall into step as he heaves up the handles of the cart and trundles off, street left. I'm impressed as only one jar falls over. We walk, and we walk, and we walk. Bill's hood is off, his gloves are off, and we little bees continue to bake.

Bill grinds to a halt. "I think we came the wrong way," he says. "I think it's back that way. It's that way to the centre, yes?"

It turns out, two of the bees have a colourful command of the English language. The third bee is still in high spirits. How?

Tarquin slaps Bill on the back. "Not to worry, old chap. Let me push the cart for a while. You look quite exhausted."

We start the trek back. I can barely see through the sweat pouring off my brow. I slow down. It doesn't stop the heat, but it eases the rubbing of the thick webbed straps over my shoulders. I plod on. I don't know what the time is now, and I don't care. When we get back to where we're supposed to be, I'm done. Bee number two is still complaining. It's been relentless and I'm in awe. I can barely breathe, let alone find the energy to moan. When Tarquin stops the cart and stacks the honey back into the drawer below, I wonder if he too is going to throw in the towel. But no, he's just being his kind, helpful and enthusiastic self, and gives Bill a leg up so he can ride back on the cart. There's not enough room for another one. Pulling my arms back into the costume, I fumble in my pouch for my phone. One hour, ten minutes to go. That's if I survive. Huffing out a sigh, I return the phone to the pouch. Only I don't. In my dehydrated state, I miss the pouch and my phone slides down the chubby leg of my costume and jams against my ankle. Fuck.

I waddle on. The next time I have the energy to raise my head, I see the welcoming sight of the bright red pillar box with an artistic cock and balls spray painted on the side. We're nearly back at the base, and I grin, triumphant. I've survived. I'm off. Tarquin stops the cart.

"Shall we just wait where we should have stayed for Flick, or go in search of water? We should take a vote. Let's have a show of hands."

"You lot can do what you want. I'm done. Finished. No amount of money is worth this hell on earth. Bill, would you call Flick again, please? Make sure I can grab my clothes from the trailer."

Flick is still unobtainable. I curse. Bill looks shocked.

"So, no point in going back," Tarquin announces, with no show of hands.

A woman appears and stops and stares at us. Tarquin beckons her forward. "Sorry, madam, we're about to take a vote, but please, take a leaflet and a complimentary jar of honey." He whips the said items from the drawer like a magician and the bemused woman wanders off. "So, show of hands. No point in going back if Flick isn't there. I vote we stay at base and wait for her to collect us. Anyone else?" Tarquin's own hand shoots up.

I see bee number two pivot to look at me and Bill mumbles that whatever we think is best is good with him.

I raise a gloved finger. "Two things. First, what if she is there but her phone is dead, and probably, more importantly, what if she herself is dead? I know she's probably sitting somewhere with her feet dangling in water and a long, long, cold drink in her hand, but we don't know. I vote we all go back to the trailer before we all die."

Tarquin's gloved hand covers his little bee smile. "Don't say that. What would Flick say?"

"Not a lot if she's dead. But maybe oh dear, if she's got a beer, or, I'm so sorry, I forgot my charger if her phone has died. Let's vote." I click my fingers and scream "FUCK!" at the top of my voice when the gloves don't allow my fingers to gain the attention of bee number two. The loud cursing did, though, and she pivots slowly.

"No offence, but I think you might have lost it. Flick isn't dead. We've still got an hour to go. She could be anywhere. I think I'll stick with Tarquin and Bill," she says.

That's it then. I'm on my own. Good, I won't have to smell them when they remove their costumes. I nod acceptance and my head swims as they set off for base. I stay perfectly still, head lowered and take some steadying breaths. Bloody hell, I'm thirsty. My head settles, and I raise it carefully. That doesn't seem too...Hottie!

I watch him skip through the traffic and hit the pavement just as Tarquin and the cart arrive at the same spot. His sexy smile lights up his face, as he graciously waves them on first, but he has to wait while Tarquin grabs him a leaflet and jar of honey. I giggle. What are the chances? I'm glad he doesn't know it's me, as he gives a cheery wave in my direction before disappearing into an alley.

Where's he going? Is there water at the end of that alley? I hurry after him. Turns out it's hard to hurry when there's waddling involved, and I reach the top of the alley as he turns left at the other end. I launch myself forwards, blinking away the sweat and ignoring the pounding in my ears. At the other end, I turn left. The road is empty. Other than a man in the back of a van, there's not a soul in sight. Bugger. I waddle on. Hottie came this way. He must be somewhere.

I scan the impressive façades of the buildings. Very upmarket for a hottie dressed in jeans and flip-flops, but, Hottie aside, one of them must have an accessible tap. However, they're all business premises and it's Saturday afternoon. There's no one I can ask. My head swims again as someone shouts behind me.

"Mind your back. You need to walk in a straight beeline." He laughs. "Buzz over to the left." He chortles again at his own humour.

Spinning towards the voice, I have to put my hand on the wall to steady myself. It's a delivery man, and he steers his trolley around me. I don't have the wherewithal to apologise. I think I'm going to...Hang on a minute! That was water on that trolley. Cases and cases of the stuff. I waddle forward, but my technique is such I don't gain enough ground, and he's disappeared into a building before I can catch him. But I'm not done yet. The front of the building in question has its windows papered over. They must be renovating. With my rotund bee belly bouncing back and forth, I bang on the door. I wait a second. Nothing, so I bang again.

A disembodied voice reaches my pounding ears. "Um. Can I help you?"

I have no idea who I'm speaking to, but I shout at the top of my voice. "I need water. Please. Water."

A familiar chuckle reaches me, but my body is in no condition to tingle.

"I read the leaflet. I'll leave a saucer out. Thanks again for the honey," Hottie tells me.

He's taking the mickey. What the actual fuck? Doesn't he realise I'm dying here? I lift my hands and bang and bang until Hottie pulls open the door, no sexy smile to be seen, and he doesn't look happy. I spot the water in the lift, and ignoring Hottie take off towards it. And then my world goes black.

Chapter 5

Christos

I FINISH MY BREAKFAST and wander back to my room. It's Saturday, and I have nowhere to go and no one to go with. I feel lonely and very cheesed off.

My marriage ending is no great surprise, not really. There was only ever a slim chance we would muddle through to our dotage. But the timing couldn't have been worse, and I've also lost my non-judgemental sounding board. Our sex life might have gone down the pan, but we still talked to each other. I know I could pick up the phone, and I know she'd listen, probably wouldn't agree with my concerns, but at least I could voice them, and Ana would hear me out. But I won't do that, not with Yorgos, look at the twinkle in my eye, Costi, listening in. Our marriage might have been doomed to failure, but he was out of order. Bastard. A sigh escapes, and I fall back on to the bed. Is he though? He's going to have to put up with some serious shit now. The Cypriot community is close. You don't step on another man's toes. My mother said neither of them had turned up to a family wedding last week and he was meant to have been one of the groomsmen. But there again, neither did I. I bet they all think I've run away because of the shame of it. The thought makes me cringe. I've never run away from anything in my life. Hence the marriage. Another sigh. Jesus, I need to pull myself together. I've never sulked either.

That thought makes me question if I'm running away from calling Cassie? I certainly haven't even considered doing it this morning. Am I sulking because she was with tall, dark and handsome? Or am I undecided because then it will be me stepping on another man's toes? Groaning, I pull myself to my feet. I have to go to work for a few hours because there are a couple of deliveries due. Not the ones we need, but anything is better than nothing. I pick up my wallet and slide it into my pocket.

And so begins another day. A movement catches my eye, and I watch as a white envelope appears under the door. As I pick it up, my phone rings. It's the project manager, George Feebry.

"George, I wasn't expecting to hear from you today. Please don't tell me we have more problems."

I smile as George tells me the plumbers need access today, and if that happens, they promise to get the water supply sorted out in the main toilets, kitchen, and, if we're lucky, the gym.

I tell him I'll be there within the hour. Perhaps if I get this launch done on time, they'll forgive my very unsettled private life. Since that initial email, I've read my contract. I'm on a six-month probationary period. Why didn't Ana wait six months before dashing off into the sunset? Once the probationary period is over, I'd have to cock up for them to kick me out, and I don't intend on doing that. I'll just have to find a way of hiding my impending divorce and deliver the launch on time. That means letting the plumbers in. I was chuffed when I found out there would be a gym. I like to keep myself fit, and the convenience of having it in the basement, and in my current financial situation, free, is a huge bonus.

Ending the call, I open the envelope. My smile drops away. The hotel is fully booked the following week. I need to be out of my room by Tuesday lunchtime. Damn. Even less time to find somewhere than I thought. Now I have only three days to find an alternative. More pressure I don't need. I was hoping to get some work done this morning. Looks like I'll be trying to find a hotel instead.

Once at the office building, I look around at the mountains of boxes as I head for my temporary base in reception. Here I can monitor the front door and direct deliveries to the correct locations, without going up and down in the lift, and I question again if it's possible to get this up and running by the end of July.

I've just opened my laptop to set a reminder to call Mark Bowman on Tuesday, when the buzzer sounds and I glance at the screen. A cheery looking chap in overalls holds up his thumb to the camera and I buzz him in.

I walk across to meet him.

"Alright, Guv? Where do you want us to start? I'm Jamie," he says, shaking my hand.

"Chris. The kitchen, no coffee machine yet, but I'll be able to fill the kettle. Then wherever takes your fancy. Do you know where everything is?"

"Yep, we put it all in. Just needs connecting. We should be done by early afternoon. Has the electrician been back in?"

"Not yet. All the sockets work, though. Just the finer details he told me."

Jamie rolls his eyes. "One of them being hot water. Still, I'm sure you'll manage. I'll grab my gear and let Bob in."

Bob and the gear arrive, and I leave them to it. Opening my search engine, I begin my quest to find another hotel. After an hour of fruitless phone calls, I drum my fingers on the desk and consider phoning Steve about the house share.

This makes me think of tall, dark and handsome, and brings me neatly back to Cassie Henderson. Actor & Entertainer. My hand instinctively goes to my back pocket, where her card sits alongside my wallet. I will call her, perhaps tomorrow. I'll offer to take her for lunch. A girl like that will not be wanting for company on a Saturday evening. Unlike myself. Not that I'd be fit for anything. I didn't sleep well, not with thoughts of what I would like to be doing to Cassie toying with me.

I need to get laid. This can't be good for my health. Perhaps I'll venture out this evening.

"Sod it. I need to occupy my mind," I curse.

"Sorry, Guv. What was that?" Jamie saunters across with his toolbox.

"Ignore me. Talking to myself. How's it going?"

Jamie jerks a thumb behind him. "Kitchen sorted, I've left Bob doing the gents, I'm going down to the gym, then we'll do a pincer movement on the ladies."

Nodding approval, I ask, "What's your estimated finish time? I might need to pop out."

"We'll be gone by two if that helps. Unless we spring a leak. Just kidding, we're too good for leaks."

I laugh as I check the details of the house on my phone, type them into the search engine on the laptop, and settle down to study the photographs. The more I see, the more I nod. The room, my room, should I take it, is on the top floor of a substantial period villa overlooking the famous suspension bridge. Sympathetic modern furniture complements the period features in the communal areas. Two bathrooms and a shower room means I won't be waiting on the landing for someone to get out of my way. The courtyard garden grabs my attention too, nice barbeque area, and a hot tub in the bottom corner. I lift my phone and punch in Steve's number. It takes a while, and I'd almost given up when he answers.

"Yes, sorry. Is this going to be quick? I'm on my way out." He sounds breathless.

"I hope so. Someone recommended I call you as you have a room to let, and I'm interested in looking at it. I'm relocating with work and am currently living out of a hotel. It's not ideal. I need somewhere by Tuesday."

He asks me a few questions, ending with, "Can you see it today? When I say today, I mean now. I'm getting ready to catch a flight, then I'm out of the country for at least a month, although my housemate should be able to show you around, but I don't know what she's up to. She works away sometimes, too. We've been ships in the night recently."

This sounded better and better. Two housemates who work away from home. I jump in. "Okay, I hear you. I'm keen, very keen, I can be with you around two. Will she be around then?"

"Who knows? What's your name?"

"Chris. Chris Baros."

"Are you a brave man, Chris?"

What sort of question was that? Does he keep snakes or arachnids? I shudder at the thought. "I like to think so, depends on what we're talking about," I say hesitantly.

Steve laughs. "Old ladies. I can leave the key with Miss Allison next door. She's your worst enemy if you mess her about or put your bin in the wrong place. She'll show you around. Touch nothing or she'll slap you. I'll be at the airport in about an hour, so if you're interested, I'll send you the necessary from there. My flight isn't until half four. I'll need one month's rent in advance, and six weeks' deposit. Once that's in the bank, I'll let Miss Allison...please never call her Mrs. Anyway, I'll let her know she can release the key, and I'll deal with the rest once I'm settled. How does that sound?"

"It sounds like you're terrified of her. How old is she?" I ask.

Steve chuckles. "Who knows? Never been brave enough to ask. Must be due a telegram from the King soon, though."

It's my turn to laugh. "I reckon I can handle her. But to be on the safe side, let's give an exact time. Say I'll be there at two thirty. I won't mess about and I'll decide while I'm there. I'll be in touch before your flight leaves."

"Perfect. Now I must dash. I have to brave next door, too. Good luck, Chris."

Getting maps up on my laptop, I look to see how far away it is. As I ponder if it's worth walking back to my hotel to get the car, Jamie appears.

"Twenty minutes, Guv, and we'll be out of your hair."

It was forty minutes by the time I'd checked their work, but it still left me enough time to walk to the property without the faff of collecting the car from the hotel, and fighting with the parking.

I buy a bottle of water from the shop on the corner and set off. The weather is glorious, and Bristol feels...comfortable. I recognise most of these streets and landmarks and I feel comfortable too. I arrive at Miss Allison's property five minutes early and smile. She can't have a problem with that.

How wrong can one man be?

Climbing the few steps to her shiny black front door, I push the bell. It's opened almost immediately by a tiny, grey-haired woman with glasses hanging from a cord around her neck. I smile at her.

"Hello, I'm Chris, I understand—"

"Arghhh."

Her scream is long and could pierce eardrums. It stops only when her mirror image appears and whacks me on the arm with an umbrella she's pulled from the stand next to the door. The second one is a little taller and places her glasses on her nose to inspect me as she wraps her arm around the one who opened the door.

"Are you Chris Baros?" she asks. This one must be Miss Allison.

"I am, I'm—"

"Silence!" she barks out the command and holds the flat of her hand towards me as she speaks to the first one. "Elizabeth, we've discussed this many times. You mustn't answer the door."

"But he rang the bell," Elizabeth explains, waving a shaky hand in my direction.

"I know he did, and I shall have words. But just because he broke the rules, it doesn't mean that you should. Now, get yourself a cup of tea while I deal with this man and I'll be back in no time. Do not answer the door should anyone else be stupid enough to call." Miss Allison shoots me a look to confirm I was stupid. "Now tell me what you're going to do."

"I'm going to make some tea, wait for you to come home, and ignore the door, if necessary, dear. Jennifer, I'm not stupid, you know." Elizabeth lifts her shoulders and tips her head to one side as though that should be obvious.

I hope my expression doesn't show my thoughts on the matter.

"I didn't say you were. We know who the stupid one was. Off you go."

Miss Allison watches Elizabeth shuffle away before rounding on me. "Why didn't you telephone to announce you were early?" she asks as she steps out to join me and pulls the door shut.

"It was five minutes, and I would have, of course, if I had your number," I explain, rushing to catch her as she marches away from me. She can move fast for an old girl but she suddenly grinds to a halt and spins to face me.

"No excuses, young man. Manners cost nothing. Come on, Elizabeth is awaiting my return." Climbing the steps, she opens the front door, pushing it right back against the hall wall. "Follow me."

Her command echoes in the hall, and I turn back to close the door. It's halfway closed before her screech makes me freeze.

"STOP!" Miss Allison marches back down the hall and pushes the door back against the wall. "Do you think I'm stupid, Mr Baros?"

"No, but...I take it you want the door open?" I hold out my hands, asking for an explanation.

"Of course I want the door open, and I want to be between you and that door at all times. You, me, door. Do you understand?"

"I do, but why?" I wait for her explanation, and although I can guess the answer, this might be the last chance I get to have a bit of fun today.

"Why? Why?" Her hands flutter about at her side. "Because, young man, you are a man, and I am a woman. I don't know you. You could be a sex maniac or an axe murderer. I am not safe in your company," she tells me.

My smile is wide. This is fun. I like her. "Me? I'm not any sort of maniac. I assure you, you are safe, and..."

"Well, you would say that, wouldn't you? I am not that easily fooled." She sweeps her hand up the hall. "That way. You're wasting time. Downstairs' convenience is on your right. It looks the same as any other, so don't go opening unnecessary doors. Straight ahead to the monstrosity they call the living area."

Leading the way and ignoring the downstairs toilet, I look around the monstrosity. Surprisingly, it looks the same as the photographs. A large, light and airy open-plan kitchen, dining and living area with bifold doors filling one wall and leading onto the courtyard garden. I walk across and look out. My hand rests on the handle.

"Don't open it," Miss Allison snaps. "You won't see anything else out there that you can't see from the window. You'll just inconvenience me a little more."

Nodding, I step away, my hands held up as though she were holding a gun. Facing in this direction, I spot a door in the far corner. "What's through there?"

"I was about to explain that. Through there is what they call the utility, it's a small room holding the washing machine, dryer, and iron, etcetera. Things normal people have in their kitchen or under the stairs. Then there's another door which leads to what they call the snug. It's a dark room with equally dark furniture, and a television as big as that kitchen table. I think they probably need spectacles and are too vain to admit it. The woman told me once they have popcorn nights. The woman is mad."

"May I look?" I take a tentative step forward.

"Did I not describe it adequately? Or perhaps you don't understand the King's English?"

"Oh no. You did an excellent job, I have a picture in my mind, I just thought—"

"I'm sure you know what thought did. Upstairs."

With no idea what thought did, I follow her back through to the hall, wondering if I'd ever complete a sentence, and the thought makes me smile. It reminds me of my mother, she always interrupts me too. Miss Allison walks past the ornate spindles and her glasses are back on her nose.

"Are you smiling? You are. Why?"

"You remind me of my mother. She doesn't let me—"

"I most certainly do not. I'm guessing your mother is Mediterranean. Greek or Turkish, judging by that nose. No, no. Greek. Baros is Greek. I stand corrected. Do I look like a Greek mother to you? No, I don't. Now stop talking nonsense and let's get this finished." Miss Allison's hand flips out as she points up the stairs, allowing her glasses to slide off her nose with a sharp nod.

"Greek Cypriot, actually. After you," I offer politely, giving a small bow. I'll make this woman smile if it kills me.

Miss Allison stills. Her eyes close, and her nostrils flare as she draws in and huffs out a breath causing her glasses to bounce. When she opens them, she speaks slowly, "I assumed English was your first language. I'll explain this again. Slowly. You man, me woman. You, me, door. Always in that order. You will go first."

My nod is brief. My bottom lip, clamped firmly between my teeth to stop me from laughing, starts to hurt, so I hurry up the stairs, waiting for her on the landing.

"Stephen's room, her room, bathroom, shower room, linen cupboard. All self-explanatory, except, of course, why one would need two bathrooms on the same floor. Up to your room."

I dare to push open the bathroom door. Again, it was the same as the photographs, but with more toiletries on show. I already know that unless my room is covered in mould, I'm going to move in. I point to the second door. "You said 'her'. What's her name? I haven't got that far with Steve to ask."

"I'm sure I don't know, but I will tell you this I don't trust her. She has far too much to say for herself for my liking. Never allows one to complete a sentence. Stephen will no doubt provide that information, if it becomes necessary." Miss Allison taps the watch on her wrist before pointing up the final staircase. "Up."

I take the stairs two at a time, and get a quick glimpse of the bathroom, which I guess will become mine. More than adequate. Miss Allison has caught me up and almost runs across to the door of my room. She pushes it open and watches me closely as I look around. I like it.

"Excellent. I'll take it. I can use that dressing table as a desk." Turning back to face her, I give her a double thumbs up.

"Why? Are you poor? Can you not afford a desk? There is always the one in the main room. As to taking it, that's to be discussed in a conversation with Stephen."

"You are correct, as always, but I need some quiet while I'm working from home. This will provide it. And I shall call Stephen right now." I pull out my phone, call Steve and hit the speaker phone icon. Miss Allison's eyebrows rise at the sound of ringing.

"Chris, that was quick. How did you get on?" Steve asks.

"I like it, I'll take it. I just need your bank details. You're on speaker. Shout them out and I'll type them in."

Details in, I transfer the money and try not to look at the balance left once I confirm the transaction.

"And there it is. It's in the bank. Thanks, Chris, I look forward to meeting you. I'll call Miss Allison and let her know you can have the key. How did you get on with Miss Allison?"

"Absolutely fine. In fact it was Miss Allison who convinced me to take the plunge. What a wonderful woman. She'll hate me for saying it, but she reminds me of my mother. Who wouldn't want to live next door to such a formidable woman?"

Steve laughs. "I totally agree. I take it she's with you now?"

"She is. Making sure I don't go into any of the rooms uninvited," I tell him with a wink for Miss Allison, which causes her eyebrows to rise again, and her nostrils to do that flaring thing.

"I should think so, too. Miss Allison, can you hear me?"

"Stephen, don't be ridiculous, you know I am not deaf. Of course I can hear you. Am I to take it I am to give Mr Baros a key?"

"If you would. Thank you for showing him around and thank you for letting the room for us. That's a weight off my mind."

"You are welcome, although I should warn you that although he was fairly well behaved, English isn't his first language, either that or he's a little slow."

It's my turn to do the eyebrow lift and I see a glint in Miss Allison's eye.

Steve's laugh is more of a snort. "Note made, Miss Allison. Chris, you didn't say when you were moving in."

"I thought tomorrow, if that's okay?"

"Perfect, I'll let…shit, I have to go. I'll call tomorrow." And he was gone.

Miss Allison tuts. "I think I should get back to Elizabeth. Here's your key. I hope you will be happy here, and that you follow a decent neighbourly code." She begins to descend the stairs.

"Miss Allison, I think I should go first, and yes, I know the rules, but on the descent, if I were a mad axeman, I could easily attack you from behind."

Her step falters for only a second. "Mr Baros, you are my neighbour now. I would never live next door to a mad axeman. The thought is absurd. Now, stop jabbering away, because I must get back to Elizabeth."

Miss Allison continues down the stairs, and there it is. I see the lines at the corner of her eye deepen, and the one visible cheek plumps up. She's smiling, and I don't know why, but that makes me feel like whatever else happens today, I'll have something to be happy about.

Back at the office, I have two more deliveries. The first is waiting for me. Literally piled up outside the door. Luckily, any dishonest passersby had no interest in plastic cable ducting. I lug it into the reception area, which makes me hot and sweaty, and I want nothing more than to go back to my cool hotel room to shower, and ponder if I really want to go out on a Saturday night on my own. That pleasure will have to wait, as I have one more delivery of water coming. An order placed when I only had running water to one toilet downstairs. But thinking ahead, I'll get it taken down to the gym because it will be useful in there.

When I track the order, I find out that it's five stops or thirty minutes away, so, with a grumbling stomach, I head for the shop down the road and grab myself a couple of sandwiches. On the way back, I bump into a bee pushing a beekeeper on a cart. I'm not kidding. I allow them to pass, and I'm rewarded with a leaflet on the value of bees and a jar of honey.

One bite into the sandwich and halfway through the leaflet, the buzzer sounds, and the water delivery arrives. Opening the door, I let him in.

"Blimey, your tracking system is excellent. Thirty minutes on the button. I don't need the water now, the plumber came, so if we can take it downstairs, I can use it in the gym as and when it gets finished. We can take the lift... oh, just a thought, as you've got a trolley. May I borrow it for a couple of those heavy boxes, and get them down there too? I won't be able to move in here soon."

"Show me what it is. I'm pushed for time. I have two more deliveries, the traffic is horrendous, and I've got an engagement party to get to."

"Machines for the gym. Literally just the two boxes. Huge and heavy, I took my eye off the ball, and they were in and out and just left there. There's a tip in it for you." I pull out my wallet and extract a note, which is snatched from my hand and shoved into his pocket.

"Done. That and a bottle of water."

He wheels the water into the lift, and I hold the door while he produces a knife, slices through the plastic and extracts a bottle. He slides it into his pocket as someone bangs on the door. I don't like the sound of that, so I hurry back to my desk while he settles the first of the two boxes on his trolley.

I check the screen. It's a bee, but before I can push the intercom button, it bangs again. I ask if I can help, and grin as it waddles about a little looking for me before shouting a response.

"Water. Help me, I need water," the bee tells me.

A laugh escapes, and I tell the bee that I'll leave a saucer of water out and thank them for the honey. The bee stills a moment before banging on the glass door so hard I'm sure it's going to shatter. I fly across reception, sidestepping the second box as it heads towards the lift, and yank open the door. The bee stops for a moment, hands up as though I'm going to attack it, then steps past me and heads for the lift.

"What the—"

Before I can complete my curse, there's a groan, and the bee launches forward before its little legs give way, trapping the delivery chap in between the two big boxes at the back of the lift. He takes it well at first, laughing and joking about a honey trap. When the bee fails to respond, he gives it a shove. It goes nowhere but now has a dent at shoulder height. I rush in and grab it from the rear, but it's a dead weight and I can't get a proper purchase.

"I think they really did need water, you know. It's too hot out there to be wandering around in this. I'll..." The lift starts its descent to the basement, and I look at the delivery man. "Was that you?"

"Yep. I haven't got time to muck about with people in fancy dress. I've got an engagement party to get to. When we get down there, I'll push, you pull and then I'll get these unloaded for you." He slaps his hands on each of the boxes. "I'll leave you to decide what to do with that." He jabs a finger at the bee.

"Whoever is in there might be dead. A little compassion wouldn't go amiss." I glance over my shoulder as the lift opens.

"Then he won't be needing my help. On three. One, two, three."

With us both working together, we get the bee out into the lobby and roll it to one side so Mr Compassionate can unload the lift. Running my hands all over its furry little body, I try to find the fastenings. As the first box emerges, I roll the bee over and start again. As the second box comes out, I shout triumphantly as I find a zip. My joy is short-lived, as I can't find the pull tab.

"I can't open it." I look at the delivery guy as he wheels the stack of water out of the lift. He hands me his knife.

"Cut it off. Mind you, if it was me, I'd have taken the gloves off first, or are they sown in?" The water slides into a neat stack next to me. "Good luck, stay there, I can see myself out."

I flick my hand to dismiss him and refuse to look at him in case I tell him what I'm thinking, because the bee is more important. I pull off the first glove as the lift door closes.

It's a girl! I'm holding a tiny, pale and clammy female hand. I pinch the skin, and it stays in a ridge before slowly settling back in place. Dehydrated, I decide, and check for a pulse. I know I should have done that the other way around, but it's not every day you find yourself with a man-sized dying bee in the basement. She's got a pulse, but it doesn't seem very strong.

Unlike mine, I reckon if I look down, I'll see my heart bouncing around. She might be alive now, but for how long if I don't get a move on? I'm not gentle as I yank off the second glove.

Bloody hell! It's Cassie.

Without thinking, I bring her hand to my lips and kiss the little scar between her knuckles.

Cassie! The first girl I've dreamed about since Sally Braithwaite, after she collided with me, having run semi-naked out of the girls' changing room at school to escape a spider. I killed the spider and got my first date. Placing her hand on the rotund bee belly, I doubt if Cassie will want to go out with tall, dark, and handsome tonight. Bloody hell, I'm smirking, and not helping her. I should phone for an ambulance, and I slap my empty pockets before remembering my phone is on the desk upstairs. There's no way I can leave her alone, so I lift the knife.

"I'm going to cut you free, Cassie. It shouldn't hurt." Pulling the fluffy fabric to one side to avoid her body, I start to saw.

Chapter 6

Cassie

I OPEN MY EYES and groan. Everything is dark, and that tells me I should be asleep, so I close my eyes and try to roll over, but something is holding me in place. The duvet must be trapped, and I don't have the energy to fight it. Probably why I feel so warm. I draw in a breath. Bloody hell, what is that smell? I bet my neighbour has bought a load of manure for her roses again. I swear she does it to annoy me. Why she hates me I have no idea, because I've been nothing but polite when I've had the misfortune to bump into her. I reckon it's because I asked her to pass me the tampons when I bumped into her in Sainsburys. I doubt witches have periods.

Hoping that I'll dream about Hottie again, I decide to ignore the smell...Hottie! My eyes open again. It's still dark, still smelly, and now there's an odd noise. Are the witches having a shed built to house the manure?

"Nearly there. A little further and I should be able to...Fuck me, you're gorgeous."

Hottie's back. I giggle, even though I know I'm dreaming. The smell, the shed, and now he's talking to me. Perhaps he's building the shed? Probably is. It is a dream, after all. I hope he's got his shirt off. Perhaps I should get him a can of cola. They all whip off their shirts for cola. Talking of which I'm parched. My tongue keeps sticking to the roof of my mouth and I can't swallow. Anyway, where's he gone? Back to sleep.

What the hell? Who pulled the duvet off me? Is Hottie being demanding? I open my eyes as my body shivers against the unexpected drop in temperature.

Eyes. Hottie's eyes. This dream is getting better. Will you look at those lashes? What sort of dream has me shivering like this? I must be in a compromising position. Oh yes, Hottie pulled the duvet off. Running a hand over my boob, I check. Yep. One rock hard nipple. I must be quivering with pleasure, weird I haven't got the tingles too. Back to the dream, they might arrive. I close my eyes.

"Bloody hell, you're going to...look, just try a little sip."

Something hard presses against my lips and fluid trickles into my mouth. Water. Not cola, water. I open my lips, allowing the flow to increase, because now, nothing else matters but quenching this thirst.

"Slowly now. I don't want you throwing up down here."

The bottle is taken away.

"More." My hand flips about in search of the bottle and is caught by his. So warm, so hot.

"Cassie, open your eyes, please," Hottie asks. My head lolls from side to side as I ponder his request. I don't want to wake up. I like this dream. "Cassie, I need you to open your eyes. I think we should get you to a hospital."

A hospital? I open my eyes. He's still there. "Am I having your baby? I missed that bit."

I get the flicker of a tingle when he laughs. "Only in my dreams, gorgeous."

"No, this is my dream. So I'm not pregnant?" I watch his eyes as they travel down my body.

"I'm going to say no. Not from this angle."

His face seems to crumple, and I want to kiss him better.

"Are you pregnant?" he asks.

Why has he started whispering?

"You tell me. You're the one building the shed to hold the manure."

"What? That makes no sense, Cassie. I'm worried about you. Do you know where you are?"

Hottie leans closer and peers into my eyes. He's worried about me, but why if I'm not in labour? I look up at the ceiling, then cast my eyes around, and see some boxes and some cases of water. Not a clue where I am. I shake my head. "Nope. But this will do. Let's get back to it. Hang on, shouldn't you be naked?"

Okay, the tingles are getting stronger, because he's now stroking my face and chuckling. I lean into his hand.

"I don't know what to do," he tells me. "I'm at a loss. Have some more water."

My eyebrows knot as I knock the water away. "Are you a virgin? How can you not know what to do? Listen, don't panic, because I'm sure you'll work it out." Hussy that I am, I spread my legs. He's patting my hand now. What's he saying?

"Cassie, open your eyes. I don't know how to help you. Have some more water."

"Not by patting my hand. You must know that much. So, that was a line about manhandling me and wobbly shoes." That last bit made no sense even to me. What the hell is going on? "Water," I demand, holding up a hand.

"Okay, but take it in slowly or you'll gag."

"I bet you say that to all the girls, virgin man." Ignoring the dimple, I snatch the water. I drink it down, toss the bottle to one side and hold out my hand again. "More."

"Okay. But take your time. If you don't remember coming here, do you remember the bee?" he asks me, and something twitches in the back of my mind.

"The bee?" I watch him nod. I could look at this man all day.

"You were wearing a bee costume. You banged on the door, asked for water and passed out. Dehydration or heatstroke, or both, is my guess. Do you remember?"

Much as I want to carry on looking at him, I close my eyes and think.

Oh no. The bee. The bee and the empty pouch. I peep at him through my lashes as it all comes flooding back. This isn't a dream.

This isn't a dream! Things just got a lot more interesting. Hottie sits holding one of my hands, his eyes full of concern. I sigh and give a little shudder. His eyes dart down my body again and I smile and wave my free hand to regain his attention.

"More."

Hottie is very compliant. I hear a rustle, a click, and he places another bottle in my hand. Taking another sip, I then lift it up and pour it over my head. That's better.

"Another."

"What are you doing?" He passes me another bottle, a smile bringing my friend's dimple into play.

"I must stink. My hair must look like I've borrowed Elizabeth's wig, and I don't like it. I can't have you looking at me like this. Just pretend I'm in a shower soaping my body." I pour the water over my head and rub it into my chest as it dribbles down. My nipples are still hard.

His eyes widen as he sucks in a breath before wiggling a little. I'm making him feel uncomfortable, or perhaps...I resist the urge to peep at his crotch, to do that I'd have to stop looking at that face.

"There's a shower here. Just over there. Might even be able to rustle up some soap. It's here somewhere." He flaps his free hand behind him. "But I'm not sure that's wise. I think we need to get more fluid into you, and maybe you should go to the hospital."

I squeeze the hand which still holds mine. "You are sweet, H. Do you know that? But as you yourself said, I'm not having a baby, and the NHS is very short staffed and very busy, so why waste their time?"

The tingles flicker again as he gives me one of his chuckles. If he actually did a belly laugh, I'd probably orgasm without him even touching me. I pour the rest of the bottle over my head before throwing it towards the others and pull on his hand to sit up properly. My brain settles back down quickly.

I might never get this opportunity again, so I go for it. "Are you going to find that soap?"

"No. If you won't go to the hospital, let me take you home. I'm sure there's someone out there worrying about you."

I shake my head and experience a slight wobble, but only for a few seconds. "No one. I'm all alone, and anyway, I am not going outside looking like this."

He's chewing his lip as his eyes sweep over me again. I need to increase the pressure. I'm wearing him down.

"Look, H, I'll sign a disclaimer if you like. Just let me shower and walk out of here with some dignity. I've been dressed like a bloody bee all day. It's the least I deserve. Now get the soap. I'm fine. You know I'll be quite safe in the shower, because you can stay and guard me."

I grin as he jumps to his feet and adjusts himself. Those jeans must be uncomfortable. He should take them off. He disappears behind a stack of boxes. I get to my feet and lean against a large box just to make sure I'm not a total liar. My head doesn't spin, and I listen as he hunts through his supplies before it all goes quiet. Where's he gone? Please don't tell me he's chickened out. Perhaps he's the caretaker? It must be gone six by now. Who else would be in a place like this at this time on a Saturday? After what feels like too long, I go in search of him. I feel a little wobbly, but nothing a giant pizza with a stuffed crust wouldn't cure. I can't find him, so I push open the nearest door. It's a store cupboard, currently empty except for a small stepladder holding some overalls and a couple of tins of paint. As I reach the next door, Hottie appears and holds up an industrial sized bottle of something.

"Eucalyptus and mint," he announces. "No dispenser."

I grin at him. "That should make me tingle, H, and I need little encouragement to tingle. You can dispense if necessary."

He grins, steps forward, and places his free hand on my hip. Instant sizzle. Instant tingle.

"Cassie, I don't know if you're always like this, or if it's heatstroke affecting you, but if you don't stop misbehaving we might find ourselves in trouble." He gives my hip a little squeeze, making me jump, and his eyes hit my boobs.

"Eyes up," I say. "Any lower and you'll see my granny knickers. I thought I was safe with them today."

Hottie steps closer, our bodies now touching. "I had to cut you out of that suit. I have seen everything already. Not as much as last night, granted. But yes, I've seen your granny knickers. It raised the question why a bee would be sensible enough to wear granny knickers but not a bra, but I decided that was unimportant, as I thought you might be dying. I was wrong, because now you want to tingle."

His eyes are doing things. So many emotions. So many twinkles, and don't start me on that dimple. It shouldn't be allowed.

"Take me to the shower." I whisper and have to clear my throat. "I refuse to tingle while I smell." Taking my hand, he opens the door next to us.

My eyes dart around the room. The floors and walls are tiled. Immediately in front is a row of hooks above a wooden bench, and to our right a row of cubicles with no doors. I look up and see the showerheads.

"You don't go in for privacy then?" I observe.

"We're not finished in here. We're not finished anywhere, as you may have noticed, but all that aside, I don't think you're shy, are you?"

"Not with the right people. I think we should test them out, don't you?" Shimmying down my grannies, I step into the shower. "H, I hope you're ready to dispense." I say, hitting the lever.

And then I scream.

Hottie grimaces. "No hot water. Waiting for the electrician to come back. It might be a tad cold."

"No shit. Dispense, H, dispense," I gasp.

He squeezes a large measure of eucalyptus and mint soap into his hands and steps forward. "Hold out your hand. I didn't think this through." His eyes don't leave mine as he offers me his gift of shampoo and body wash.

My lips twitch a smile as I step out of the flow of cold water, which I'm now used to. "That wasn't the deal." A laugh escapes as I watch his Adam's apple bob up and down, before looking down at his obvious approval. He shifts, knowing I know what he wants. "Come on, H, I know that someone who looks like you definitely isn't a virgin. Soap me up."

"I think the deal was I would watch you soaping up. But if you insist, bend your head this way." He soaps my hair, his strong fingers massaging my skull, and it's as sexy as if he were soaping my body. "Rinse," he commands.

I step back under the flow of water, and he follows me to rinse the soap from his hands; the water soaking the sleeves of his shirt.

"People would pay money to watch soap flow down your body," he tells me.

I risk opening an eye to see him adjusting himself again. So much fun. I step out of the flow again. “Next.” I’m using my deep, throaty, Nigella voice now, and he holds out the bottle.

“Hands,” he croaks.

“Oh, I think your hands are the ones I need,” Nigella tells him.

“Fucking hell. Two minutes.” He disappears around to the coat hooks. When he reappears, he’s naked except for his boxers and I wonder how they’re keeping control of what I should be able to see in the flesh.

“Are you shy, H? They need to go. After all, I’m at a disadvantage.” I point at my foof. Grateful I’d waxed recently.

His thumbs hook into the top of the boxers, and he pauses. “Are you sure? I mean, you did pass out, and I don’t want to take advantage of you. Or for you to have any regrets. You need to remember I offered to walk away.”

“H, get your knickers off and bring the soap!” Yet again, he obeys my command. Bloody hell! He’s a compliant Adonis. “Tell me that won’t disappear if you step into this cold shower.”

He’s laughing as he strides forward and pulls me to him. His mouth finds mine, his hands find everything else. All the tingles!

When he’s finished with my mouth, he’s on his knees between my legs and I’m not convinced they’ll hold my weight for much longer.

“You forgot the soap,” I gasp, grabbing his hair tighter and resting my shoulders against the partition wall for support as the tingles turn to fireworks.

“That’s because we’ll need it later.”

He laughs against my skin, the vibration sending a jolt through me, and then he’s suddenly back at my face, his nose brushing clumsily, then tenderly, against mine. I never thought noses could be erotic, but God, this one is.

“You’re something else.”

His voice rumbles low in his chest, and the sound seems to sink straight into me. His hands grip my waist and he lifts me up. I wrap my legs around him, my heart hammering against his. His laughter fades, and his eyes catch mine — steady, searching, almost undoing me.

“Ready?” he asks.

I nod, breath caught.

"You're sure? Say it."

"Yes," I whisper and hold my breath.

He presses into me, and every nerve sparks alive. Heat coils low in my stomach, rising fast, dizzying. My breath shatters into fragments as I cling tighter, body straining toward his. Each movement pulls me deeper, the pressure building like a storm I know I won't survive — and don't want to.

My tingles have got tingles and I can't wait for the fireworks to start up again.

H does not disappoint.

When the fireworks are over, we soap each other while catching our breath. My fingertips are prune-like, and I'm sure I'll get pneumonia, but I don't care. That was special. No, more than special. It was one of those moments that needs to be bottled and opened when you're in your dotage and you wonder if you've done enough with your life. That was enough. More than enough, and yet I want more. I place my hand on the lever.

"Done?" I ask as he grins at me.

"Only for now."

I turn off the water and kiss his nose. "Was the correct answer. Where are the towels?" I watch his eyebrows rise. "Please tell me you have towels."

He shrugs. "We're nowhere near ready for towels yet. I didn't think about getting dry. Even the hand dryers don't work."

My stomach rumbles and I clamp a hand over it. "Okaaay," I drag out the word. "You order us some food and we'll drip dry while we wait."

"You know I meant it when I said you're something else. Do you know that? I've never met a woman like you. Come on, I've got sandwiches upstairs. They'll do for starters." Taking my hand, he leads me around to the bench, where he pulls on his boxers, before picking up my granny knickers. He laughs at my expression. "I'll take that as a no. Here you go." He pulls his shirt over my head and takes his time to roll the sleeves to the proper length. It swamps me, but feels right. Appropriate. And it smells of him. "Perfect," he says, and his kiss is soft.

The air between us vibrates, taut and electric, but I'm starving. "Save your tingles for later," I tell him. You said you had food." I reluctantly push him away and pull open the door. As we approach the lift, I catch sight of the bee costume. "It put up a fight, then." I giggle. "Tell me the gloves survived. I was going to acquire those."

"Fought to the death. You want the gloves? Why? Some kind of souvenir? Will they remind you of me? Perhaps I should keep one, not that I'll ever forget you."

Hot and sweet. Of course they'll remind me of him!

"They will now. Originally, they were just an accessory for my silver dress. But I won't need them to make me think about you," I say as he recovers the gloves. "Thanks. Now where's this food?"

H is a total gentleman and only eats the half of the sandwich he's already taken a bite out of and then produces a protein bar from his laptop bag just for me.

"Not as good as a large pizza with stuffed crust, but thank you for feeding me, H." I'm sitting on the desk. H is on the chair and my toes rest on his knees. I tap them, and he runs his hands up my calves as he speaks.

My thoughts are scattered, my body thrumming with a pulse I can't slow. The tingles are back.

"My pleasure. Today has been the best day I've had since I can remember. I'd like to feed you properly. Can I take you out tomorrow?"

The tomorrow element suggests we won't be together tonight. I want a replay and definitely sooner than tomorrow, but I return his smile. "But of course. I don't have mind-blowing sex for just a sandwich, you know. I think that was worth at least a Sunday roast and maybe a midweek pizza."

His hands stop moving and he takes hold of my knees. He looks serious. I brace myself in case I've pushed my luck by suggesting two dates.

"Cassie, let me tell you, that was worth so much more. Mind-blowing. Hmm. Yes, I can agree with that, although I think we should give it another go, you know, to test your theory. But you're selling yourself short. I don't think I'll live long enough to take you out for all the meals you'll deserve. But like I say, I think we need to test your theory. Let the science decide."

"I agree. I love chemistry. When?" My heart is doing a little salsa around my chest. He likes me.

He clenches his fists and holds his arms aloft as though he's just scored the winning goal, and my pulse begins to race again.

"I feel like I just won the lottery. Whenever you like. I'm free tonight," he suggests.

I grin because that would have been my suggestion. Why Joel would think I wasn't interested, I don't know. Can't wait to tell him about this.

And then I see it.

A wedding band.

The bastard is married.

The tingles stop and the chills are back. I close my eyes and shudder before I take a last look at his lying, cheating face. And those beautiful eyes. He notices the look on my face, gets to his feet and steps forward, holding out his arms. I shake my head. Don't go crazy, I tell myself. Not yet. There might be an explanation.

"When did your wife die?" I ask.

He frowns. "She didn't. Why would you think that?"

I nod. "Ah, so you're still married."

"Technically, but—"

Now I can go crazy!

I should have known it was too good to be true. I pull back my arm, the fist already clenched, and I punch his wonderful, a bit on the large size, nose. Only my shot is off, because I'm so fucking mad. I catch him on his perfectly plump top lip. My knuckle collides with a tooth, and I yelp. Hoping against hope that it hurt him more than it did me.

He runs his tongue along his lip, looking for damage. "Cassie! Fuck me, you can punch. I'm not married, not really, because—"

I slide off the desk and march over to bee costume number three and yank it up, rummaging in the legs for my phone as I shout at him. "Not really married, but you still wear the ring. Not really married because you want to fuck girls who collapse at your feet. No, no, I take that back. I'm sure the collapsing and vulnerable bit isn't required. Yeah, I've heard about those not really marriages."

"HEY!" he booms. "I asked you if you were sure. I asked and I asked again."

"You did," I say through gritted teeth as I hit the call button, "But not with full disclosure. You didn't say, can I fuck you although I'm still married? Did you? DID YOU?" I scream at him.

"I AM NOT—"

He stops bellowing back at me as I greet Joel. "Joel, I need you to come pick me up and take me home."

"Why?" Joel asks.

"Because I'm asking you to. I've done something really bloody stupid, and I need you to come and get me and take me home."

"How stupid? Can't you get an Uber? I'll send you some money. I'm in the middle—"

Whatever he was doing wasn't as important, so I jump in.

"No. It's not the money. I'm virtually naked, I need to get home, and I want you to come and..." My voice breaks and I gulp the sob back down. "Forget it. I can't argue with you."

"Cass, are you crying? You don't cry. Don't hang up. I'm on my way. Where are you?"

I hear the concern in his voice, and the first tear escapes. Damn, I was saving the tears for later, after a bottle of wine, and after the knowledge that what I'd just experienced would never happen again had sunk in. I flip it away with an angry swipe of my hand as another arrives.

"I don't know. In town somewhere."

"You're naked, crying and you don't know where you are? Cass, what the hell has happened? What's going on?"

I hear the clunk of a car door.

"I'm in the car. Where am I heading?"

I have to look at H. He looks magnificent. Hands on hips, his muscles tense as he marches back and forth in his boxers. He slows down as he realises I'm looking at him.

"Oh, I can speak now, can I?" he spits at me.

"Sarcasm? That's what you think is appropriate? Fuck off, H. Where are we?" I sniff.

For a moment I don't think he'll tell me, but he thinks better of it, and gives me the address. I pass this on to Joel.

"Who's H?" Joel asks.

"I'll tell you later. How long will you be?"

"Five minutes. I'm only up the road. I'll text when I'm outside."

"Thank you." I hang up, lower my head, and let the tears and relief flow. I don't know how, but when I look up, H is standing next to me. He runs his hands up my arms and I curse silently at the shudder that runs up my spine. "Get your hands off me," I hiss.

"Don't cry. You're breaking my heart. My marriage—"

I thump my hands onto his chest and push him away. "Fuck off. I don't want to hear it."

"Why won't you let me explain?" he asks.

My phone pings. A glance at the screen tells me it's Joel. "No need. That ring on your finger says it all." Turning away, I walk to the door and grab the handle: I pull, then push, and pull again. The bloody thing won't open. "Let me out of here!"

"Push the button," H snaps as he walks towards me, but before he can reach me, I've hit the button and escaped.

Chapter 7

Christos

I WATCH TALL, DARK and handsome, who I now know is Joel, jump out of the car and wrap his arms around her. My fists clench at my sides as I watch him comfort her. I already think that should be my job. What the fuck just happened? It's no exaggeration to say that was the best sex I've ever had. But even as I think that, I know it was so much more than just sex. We connected, and that connection started last night. I've never experienced that before. Why wouldn't she let me explain? The ring on my finger is just a prop these days. A lie for anyone who might question my marital status. Which, of course, she did, and with devastating results. Had she let me explain, it would be me with my arms around her, probably deciding where we would spend the night.

My shirt rises as he turns her around and I get a glimpse of her perfect arse before he whisks her around to the passenger side and opens the door for her. A gentleman. As he returns, he notices me standing there and pauses as he squints at me. His head moving up and down, taking in my lack of clothes. I pull my shoulders back and lift my chin. Fuck him and fuck his judgement. I've done nothing wrong. When he's back in the car, he jerks his thumb towards me. Perhaps he remembers me from last night, or perhaps he's asking who H is. I hadn't got that far as to ask what it meant. It was cute. I liked it.

The car pulls away and I step back, pushing the door closed. This isn't the end. I still have her phone number. I'll call her and explain later, but I'll let her calm down first.

For the next hour, I clean up. As I hose down the shower cubicle, I remember she's still wearing my shirt. I'm going to be walking back into the hotel bare chested. Well, fuck them too. I'll be out of there tomorrow.

Before I switch off the lights, I snatch up her gloves and granny knickers. I'm going to return those one day, and it had better be sooner rather than later. For the time being, the mutilated bee body can stay there.

Back at the hotel, I ignore the stares as I cross the foyer and go straight to my room. I dress and head out to a local restaurant and eat what was probably a decent meal, but one I have no appetite for, and return to the hotel bar. Jake is on duty. The bar is empty.

"The usual?" he asks, holding up a glass.

"Yep, and keep them coming." I climb onto a stool.

"Bad day?" He places my drink on a coaster, squinting at my lip, and steps back as I throw my hands into the air.

"Only the fucking best. And then the worst. I'm probably not going to be the best company tonight." As I speak, I wonder if I should call her now.

"A woman." Jake nods knowingly. "Was she married? Did her bloke catch you at it? Do you want to talk about it?"

"That's a lot of questions. I don't know if she's married, but I doubt it. We didn't get around to talking, not really. Why did you ask that?"

"It seemed obvious. You walk in here with a thick lip, saying you had the best and then the worst day. My guess was some hot sex and then her husband came home. Fisticuffs ensued, and now she's called it a day. Probably for the best." Jake is wiping down the bar and pauses in front of me. "How did I do?"

"Wrong on every count. She gave me the thick lip, caught me unawares. It was the very last thing I expected. Although I concede the sex was something else." My smile is momentary as I wince at the pull on my damaged lip. "And trust me, it's not for the best. Why do you say that?"

"Because you're married." Jake grimaces and waves a finger at me. "None of my business, but is that what happened? Did your missus turn up?"

"I am not fucking married! But she wouldn't let me clarify my situation. Never even had a fighting chance!" I hold up my hands and jab a finger at my wedding band. "Like you, she sees this and jumps to con—" I stop speaking as someone punches my shoulder.

"Fabulous. So now you're talking about me. I thought I'd find you here." Cassie looks at Jake. "Believe nothing he says. He's a lying, cheating bastard."

I've recovered from the shock enough to slide from the stool and face her. "Cassie, let me get you a drink. We need to talk."

She waves a finger at me. "Oh, that ship has sailed, buster. I want my bee back. Bring it here. I'll pick it up from reception." She looks at me through puffy eyes. The crying wasn't really my fault. But I should comfort her. When I take a step closer, she steps back. "Don't you dare. No, don't speak, or I might just be on target next time. God knows how I missed a nose that size. Like I said, leave the bee at reception tomorrow. I have to return it."

"And what about my shirt?" She's still wearing it over a pair of leggings. If she hated me that much, surely she would have slung it at me as soon as she saw me. To my surprise, she starts to unbutton it.

"I forgot. You can take it now." She's on the last button and I step forward and catch her hands. She's naked underneath. There's only me and Jake here, but still.

"You gave Bob an eyeful of your foof last night. Traipsing out there topless might just finish him off." I let go of her hands and secure one button before she slaps my hands away.

"Don't touch me. I'll bring the shirt back tomorrow when I pick up the bee."

"That bee will never buzz again. Are you sure that's why you're really here?"

Cassie tuts at me and shakes her head. "You arrogant bastard. I'm here for the costume. If I don't take it back, I don't get paid. I need the money. So, yes, H, I'm here about the bee. I'm broke. If I wasn't, I'd be happy never to see you again."

I catch hold of her hand again. "We both know that's not true. But I can't do that. Let's get it now, because I'm leaving here tomorrow, so—"

Although I have hold of one hand, she makes a fist with the other before swinging it towards my face. This time it finds the intended target, and releasing her hand, I raise mine to my nose. It's bleeding.

"What, you thought you'd get another session in before running back to the wife? Up yours, H. Fuck. Off." I hear the catch in her voice. From the corner of my eye, I see Jake hold something towards me, but I ignore him.

"For the last time, I—"

Cassie reaches past me, lifts my drink and throws it in my face, before banging the glass on the bar. "I have regretted many things in my life. But meeting you comes in at number one." She holds up the flat of her hand as I begin my protest. "No, no. No more words, H. Have a nice life."

And then she's gone. Jake hands me the pile of clean napkins as I climb back on the stool.

"You didn't say it was her. I understand why it was the best day now, and I reckon a thick lip and a bloody nose are probably worth it. You should have gone after her. Another?" Jake doesn't await my reply. He drops ice into a clean glass and turns away to the optics. He places my drink on the bar. "On the house. If you're not married, although I would say if you're not, take the bloody ring off, why didn't you go after her?"

"Because I need her to listen to me, I need a fighting chance. She's clearly not in a listening mood. I'll call her tomorrow."

"She would have listened tonight. You just needed to press on."

I take a large swig of my drink. "Press on with what?"

"Explaining, winning her back. Whatever her mouth was saying, her body didn't look like it was agreeing with her words." Jake holds up his hands. "A blind man could see them."

I frown. "See what?"

Jake clears his throat. "Just remember, I'm only human. When you rebuttoned her shirt, her nipples stood to attention, and she leaned forward. I can't believe you didn't notice! Are you sure you're not married?"

"Yes, technically I'm married. But not for much longer. My wife left me for a man I thought was a friend. And I didn't notice her reaction because I was looking into her eyes." I empty my glass. "Another." When Jake places the drink in front of me, he drums his fingers on the bar. I can see he has something to say. "What? Just say it."

"Tell me to sod off if you don't want to answer, but I have to ask: you didn't do the 'my wife doesn't understand me', or a variation of it, did you?"

"I couldn't get a bloody word out. She asked if she was dead and I said no. She whacked me and called the bloke she was with last night to rescue her. You saw what she's like. She's totally unreasonable. Impossible."

Jake gives a sage nod. "Like I said, you should have gone after her. In my experience, sex is wild when they're mad."

"Thanks for that. Just the ticket to make me feel better." I finish my drink and slide off the stool. "I'm not going to be very good company. Fill that up, I'll take it with me."

Jake nods again. "I have so many questions, not least the bee thing. Oh, and the why you're wearing that ring, but I'll let you go. Tonight will be one of the great mysteries of my life."

I give a laugh, and my entire face hurts. I shake his hand. "Nice meeting you, Jake. I'll bring her back in one night and let her explain."

"Fighting talk. I like that. Good luck."

"I shouldn't, but I think I'm going to need it."

Back in my room, I clean my face cautiously. It's not that bad to look at, but it's bloody painful. I down my drink, clean my teeth carefully, fall into bed, and sleep fitfully throughout the night. I will never look at a bee in the same way again.

Chapter 8

Cassie

I STORM OUT OF the hotel with my head held high. Why does he have to be so gorgeous? I almost stayed to hear him out, but common sense has always been my strong point, and with the barman listening in, I wasn't about to listen to the lies he would spin to convince me out of my knickers again, much as I wanted to be convinced.

"How did it go?" Joel asks as I climb into the car. "You're going to cry again, aren't you? You should have let me go in."

"I wanted to look him in the eye and tell him to fuck off, and I did." I sniff, rubbing my knuckles into my eyes to stem the tears. "The bastard wanted me to go back into town and collect the costume. He's refusing to give it to me otherwise. I told him he just wanted another session."

"You were tempted, weren't you? That's why you're upset." Joel's tone isn't judgemental, nor is it teasing. It's more a statement of fact.

"Of course he tempted me. I knew he would, but I was hoping my anger would douse the flames, or maybe even...I don't know, exorcise him in little. All it did was confirm what might have been. What I was losing, because that's what it feels like. Like I've lost someone. It was so special, Joel. Magical almost. And that's why I'm upset. Had I known he was married, I would have been embarrassed about my state of undress, thanked him for saving me, and gone home, sad that the one man I've been attracted to in months was already taken. Never knowing what I was missing. But he didn't tell me, so now I do. Ah, shit Joel, I don't think I'll ever find that again." I blink away the tears. "Take me home. I need to wallow in my misery. I'm broke and broken-hearted. Why didn't he tell me?"

"Can I be honest with you?" Joel shoots me a quick glance.

"No." There's silence for a while. I know he's going to tell me something I don't want to hear. But the masochist in me gives in. "Go on then, spit it out."

"You're blaming him to make yourself feel better," Joel says and falls silent again.

"Explain. How the hell did this become my fault?"

"He didn't lie. You didn't ask, you didn't notice the wedding ring. He wasn't hiding it, was he? From what you told me, you were a very willing partner. Who made the first move?"

"That's got nothing to do with it!"

"So it was you."

"Yes, but I was suffering from heatstroke. So it doesn't count." I really don't like the way this conversation is going, and I fold my arms, defensively, across my chest.

"Ah, so he took advantage of you, knowing you weren't fully in control of your faculties. You're right, he's a bastard."

"Well...no, but still." I'm pathetic, I'm beginning to realise that now.

"Want to elaborate on, no?"

"He asked if I was sure. Several times, bloody hell, Joel, he even said he didn't want me to do something I'd regret. But I defy any woman to walk away from what was on offer. Even a nun would drop her knickers if they were feeling what I did. The married bit was more important, though. He didn't say you might be suffering from heatstroke, and I'm married, are you sure?"

Joel merely nods and doesn't pass comment as he pulls up outside my house.

"No more words of wisdom?" I ask.

Joel pouts and his shoulders twitch. "Not really."

"Just say it. I couldn't possibly feel any worse. I know you want to say more."

"Okay, you asked, but based on what you've told me, he did nothing wrong. Quite the opposite. He tried to save you from yourself. He was a gentleman. But a gentleman who is also a bloke, who faced with a very attractive, naked, if you ignore the granny knickers, woman, offering it on a plate, and insisting on magical sex, he caved. Is that his fault?" Joel rubs his hands over his face.

I know he's hiding a smile at this latest predicament of mine, but when he lowers his hands, he looks me in the eye, his face deadly serious. "Am I taking you back to the hotel where you can apologise and take advantage of him again? Or am I coming in and getting drunk watching you get drunk?"

I run over our conversation. Is Joel right? Everything he's said is true. But he's ignoring the fact that H is married. Then the realisation hits and I gasp. "It's your fault. Not mine. Not his. Yours."

Joel throws up his hands. "How the hell did you make this my fault?"

"You knew. You knew, and you didn't tell me," I accuse.

"Knew what?" Joel demands. "That he was married?"

"Yes. You came back from the bar, told me he was hot and I wasn't interested, but you didn't tell me why. Your. Fault." My arms are back across my chest, punctuating the seriousness of his error.

Joel wags a finger at me. "You're being ridiculous. And you went home. How the hell was I supposed to know the very next day you were going to dress up as a bee and throw yourself at him in your granny knickers?" He's laughing now and if I wasn't heartbroken I suppose I could see the funny side, but I am and I refuse to be cheered up.

"Stop laughing. I'll forgive you, but in future you tell me the important bit first. In the future, that conversation will be, he's married. Hot, but married. No misunderstandings that way. Understand?"

"Yes. Noted and underlined. I will never put you in that situation again." His lips twitch, but he holds back the smirk. "What are you going to do about the costume? Three hundred quid is a lot of money."

"I told him to leave it at reception for me. He said he couldn't because he's leaving today. Going back to the wife, no doubt, so I hit him again. I'll call the hotel tomorrow and see if he's as much a gentleman as you make out. If he doesn't, well...I don't know."

"Do the audio audition. Come on, Cass, you'd be helping me out too. I'll come round on Monday and we'll do it then. You never know, they might not like it."

"How dare you! Of course they'll like it. I'm an actor, you know!" I punch him on the arm. "I'm going in now. You go and find some fun somewhere, because I won't be good company."

"So that's a yes." Joel leans across and kisses my cheek. "I'll see you on Monday."

Once in the house, I snatch a bottle of wine we didn't drink from the table and take it to my room and sit cross-legged on the bed and run over everything that's happened as I swig from the bottle and list the facts. I do like a good list.

My conclusions:

I almost had the love of my life. Probable fact. (I'm an actor, I'm allowed to be dramatic.)

It was the best sex I've ever had or am likely to have in the future. Fact.

Joel is at fault, he should have told me. Fact.

H is at fault, he should have told me. Fact.

Finally, I'm at fault because I didn't ask. Fact.

Nor did I notice the very obvious, and not at all hidden, wedding ring. Fact.

But I slept with a man I didn't know. I didn't even know his name, and I still don't come to that. Fact.

I did all the running, but in my defence, he was very suggestive last night. Fact.

He is very sexy. He knows what a girl needs. All facts.

But the facts don't help. Because despite knowing all this, I still want him. And that's wrong. I know the destruction that giving in will cause, because I've lived through it, but I still want him. Perhaps it's just as well he's leaving tomorrow. But I don't want him to. Another fact!

And now I'm crying again. I'm pathetic. Fact.

Chapter 9

Christos

AT SEVEN, I GIVE up any pretence of sleep, go down and have breakfast, convincing one of the servers he wants to help me load the car once the breakfast service is over. By eleven, I'm driving the short distance to my new home.

I park outside, on double yellows and open the hatchback. Unlocking the door to the house, I shout a hello, wait a few seconds, and getting no reply, I unload the car, piling my belongings in the hallway. I'm about halfway through when Miss Allison appears.

"Mr Baros, I need a word."

"Miss Allison, what a pleasant surprise. How are you and Elizabeth?" I'm already grumpy and tired and could do without further irritation, so I'm going for charming.

"We'd be happier if there wasn't a car parked illegally outside our home."

"I'm sure, but I won't be long. There's not much left to do, and then I'll park somewhere sensible. Are you enjoying the sunshine? I'd rather there was a bit of a breeze. It's too hot to be lugging boxes about." I pick up the next box and step around her, taking it into the hall. "So you and your sister are well?" I'm wondering why she's not answering me. She's just standing there staring and sucking on a lemon. As I return to the car, she steps to block my way and lifts her glasses to her nose to peer at me.

"I had come out to thank you for the flowers. It was thoughtful, but now I'm not sure."

I haven't got a clue where this is going, so I smile at her. "You're most welcome. It was kind of you to take the time to show me around. I hope you liked them."

"Oh, that wasn't for you. That was for Stephen. Are you a thug, Mr Baros?" she asks, allowing the glasses to swing from their chain.

"I most certainly am not, so we're building quite a list." As I can't get past her without being rude, I list them off on my fingers. "Not a sex maniac, not an axe murderer, not a thug. Excuse me. I'd better get this done before a parking attendant appears."

"Oh, you won't see one of those on a Sunday. Which is the most ridiculous state of affairs. Sunday is the worst. Sightseers. Our bridge is famous, as I'm sure you know." Miss Allison flicks her hand towards the majestic bridge. "But you are avoiding the subject. What happened to your face? It appears you have been fighting."

Ah, that's what she was staring at. I clasp a hand over my chest. "Me? I'm offended that you would think that. I have not. We're renovating at work. I had a mishap in the shower." It's as close to the truth as she's going to get. She doesn't look convinced.

"You have a shower at work?"

"I do. There's also a gym, or there will be once we get finished."

"I'm not going to ask what you do. It all sounds most unsavoury. I think, Mr Baros, you should stop dawdling, get that car unloaded, and stop breaking the law. That's an accident waiting to happen. I must get back to Elizabeth. She's in the garden and can get quite carried away with the secateurs if not monitored." Miss Allison gives a sharp nod and leaves me to it.

Half an hour later, the car has been unloaded, parked legally, and I'm standing in the hallway looking at the boxes. I've got two flights of stairs to lug them up and I reckon it will take me at least ten trips. It's far too hot to be doing this. How Cassie managed in that bee costume yesterday is anyone's guess. No wonder she collapsed. And here I am again! Back to thinking about Cassie. Stomping into the kitchen, I locate a glass and fill it with water. I leave it on the hall table, lift the first two boxes, and take them to my room. Once there, I strip off my clothes and pull on a pair of shorts before returning to the rest of my belongings. It takes far too long, but I have only one mishap when a box slips from the pile on the first landing. My room now looks like a bomb has hit it, but that's enough for one day.

I need a shower, which reminds me that I've got no toiletries. I make do with plain old water and add shopping to my mental to-do list.

Once I've freshened up, I refill my glass and wander into the garden. I head for the top corner where the trellis provides some shade, take a seat, and decide now is the time to call Cassie and make her listen to me. Before I can dial, there's a piercing scream from next door, and having heard it before, I know it's Elizabeth. I hurry to the wall that divides the two gardens, and balancing on a large pot containing very prickly rosemary, I peer over.

"Mr Baros! I would never have shown you around if I'd known you were a peeping Tom! Get down! We value our privacy." Miss Allison is walking towards me, with Elizabeth cowering behind.

"I heard a scream. I thought Elizabeth may be—"

"As you can see, she is perfectly well. A spider. That's all it was, a spider. It does not warrant an invasion of our privacy." The nostrils are flaring, and the hand is flapping.

"I was simply trying to help, and—"

"No help required. Please remove your being. I haven't got a cardigan on."

It's a losing battle, so I offer more unnecessary apologies and return to my seat. It's too hot. Perhaps a dip in the hot tub would work. I'm sure it doesn't need to be heated. I don't really know how they work. Ana hadn't got that far down her list of acquisitions. I lift the cover and stare at the controls, pushing a couple of buttons. The water churns, and I dip my hand in. Perfect temperature. I place my phone on the side and climb in, only squeaking once when the cold water hits my manhood.

I shake the water from my hands and call Cassie. Her muffled voice grunts at me.

"Who is this?"

"Cassie, it's me. Um...H. Why do you call me that? Anyway, I don't care. We need to talk."

"Fuck off."

Despite her words, she doesn't hang up.

"You don't mean that. You know we need to talk. Let me take you out to dinner and explain."

"I don't need an explanation. What I need is my bee back."

She sounds odd.

"I'll bring it with me," I tell her. "Have you got a cold?"

"Um, no. Oh, it's hay fever. Not that it's any of your business. Drop the bee to the hotel, and...how did you get my number, and how do you know my name? Joel? Bloody Joel. I'm going to bloody kill him."

"No, I..."

I stop speaking when she hangs up, but call her straight back. It rings twice before going to her answer service. I'm guessing she's rejected me, or more likely is giving Joel an undeserved telling off. I leave a message.

"There's no point in avoiding me. I won't give up. You can have your bee costume back, but I'll be delivering it in person. I'd like to do that over a meal, or even just a drink, but you will listen to me, and we will absolutely test your theory. Call me."

I place my phone on the side and dunk under the water. It feels like I'm making headway. We almost had a complete conversation, and my face didn't get damaged. I wonder who taught her to punch? She's got a pretty good shot. My text alert sounds and I grab my phone. It's from Cassie:

I've listened to your message, you're too sure of yourself. All I want from you is my bee back. Let me know when you've dropped it at the hotel. No calls, no meal, no drink, nothing but the bee. Text me.

I reply immediately.

Ah ha. You didn't mention the tingles. You still want the tingles. Me too. That was fucking hot. But it was more than sex. We both know that. I'm not taking the mutilated bee to the hotel. I'll drop it off to you. Where do you live?

I know it's a long shot, but it's worth a try. I watch the little dots dance about as she types a reply.

Like I'd be stupid enough to give you my address. The tingles are but a distant memory. The bee, however, is much needed. Leave it at the hotel, H. Don't be a super bastard.

Liar! I've hardly stopped thinking about our mind-blowing meeting. I was going to start a little sexting with you. I've never done that before. Fancy giving it a go? Bet I can make you quiver. Shall we try it? I'll start. Put one hand between your legs, the other on one of those glorious nipples ... imagine my breath on your neck.
How does that feel?

As the little dots do their stuff, I adjust myself, grateful Miss Allison and Elizabeth can't see what simply texting Cassie does to me. Her message arrives.

Looks like you have too much time on your hands, but I, on the other hand, am busy. You carry on and pleasure yourself; I don't need to. Better still, get the wife involved. I think you must be neglecting her. Let me know about the bee. Any more of this nonsense and I'll block this number.

I start to type my response when there's another scream from next door. Followed by a call for help. I tilt my head and listen. Someone is whimpering. Leaving my phone, I run across to the rosemary pot and stick my head above the parapet. Surrounded by broken pots, Elizabeth is lying on the ground, her arm trapped beneath her. A small stepladder lies on its side next to her. Miss Allison hurries up the path towards her and spots me as I pump myself up and get a leg on top of the wall. I pause.

"I was coming over to help. Is that okay?" I ask. It should be a stupid question, but there's a broom and a rake propped against the shed. I've had enough injuries for one weekend. Turns out it was.

"A stupid question, Mr Baros. Why are you dithering?" Miss Allison drops to her knees, wincing as one finds a piece of the broken pottery. "Elizabeth, dear, where does it hurt?"

"Everywhere," Elizabeth wails as I drop onto the lawn.

I head for the shed and collect the brush leaning on the door. "Move back Miss Allison. Let's not move her until we've cleared this out of the way" Miss Allison merely nods, a miracle in itself, and I sweep the area clear while Elizabeth whimpers. Once done, I kneel next to her. "I'm going to move you, Elizabeth. Is that okay?"

She ignores me and looks at her sister. "Is it? Is he a doctor?"

"He is dear. A near naked one, but we'll deal with that once we've sorted you out. Proceed, Mr Baros."

I turn a wailing Elizabeth onto her side and wait while she catches her breath. Her wrist is already swelling, and I'm guessing it's broken. I move behind her head. "We need to sit you up. Hold your right hand against your body. Can you do that for me?" She does and I sit her up. She lets out another scream, and I give her a moment before I place my hands under her arms. "Now we're going to get you up on your feet. Are you ready?"

"I think so. Don't let me fall again." Her face is white, and she's shaking all over.

"I won't. One, two, three." I lift her to her feet. She's so tiny, it's like lifting a child, and taking hold of her good hand, I wrap my other arm around her back. "Let's see if we can get you into the house and make you more comfortable while we assess your injuries."

I help her take a step forward, and she screams again. "I can't. Sorry, doctor, but I can't. It hurts," she cries out.

"Then I'll carry you in, and Miss Allison can call an ambulance." I lift her into my arms, and she giggles.

"Oh my. Jennifer, can you see me?" she asks. "A naked doctor has me in his arms."

"Of course I can see you. Be serious, Elizabeth, you have injuries. This way, Mr Baros."

Miss Allison leads the way to a farmhouse style kitchen, which houses an aga that looks older than the house. There's a wing-backed chair by the door and I place Elizabeth in it, while Miss Allison pushes the foot stool closer. I look at the ankle and, unlike her wrist, I can't see anything obvious.

"We should call an ambulance. I think she's broken either her wrist or her ankle or both," I tell Miss Allison.

"Yes, I agree. Carry on. I shall listen."

"Oh, I don't have my phone on me. It's in the other garden."

"Then follow me. I can't leave you alone with Elizabeth. She hasn't got her stockings on. Why are you naked? Are you an exhibitionist?"

"I was in the hot tub. I wasn't expecting to leave the garden, so—"

"In this weather, are you mad? Sit." She points to the chair next to the telephone table and lifts the receiver with a shaking hand.

"Would you like me to do it?" I keep my voice soft. "This has all been a bit of a shock."

Miss Allison nods and I lead her to the chair and then make the call.

After a very frustrating conversation, I turn to Miss Allison. "It's going to take hours. This isn't a big enough emergency, and they are very busy with the current heatwave. They've asked that, if possible, we take Elizabeth in the car. Would you like me to drive you, or would you rather wait?"

Her hands clasp her face, and she shakes her head. We enter into another few minutes of pointless conversation before she agrees the car would be best. I tell the operator that an ambulance won't be needed and hang up.

"You will put some clothes on, won't you?" she asks.

"I'll do that right now. But I'm going to have to go back over the wall. Do you need to escort me through the kitchen?"

She grins at me. I kid you not, a proper full smile, dimples in her cheeks, the full works. "I think I can trust you. Elizabeth and I will make ourselves decent in your absence."

Using the steps Elizabeth fell from, I hop over the wall, collect my phone, run up to my room, quickly change my wet shorts for jeans and pull on a polo shirt. I doubt Miss Allison will approve, but I'm not putting a suit on. Grabbing my keys and wallet, I leave by the front door. Knowing my afternoon and probably my evening are going to be spent at the hospital, I sigh out my frustration. This is not the weekend I was expecting after rescuing Cassie from her bee outfit. I had a far more entertaining day planned out.

I was right. It's eight o'clock, and we're still here. The nurses, who were sweet to us at first, now only come near when necessary. Miss Allison doesn't encourage small talk. I've done my bit and kept them supplied with drinks and questionable sandwiches. I've even managed a call to my mother, and under duress, taken a photograph of the sisters sitting in the little cubicle to convince her I hadn't intentionally ignored her earlier calls. She calmed down then. Although she wasn't happy that I'd found a shared house to live in, and she gave me a list of things to look out for: sex maniacs, junkies, thieves. Miss Allison was too far away to hear, thank goodness, or she'd have had more deviants to add to her list and grill me about.

The doctor reappears. He looks as knackered as I feel.

"The good news is that although the wrist is broken, the ankle is only sprained. We'll get that strapped up for you, but we can't plaster the wrist until the swelling goes down. As Elizabeth can't walk or use her hand, and you tell me she wouldn't cope at home, I've arranged for her to have a bed for the night. The nurse will be along in a minute to wheel her up to the ward. Visiting time is over, so you'll have to say your goodbyes here."

"Are you telling me I can't stay with her?" Miss Allison asks.

"I am. She'll be perfectly safe. You can come in and see her tomorrow," the harassed man answers.

There's more back and forth, but I zone it out. I'm starving and I still haven't got back to Cassie. She probably thinks I've taken heed of her threat to block me. Although I don't believe she would. I hope she won't.

Back in the car, I convince Miss Allison that having a fish and chip takeaway on a Sunday night is perfectly acceptable, particularly in times of stress. She caves in, and we eat it in relative silence at her kitchen table. I don't really want to leave her alone; she looks tiny, pale and lost, but when she slides the plates into the sink, and tells me I should go, I jump up.

"If you're sure. You have my number now. Please call if you need me. I'll be going into work first thing, then I'll come back around ten and take you to the hospital. We'll plan what happens then once we know what's happening with Elizabeth. Luckily, work hours are fluid at the moment."

"Thank you, Mr Baros. I am in your debt. She will be okay, won't she?"

Miss Allison stiffens as I pull her into a hug. "She'll be fine. It's one night, and you did everything you could to make her understand what was happening. You never know, she might surprise you."

"Yes, you're right. Why are you hugging me? I think you should unhand me." Her words don't hold their usual sting.

I release her and step back. "Because you needed it. Never underestimate the power of a good hug. Goodnight, Miss Allison."

"Goodnight, Mr Baros." And there it is, another smile. I've given up asking her to call me Chris, but I like making her smile.

I'm exhausted, but I need to shower, and I'm grateful the house is quiet when I get home, because I don't think I have it in me for polite conversation with a stranger. I strip off, grab my towel, and head to the shower room. Damn it. Still no toiletries. All I have is my razor and shaving foam. I tiptoe down to the next landing and go into the bathroom. Oh god, it smells like Cassie in here. I pick up the nearest bottle. Yep. Strawberry body wash. It'll have to do. If I'm going to dream about her all night again, I might as well smell like her, too. Glutton for punishment, me.

When I get back to my room, I send a text to Cassie.

Goodnight, my little bee. I hope you're thinking about me. I'm not only thinking of you, but I can smell you, too. It's not eucalyptus and mint, because I'm not sure I could cope with the tingles, but strawberries remind me of you, too. Just typing that is making me hard. I need to see you, to speak to you. Let me know where and when. Love & Lust H xxx

I flop onto the bed, wondering if she'll reply. She does.

You woke me up! Not impressed H. If I can conjure up the smell of boiled cabbage and old boots, I might get back to sleep thinking about you. Cute that you've got a nickname for me. (NOT) I want my little bee back. Let me know when you've dropped it at the hotel. I really do need the money, and Joel tells me you're a gentleman. I beg to disagree, but if he's correct, prove it. Anything else is not happening.
No lust, and certainly no love, Cassie. (Note the absence of kisses)

Liar! I set my alarm and try to sleep.

Chapter 10

Cassie

I DON'T KNOW HOW long I carried on drinking and crying, but I have the headache from hell as I drag myself out of bed. I rummage in the bathroom cabinet and find the last two paracetamol, which is pretty impressive given I can barely open my puffy eyes, then I drag myself back to bed. It's Sunday, I have nothing better to do, I might as well wallow the day away. At some point, thinking about H and my lack of funds stops becoming so important, and I drift back to sleep.

What the hell was that? I sit up, causing my head to swim, and listen, or try to. It's difficult to hear anything with my heartbeat echoing in my ears. There's movement outside on the landing. There are footsteps going upstairs. Are we being burgled? Probably not, because they're on their way back down. I creep out of bed and lock my door. Then freeze. Whoever it is, they're on their way back up. I look at my chest of drawers and wonder if I have the strength to drag it in front of the door. No need, they've gone upstairs again. Oh? They're coming back down again. What the hell?

The front door slams, and I stand with my ear pressed against the door. Have they gone?

Note to self: Fear is an excellent cure for a headache. My heart might be threatening to explode, but at least my head is no longer pounding.

Knowing I wouldn't relax until I'd investigated, I open the door and step out onto the landing, ready to dash back in. But when I hear nothing further, I decide to see what was going on upstairs. Then it occurs to me that perhaps Steve is home? Did he miss his flight? I tiptoe to Steve's door and tap on it. When I get no reply, I open the door slowly. Empty. Just a dent on his bed where his bag must have been.

Taking the stairs two at a time, I hit the upper landing in record time. Everything looks normal. I check the bathroom and end up at Jerry's old room, and taking a deep breath, I knock on the door. I'm not in the mood to meet new people, because look where that gets me, and I must look a sight, but this mystery needs solving. No reply, so I push the door open. Boxes. Boxes and suit bags laying across the bed. It would appear I have a new housemate.

The door slams again. Shit. Whoever my new housemate is, they're back. I fly back down the stairs and shut myself in the bedroom. I'm really not in the mood for meeting someone new. Tomorrow will be soon enough.

Throwing myself on the bed, I grab my phone and text Steve.

I've just had heart failure as someone was banging about in the house. My investigation tells me someone has moved in? They've gone again now. What's going on? Who is it? Will I like them?

I wait for his reply, and when it doesn't come, I fall back to sleep. I'm woken by my phone ringing, and see it's an unknown number, so I snap out a greeting as I snuggle back down and close my eyes. In seconds, I bolt upright, my eyes wide open. It's H.

H wants to talk, and he wants to take me out to dinner. Despite the rumble in my tummy caused by the mention of food, I tell him to fuck off. I tell him I want my bee back. He thinks I'm ill because my nose is still blocked from all the crying, so I tell him I have hay fever, and demand to know how he got my number. Joel! It must be Joel. I hang up and call Joel.

"Cass. How are you feeling today? Because I've got a mammoth hangover, but I'll try to be sympathetic. I'm off tomorrow for a couple of weeks, but we'll do the audition first. I'll treat you to a McDonald's now if you're up to it."

He sounds cheerful. That won't last for long.

"Did you tell H my name?" I demand, ignoring the offer of food.

"No. Oh, wait. Probably. I thanked him for picking you up when you fell at the hotel. Said something like thanks for helping Cassie. Why?"

"When did you give him my telephone number?"

"I didn't." Joel yawns, sounding bored.

"You must have. Someone did. He just called me."

"He did?"

Now I've got his attention.

"He did. Yes. So, are you still saying you didn't give him it?"

"I am. But get to the important stuff. What did he say? Did you apologise?"

"WHAT? No, I didn't apologise! I did nothing wrong. Let me tell you, he'll be forever grateful for what I did."

"What, the thick lip and the nosebleed?" Joel laughs.

"Well, perhaps not that, but the other stuff. Why did you give him it, Joel? It's hard enough getting him out of my brain as it is." I fall back on my pillows with a sigh. "Do you think he'll call back?"

"You hung up on him, didn't you?" Joel accuses. "You're your own worst enemy. Do you know that?"

"I did, and I'm not. It's called self-preservation." I'm pouting now, pouting with my eyes shut because they're so sore. I need an ice pack or something.

"It's called cutting off your nose to spite your face. Talk to the man. Listen to what he has to say. He's not giving up by the sound of it, and if it's over the phone, your granny knickers will stay put. Look, I need food. Do you want to come?"

"No thanks. Still wallowing and I can't open my eyes. But think about this, if you didn't give H my number, who did? There is no one else, so I know it's you, but I forgive you. I know you probably thought it was for the best."

"Cass, I'm going. I didn't give him your number. Perhaps he looked at your phone while you were with him."

I think about this for a second but dismiss it. "No. It was still in my leg."

"Yep, you've lost the plot. Did you hear what you just said? Yes or no to food. I can't have ridiculous conversations. I'm getting hangry."

"No."

Joel leaves the conversation, and I listen to the message H has left. The man is trying to blackmail me. He's taking bee number three hostage unless I go out with him or tell him where I live. We'll see about that! I can't speak to him, I might cave in, so I send him a text demanding the return of my bee. We then have an exchange that leaves me hot under the collar of his lovely smelling shirt, which I'm still wearing. He tells me the sex was hot, as if I didn't know that! He says that he'll never forget my tingles, nor will I, but I'm not telling him that. Then he says he's going to sext me, and tells me to touch my foof, and I almost do, because guess what? They're back. So I decide to make him text me what I wouldn't listen to. I tell him to sext his wife, hoping that he'll explain why he's wearing that bloody ring, but isn't really married.

But he doesn't reply. So I wait. But nothing. I knew it. I expect he's sexting her. Any port in a storm and all that. Bastard.

Was that a scream? It was. And a shout. It came from the garden, so I hurry to the window and wince as the light hits my sore eyes. It appears a naked man has just jumped into next door's garden. He looks a little like H. Stop it! I've got it so bad. I'm hallucinating now. But whoever it was, good luck to him. He'll probably be in a cauldron in the next five minutes. Brave man. I turn away when my phone pings a message alert. H! I rush back to my phone. I'm disappointed.

Hi Cass, sorry about the lack of warning. I've had a nightmare. One of the crew's luggage didn't arrive. But yes, we have a new housemate. His name is Chris, and he's moving in today. Can't tell you much more. I haven't met him. Miss Allison did the viewing. He seemed nice over the phone, though. I'll call you in the week. But have to dash, need to see if we can rent some audio equipment in the back of beyond. Steve x

He's never met the man, and he's allowed him to move in with a vulnerable, innocent young woman? Okay, not innocent, but still. It means my financial situation just got a little better. And why hasn't H come back to me?

I stop thinking about H for a few seconds when I hear my new housemate fly up the stairs. He survived! I really should introduce myself, but I just can't. Not until I look and feel human again. Maybe later. His bedroom door just slammed. He's on the move. Back down the stairs, I'll starve to death at this rate. Why can't he just go...oh he did. The front door just slammed. Just as well I'm not sleeping, or he'd be waking me up. I'd better grab some food while he's gone.

That's better. I've showered, and I'm now going to tuck into cheese and digestive biscuits, while listening to the oldies radio channel. My mum used to love it. Makes me weepy, but then I'm in a weepy sort of mood. They knew how to write a love song in the old days. When I've demolished the pack of digestives, I head back to the kitchen. There's a cucumber in the fridge with my name on. I smirk, wondering what H would tell me to do with it. Well, sod him. These puffy eyes need it more than his venture into sexting.

Joel sends me the audition script for the audio book. It's corny, and yes, I was right, pornographic. I'm as broad-minded as the next person, extramarital liaisons excepted, but I have to admit in my mind I'm imagining it's me and H cavorting from one scene to the next, but I don't want to act it. Although I'm a pretty talented actor, even if I do say so myself, but I can't channel sexy well. I know my limitations. At the click of a finger, I can do happy, desolate, angry, evil, and all the other emotions required of me, should I ever get another job, just not sexy. But I'm broke, so I have to give it a go.

I wish H would give me back that bloody bee. I doubt the agency will give me more work until I return it.

Oh god, now I'm thinking about H again. I drift back off to sleep, my phone on my chest. I'm awoken by a text from H and smile at the message. He's got it as bad as I have. But I'm not married and am allowed to have *it.* Ah, he's thinking about me, even calling me his little bee. Ooh, I wonder if he's stroking himself as he...stop! This can't go on.

I bang out what I consider to be an amusing but sarcastic response and set my phone to silent. I need to get some sleep tonight, and getting into a conversation with H, however amusing and tingle arousing is not on the cards. He'll probably haunt my dreams anyway.

Chapter 11

Christos

I WAKE UP LONG before my alarm goes off, and pulling on my shorts, I head to the kitchen in search of coffee. I must hit a supermarket today, because I feel guilty using my housemates' supplies. But use them I do, and I make a pot of coffee and sit at the table, going through my emails, while eating a bowl of sugary cereal. I'm guessing I'm home alone, because nothing has changed since I was here yesterday. I load the crockery into the dishwasher. A single plate and knife are in there. Perhaps someone came in while I was out, so I need to keep the noise down. I send a text to George to let him know my movements, and head for the shower.

When I leave the house, I'm smelling like Cassie again, and before I drive away, I text her.

Good morning. I'm guessing you're still in bed, and the thought that I'm not there with you is killing me. Look forward to hearing from you later, but in the meantime, you'll be in my thoughts.
Love & even more LUST (it's been too long, little bee) H x

I'm regressing into a fucking teenager. But at least I'm smiling as I drive through the still quiet streets into town.

My first job is to move the bee costume, so I park outside the office and get it into the car before I do anything else. The fitters and electrician have promised to attend today. If they get their stuff done, I can bring the IT guys back in. Once the IT is up and running, I can get staff in and trade properly, however bad the office looks, but I know Gemini will want both. Some contractors arrive and I let them in and answer their questions as best I can, then pull out the plans and wander from room to room. Making notes, before checking the time and calling George as promised.

"So I've done the rounds. We have three key areas that need prioritising. First reception, public facing areas need to look the business. Next are the toilets and shower areas. Staff and clients alike need privacy and comfort while here, and almost as essential, are the boardroom and the main office. I know you think we should get my office done, but really I think that's the last on the list. If we get the boardroom sorted, we can see individual clients and hold meetings. My office can wait, as well as all the other smaller rooms, because having somewhere comfortable for the staff to work is more important. I can perch anywhere. If I'm honest, I can't see me sitting in all that splendour, so that can go to the bottom of the list. What do you think?"

We bat the pros and cons back and forth and come to an agreement for the best way forward. When George tells me he's on his way, I panic. If I don't get a move on, I'll be late for Miss Allison. I call her from the car and tell her I'm on my way.

"Thank you. I'll be waiting. I've spoken to Elizabeth, and she wants to come home. We need to make it happen. A united front if they give us any trouble, Mr Baros. Agreed?"

I agree because I don't know what that will entail and arguing is pointless.

"Thank you. I've a lot to thank you for, Mr Baros, and I've left a token of my thanks with the woman. Hopefully, it will be waiting for you."

Five minutes later, I arrive to find Miss Allison standing on her doorstep. She looks at her watch, and I glance at the dash. I'm two minutes early.

When we arrive at the hospital, we hear Elizabeth has had a disturbed night and the rehabilitation nurse is concerned that she won't be able to manage at home. Eventually, Miss Allison, and me by default, agree that a bed can be set up in the living room so she won't need to climb the stairs, and a district nurse can come in every couple of days to check on her. I'm responsible for moving the spare bed downstairs. Elizabeth is packed up and I take them home. Elizabeth is dozing in the chair before I can escape.

"I understand that you have to work, Mr Baros, but as long as the bed is moved before bedtime, we'll let you get back. I wouldn't be surprised if they don't send someone to check on us."

"What time is bedtime?"

"Nine thirty as a rule. Will that be acceptable?"

"It will. Now, before I go, I also have to get some shopping in. I can't keep borrowing from my housemates. Is there anything I can get for you?"

Ten minutes it takes to write a four-item list. I shove it in my pocket and head for the supermarket. When I return, I hand her the groceries, and head next door to unload mine. I've probably bought too much stuff, but I'll let 'the woman' know she can help herself. As I enter the kitchen area, I see two mugs, two plates and a lot of crumbs. She's had company. Next to the hob is a floral cake tin with a card on top. It's for me. I peep into the tin. It's a sponge cake. I open the card, its message short and sweet.

Mr Baros, thank you.
You have been most kind, a true gentleman.
A token of our thanks.
Jennifer and Elizabeth.

I stand the card on the table and unpack my groceries. The fridge is looking a lot healthier now. Taking the bag holding my toiletries, I head upstairs. As I pass my unknown housemate's room, I hear a groan. It's definitely not a groan of pain and I slow down.

"You like that, don't you?" a deep voice asks.

"Yes!" comes the breathless response.

"And this?"

"Ooh, yes. I need you. I need you now. Fuck me. Fuck me hard."

Wow. She's got one husky voice. I can't wait to see the face that goes with it.

Okay. This is so wrong. I shouldn't be here, quite apart from the privacy she deserves, I've never met this woman. I'll never be able to look her in the face. Yes, she has one hell of a sexy voice, but I need to move away, and I'm one step closer to the stairs when she giggles.

"For fuck's sake, Cass. Take this seriously. Can you do that?" the deep voice demands.

I turn back. Cass?

"I think so." Cassie giggles again. It is her! And I'm walking towards her bedroom door. For one second, I think I'm going to burst in there.

Cass. Cassie Henderson. Actor and Entertainer! My Cass. What are the chances? Seems like she got back on the horse again quickly.

"Okay, let's try something else. Pretend I'm H. I know you can do that. Are you ready?"

It is my Cass! How can he want her to pretend she's with me? Despite my confusion, I smirk. She must have been flattering about me. I step closer. To hell with it being wrong. My ear is practically resting on the door.

"Get on with it," Cass snaps.

I don't think she's feeling it. Poor bloke. The smirk is back; she was feeling it on Saturday.

He clears his throat. "Tell me what you want. Do you want me to eat your pretty... Oooo. Look at that, you're all ready for me."

He has a really deep voice. I must sound like I'm squeaking in comparison. But she didn't snap at me. Punched me, but that was after.

"Oh my god. That's it, do that again. Oh, Oh, I think...I think...Yeeeesss."

I've had enough. And so has she by the sound of it. I clear my throat with an exaggerated cough and stomp up the stairs as noisily as possible.

There's a note on my door.

Dear Roomy,

I'm big on sharing, but it is polite to ask. I had to drip all the way up here to recover my body wash.

If you need to borrow things, please put them back from whence they came.

I sound like a bitch now. I promise I'm not. Anyway, looking forward to meeting you.

Cassie x

PS: And put the cover back on the hot tub. (Still not a bitch) and hope to meet you soon. x

Oh, she can give kisses to a total stranger. Nice. I deposit my toiletries, except for the body wash I brought home from work. That I take down to *her* bathroom and put it in there. She can tingle away. With that thought in mind, I stop mid-landing and tilt my head towards her door. They're still at it. My coughing and stomping had no effect.

"Oh, yes, yes. I never thought it could feel like this, so hard, so deep." Her breath catches. "I'm going to...Yesss!"

"Finally. Come on. I need a drink. Pass me my phone," Deep voice says.

What? I mean, really? He's a dedicated romantic, I don't think. Still, he pushed her buttons. Who needs romance, I guess. I can't believe she's accepting his attitude. Perhaps she's trying to forget me. Shit! The door's opening.

"Tea, coffee, or something stronger?" Deep voice asks.

I'm halfway down the stairs, so I don't hear her reply. I reach the hall planning to make a fast exit, but bugger, if my keys aren't in the kitchen, so I head that way as he gallops down the stairs. He really needs that drink. Double shit! Pulling out a chair, I sit at the table and pick up the thankyou card. My back is to the door as he breezes in.

"Hi, you found it then. We were tempted to tuck in but thought that might be rude as we hadn't even met. I'm Joel. I don't live here. Just a friend of..."

Joel? Has the man got no pride? I jump to my feet and spin to look at him.

Joel slaps his hands on his head and grips his hair. "You! You've got to be kidding. She's going to kill me. Oh, my dear god. You?"

Cassie walks in behind him. "Who's going to kill who?"

She spots me. There's a moment of silence before she loses it.

"What the fuck? What are you doing here? Joel, is this your idea of a joke? I mean, what the actual fuck? This is not funny. Get out of my house." She jabs her finger at me.

"Can't do that, because I live here. No joke. Hilarious, don't you think? Of all the house shares in all the world. How are you, Cassie? Keeping busy? Having fun?" I ask as I realise she's still wearing my shirt. She's just shagged another man and puts on my shirt afterwards. Priceless!

Cassie points at the card. "You're Mr Baros? Can I assume Mrs Baros will move in too? How cosy. Can't wait. How we'll laugh."

I step towards her and jab a finger back at her. "Pot and kettle, Cassie. I need to get back to work. Excuse me." I snatch up my keys and push past her. She chases after me.

"Oh, no you don't. Where's my bee?"

"Dead and buried." I pull open the door and step outside. "You are quite a girl, Cassie. I'm disappointed in you, and a little hurt."

"And what does that mean, H?" she demands, following me out.

I look her up and down. She's still got those legs sticking out of my fucking shirt. "Think about it. Why are you wearing my shirt?"

"Because it was there. Where is my bee?"

Miss Allison appears on the doorstep. "Is everything alright, Mr Baros?"

I drag out a smile. "All good. Cassie is just wearing my shirt by mistake."

"She could do with wearing a lot more than that. She's practically naked. I was going to suggest you join us for dinner tonight. I'm sure after a day's work, and sorting out Elizabeth, you won't want to cook."

Miss Allison is speaking to me but still looking at Cassie. Cassie's head is swivelling back and forth, a look of shock on her face.

"Perfect. What time should I arrive?" I ask.

"It will be ready by six. But you may come as soon as you like. Did you get our gift?" The question is for me, but she's still looking at Cassie.

Cassie pulls her shoulders back, and despite the conflict, my eyes stray to her breasts as she steps forward. "He did. Did you think I would eat it before he got home?"

"I didn't know. Anything is possible, because this morning I wouldn't have thought I'd be speaking to you while you were naked in the street. I will see you later, Mr Baros."

Cassie flips up the front of the shirt. "I have knickers on. Big knickers."

Now Miss Allison looks at me. "I told you she was odd. I'll see you later, Mr Baros." Miss Allison takes her flaring nostrils inside and closes the door.

"Don't smirk. Where's my bee?"

Cassie moves to jab me with her finger, but I grab her hand and half drag her around the corner to where I parked the car. The hatch flips open as we approach. "I brought it home, because I didn't want someone to throw it away, because you said it was important. Do you want to take it now?"

Cassie's cheeks are a little pink, and she shakes her head. "No, I'll get it when you've finished work. Although I don't know how I'll take it back. But don't worry, I'll ask Joel."

"Get in the car," I tell her.

"What?"

"Get in the bloody car. We'll take it back now. I think Joel has done enough for one day, don't you?" Now I know I'm losing the plot. I've just heard the man bring her to orgasm several times but feel jealous because he's going to help her with the bloody bee.

"I can't. Look at me, I'm not dressed."

Unable to resist, I look her up and down. "You have your granny knickers on. You showed the entire street that. How many pairs of those do you have, anyway? Get in the bloody car. Now."

Cassie grins and gets in. "It was a pack of three."

"Where are we going?" I ask and start the car. Luckily, it's not far, and ten minutes later, I'm helping her drag the bee into a lift.

"Cassie. You got it! Thank you. Is it alright?" An attractive lady, with purple streaks in her hair, comes out from behind the desk and inspects the bee as we drag it out of the lift. "Oh dear. It's damaged." She looks up at me and smiles. "Oh, hello. Are you after work? I'm Jan, I'll be with you in two minutes."

"No, just helping the lady."

"Really?" She looks me up and down and flashes Cassie a grin. Before returning her attention to the bee with a shake of her head. "I don't think they'll pay, Cassie. Not with it in this state." Jan sucks in air between her teeth and grimaces.

"They'd bloody better. I nearly died, Jan." Cassie's hands fly to her hips, and reveal a glimpse of her knickers.

I grin at Jan.

"Don't exaggerate. I'll do my best. You know that, Cass." Jan doesn't sound convinced.

Cassie walks into the centre of the office and bellows, "GLEN!"

"Bloody actors." Jan rolls her eyes.

After a few seconds, a tall blond bloke appears and grins when he spots Cassie. He walks over to her, loops his hand around her back, and kisses her upturned cheek.

"You look amazing," he says, pulling her in for a hug.

I clear my throat, and he glances at me with raised eyebrows as Cassie explains she's here to return the bee costume and expects payment in full. The bastard slaps her backside and tells her he'll do his best. He looks as though he's going to walk away. I step forward.

"Do you know who I am?" I ask, wishing I was a couple of inches taller.

"I don't. Should I? I'm Glen." He holds out a hand, which I ignore.

"I'm the man who saved her life. The man who had to cut her out of that thing when she collapsed, dehydrated and suffering from heatstroke. I'm the man who had to sit with her until she was well enough to move and take a drink. It was touch and go. I've asked to see the health and safety plan, and she tells me the plan was a bottle of water in a pouch. There were no planned breaks, no support, no first aid. Nothing. She was lucky she found me, very lucky." I cast a glance at Cassie to confirm this. "If the money isn't in her bank by the time she gets home. You'll be hearing from my solicitor. What sort of business are you running?"

Glen nods. "I understand what you are saying, but our client is—"

"Your client is your concern. Cassie's contract was with you. You were responsible for her wellbeing, and you are responsible for paying her." I purse my lips. "Although, perhaps not. Let me see the contract." I hold out my hand.

Glen looks sheepish.

"I thought not." I glance at my watch. "Ten minutes. Cassie, this way."

Cassie winks at Jan and gives a little wave. "None of this was my fault. I still want work," she calls as I hit the button for the lift. "Well," she says, as we step inside. "That was quite a performance. I'm impressed, H. Thank you."

"Thank me later, when they've paid you."

Cassie goes pink and looks at her feet. "Will I see you later?"

"Do you want to see me later?" I take a step closer.

Cassie shrugs. "Don't know how we can avoid it now that you're living with me. Um, I mean sharing." I see her lips twitch.

I lift her chin with my finger. "Then I'll see you later. Not sure what time as I have stuff on. But for now..."

I lean forward to kiss her as the lift door opens. A young woman coughs, and I step away. I take Cassie's hand and lead her back to the car.

"We need to talk," I tell her.

"Yes. I know. Tonight, after you've finished at the cauldron. I'll wait for you."

I glance at her and see her flush again. "Cassie Henderson. Actor and Entertainer, are you blushing?" I tease. "And the cauldron? They're not that bad. They're just a little eccentric."

"To you. Since I've been here, I've been attacked several times, and humiliated, and don't start me on the accusations. Steve gets on okay with her, but he's never been invited to dinner. You've only been here two minutes and look at you."

"You didn't answer the question about the blushing." I reach across and place my hand on her thigh and love her little gasp. "You weren't shy on Saturday." I also want to mention her shenanigans with Joel, but that would let her know I heard them.

What am I doing? Am I just writing that off? I can't, can I? That said, it's none of my business. But if this goes where I want it to, I'm going to have to find out. I leave it shelved for the moment.

"Tell me what you're thinking. Right now. What are you thinking about?"

"You. I can't work you out. You're an enigma, H. But let's talk later. We're nearly home."

I nod and give her leg a squeeze and am rewarded by another sharp intake of breath. "As you wish." I pull over before we get to the house and her head jerks towards me.

"You're not going to make me walk from here, are you? Come on, H. That's not fair."

"No. I promised Miss Allison I wasn't a sex maniac, so I didn't want her to see."

"See what?" The flush is back, and it's the sexiest thing. This girl was ripping my clothes off two days ago, and I tell her that. With a little encouragement, I help her climb over the handbrake and she straddles me. The heat emanating from her causes me to twitch a response.

"Anyone could walk past," She says, her eyes wide.

She's glances around, and I grab her neck and bring her lips to mine. As our passion deepens, she keeps giving these little moans as she rocks her hips. I know I'm going to lose control so I reluctantly push her away. This is not the place.

"To be continued," I whisper.

Cassie runs a finger down my nose. "I love your nose. Sorry I punched it."

"You're the first person who's ever said that. You're forgiven if you promise not to do it again." I help her back into the passenger seat, make myself more comfortable, which is becoming an increasing necessity, and start the engine. "I'll be home by nine thirty at the latest. Promise you'll wait up."

"I'll be there."

She's smiling. I don't know what the hell that was with Joel, but my smile is bigger.

My phone rings and my dash tells me it's George. "Work. Stay quiet a moment." I take the call. "George. How's it going? I'm on my way back. Something came up." I grab Cassie's hand as she slides it up my thigh towards my crotch with a breathy giggle.

"Then it will wait until you get here. See you in a minute." George hangs up.

"Sorry, couldn't resist. What do you do?" Cassie asks. "I thought you were the caretaker. But with today's shirt, tie, and suit trousers, I'm guessing not."

I laugh. "Not quite. It feels like it at the moment, though. Easiest way to describe it is to say I'm in finance," I reply and see her nose wrinkle. "What was that look for?"

"Too long a story, H. Let's park it for now. You have to get back to work. The short story is that my father was in finance. Might still be for all I know. He was a total bastard. You won't be a total bastard, will you, H? I'm taking a risk here."

"Never have been and I don't intend to start now. I'll see you later. Before you go, check and see if they paid you."

"How? You abducted me." She smiles. "Not that I'm complaining, but all I have with me is your shirt, my granny knickers, and my flip-flops. No phone. I'll check as soon as I get in and message you."

"Will Joel be there?" I ask, wondering if I should go in. Perhaps I need to stake a claim.

"I doubt it. He's got a show up in Birmingham for the next ten days. He'll be back at his wondering what to pack. Why?"

"I'm probably overstepping the mark, but I don't like the thought of you being alone with him." I stare straight ahead, willing myself not to challenge her about this morning's activities.

Cassie throws back her head and laughs before kneeling up on her seat and turning my face to look at her. "H, are you jealous? I promise you Joel is not competition for you. Not even close."

Then she kisses me, and I believe her. She pulls away. "I wonder if the coven was watching, and after you tried to avoid it. Make sure they eat the same as you. Don't take the first bite."

"Wait for me." Laughing, I watch as she runs to the door and catch a glimpse of her grannies. Then I smile all the way back to work, still wondering what the hell I'm doing, because it's not the old ladies next door that have me under a spell.

Chapter 12

Cassie

I SLAM THE DOOR shut behind me and do a happy dance in the hall before going in search of my phone. I find it on the kitchen table, along with a note written on the back of an envelope. It's from Joel.

Cassie,

Where the hell did you go? I'm guessing with H. I was worried that he might have abducted you but also thought you might be shagging him somewhere of your own free will, and without a thought for me.

If I don't hear from you by two, I'm calling the police.

Call me.

Jx

I send him a quick message telling him H did abduct me, there was no shagging (yet), and all was well. I promised him a call later. He sends a thumbs-up as an acknowledgement.

My bank app tells me the money is in my account. There's not much of it left because of the overdraft that proceeded it, but H is now officially my hero. I text him.

The money was there, I can now buy you a drink as a thank you. Please don't be late, although I can't promise to wait up, I might be in bed. We can talk after.
Cassie xxxxxxxxxxx
(making up for yesterday)

I have a couple of hours to fill, and as I'm intending on entertaining in my bedroom tonight, I give my room a good clean, change the bedding, collect all my stray clothes and head downstairs with an armful of washing. As I put a load on, I hear the doorbell ring. I'm still only wearing H's shirt but given I've been out and about in it today, I open the door with a smile. I'm greeted by a short, attractive, middle-aged woman holding an overnight case. She forces a smile as she looks me up and down. I wish people would stop doing that!

"Hello. Can I help you?" I ask.

"I'm here to see Christos." She makes to step into the hall, but I hold my ground.

"Christos?" I shrug. "I'm not sure who that—"

"Christos Baros. My son. He lives here. I know that because you are wearing the shirt I bought him for Christmas." This time, I allow her to enter the house.

Shit. How do I explain not knowing his name? "Of course, of course. Come in." I coo, despite the fact she's already halfway up the hall. "He's at work, I'm afraid. Was he expecting you?"

Mrs Baros places her bag on the floor and looks around before returning her attention to me.

"Does a mother need an invitation in this house?" she asks.

"No, of course not. But tonight he's going to be working for the wi...old ladies next door, and then he's eating with them. I'm not expecting him home until nine thirty, although he might be earlier, of course. Have you phoned him?"

"I'm here to surprise him," she tells me and pulls out a chair at the table.

"I'm sorry, I'm being rude. Can I get you a drink? Have you had far to travel?" I hurry round the table and hold up the kettle.

"Water, thank you." She accepts the glass of water and pats the table. "Sit with me. Tell me about yourself."

Bloody hell. I'm not equipped to deal with the mother of my very new, but hopefully long-term lover, and for a moment, I consider lying and telling her I have somewhere to be. But she has this look about her, and when she pats the table again, I pull out a chair.

"Not much to tell. What would you like to know?"

"How long have you known Christos?"

Her smile is charming, but I'm not falling for that. I can also see her eyes. This woman is on a mission.

"I met him on Friday. So not long."

She nods. "Aha! And why are you wearing his shirt? Today is only Monday."

Bam! Straight between the eyes. I probably look like a rabbit caught in the headlights, but she'll have to be quicker than that to catch me. "I was in the utility room doing my laundry when you rang the bell. As I only had my knickers on, I grabbed the first thing to cover me."

Another knowing nod. "So you walk around half naked when you share a house with a man?"

"Not usually, and it's two men. Both were out, and neither expected back. I took a risk." I swear if she nods again, I'm calling H. She surprises me by barking out a laugh. Her dimple is in the same place as his. When she relaxes, I can see the family connection.

"I doubt they would complain. When he was a teenager, he had pictures of girls wearing less than that on his wall."

I tut and roll my eyes. "Teenage boys. They'll never change. It's the hormones."

"This is true. But now he is a man, a married man. His hormones should be under control, don't you think?" She takes a sip of her water. Watching me over the rim of her glass.

She still thinks he's married! I'm seething again, but true actor that I am, I keep my face expressionless. "I do. But I thought his marriage was over. Why would he be here on his own if he was married? Sorry, that's none of my business. That's for...Christos to tell me."

She rubs her forehead and her shoulders slump as though she has the weight of the world on them.

"I agree. He shouldn't be here. Why? Because he ran away, and who can blame him? But he didn't even try. I understand that because I'm his mother, of course I do. But he should come home and put it right. The shame of it."

"I thought he had a new job here?"

"Yes, of course he does. He's not stupid. But Ana should be with him. He should have made her come."

The tutting and shaking of her head is now continuous. I need to get more information. This doesn't sound good. I feel sick.

"He didn't want her to come? He left her?"

She bangs the table with the flat of her hand. "No! My Christos is a good man. He would never abandon his wife. She didn't want to come. She left him. But he didn't even try."

My heart soars and I hope my smile isn't too big. "Perhaps he didn't want her to."

"What has want got to do with it? They're married."

Mrs B flips a hand, dismissing the conversation, but I've heard enough. She left him; he didn't want to fight for her. So why the ring? I'll ask him, but she's asking me another question.

"And what is it you do? Do you work?"

"Oh, yes. I'm an actor. I've just finished a production at the Hippodrome, but my next job doesn't start until July."

Another nod and another 'Aha' and then she falls silent as she considers this.

I have to fill the silence. "How long are you here for?" I ask with a smile.

"That depends on Christos. He never even told me he was coming here. Had to hear it from Stella. So, where are your parents? Are they close by?"

"No. I don't know where my father is, and I don't care. He left when I was still at school. My mother died." I look her in the eye. "I don't like talking about it."

Her hands clasp her cheeks. "Oh no. That is so bad, I am sorry. We lost my husband when Christos was too young. Only nineteen and just starting life as a married man, a boy needs his father for guidance. Perhaps if Papa had been around this nonsense with Ana wouldn't have happened."

Nineteen! She's telling me they got married when he was only nineteen. What boy knows his own mind then? No wonder it didn't last. I feel the need to defend H.

"But you were there. You did your best, I'm sure. My best friend has only met him briefly and called him a gentleman," I snatch up the card from the witches, "and look at this." I thrust it into her hands. "That's the old ladies next door. One of them had a nasty fall. He took them to the hospital, and tonight he's going to make a bedroom downstairs for one of them. That's why he's having dinner with them."

Mrs B's eyes widen, and she pulls her phone from her bag.

"Wait," she says as she's tapping away. It takes a while, but when she turns it to face me, it's a photograph of two tiny old ladies looking very sorry for themselves. I know with Miss Allison it's all an act, but Elizabeth looks like she's shrunk. "This is them?"

"Yes." I point to the adjoining wall. "They live next door."

Mrs B falls silent for a moment before banging the flat of her hands on the table and pushing herself up. "They should not be cooking for him. Take me to meet them."

Do what? They hate me! Think of an excuse! "Oh, I'm not sure. I don't think they'd like visitors, particularly as Elizabeth is indisposed." My head is moving like a nodding car dog. "No, I don't think they'd approve."

"My son saved them. They can tell us that if they want. But you might be wrong." She looks me up and down again. "Take me to Christos's room. I will unpack and freshen up while you get ready. I don't think you want to greet them in his shirt."

So, I take her upstairs, shift a couple of his boxes for her, show her where the bathroom is, and am now sitting on my bed wondering how the hell I'm going to carry this off. Miss Allison is never backward in coming forward and will not be intimidated by Mrs B. Shit! I pull off his shirt throw it on the pillow of my freshly made bed. That won't be seeing any action tonight. Not with his mummy upstairs. Pulling on my robe, I go to my own bathroom.

Good old H. He knows how to cheer a girl up. The industrial sized eucalyptus and mint shower gel sits on the corner of the bath. I open the lid and sniff. So many memories, but I must crack on, I doubt she's going to wait while I fantasise about what should have happened tonight.

I towel dry my hair and muss it with my fingers. It will have to do. My wardrobe stands open and I stand naked, staring at the totally inappropriate clothes for a visit with Mrs B and the witches. That's if they let me in, of course. I jump when there's a knock on the door.

"It's just me," she calls as though someone else might have sneaked into the house.

"Two seconds." I yank the Laura Ashley from the hanger and pull it over my head, before hurrying to open the door. "Nearly ready," I tell her.

Her lips are pursed, and it looks as though she's holding back a smile. "You are ready. You look perfect. Pop your shoes on." She points at my flip-flops. "Very summery."

Like a child, I do as I'm told. My stomach is doing somersaults at what comes next when she clears her throat. I look at her and she's holding up a pair of my granny knickers.

"Are these yours?"

"I don't think so. Where did you find them?" I know I'm blushing. It's a curse I live with.

"Under his pillow. I lifted it for my nightie." Her eyes stray to my bed where his abandoned shirt and the matching knickers lay. "So, not yours?"

I blow out a very long breath, and give a big shrug, my shoulders touching my ears. "I don't know. Our laundry did get mixed up."

"Aha." Walking into the room, she sweeps up his shirt and my other knickers and drops all three into the washing basket. Tapping the lid, she nods. "All ready for the next mix up. Shall we go?"

I have no underwear on. Luckily, as previously mentioned, I can get away going commando with this dress, but all I can think of as I follow her down the stairs is that H was sleeping with my knickers under his pillow. My smile is wide as I grab my keys and head next door.

Miss Allison opens the door. "You're dressed. May I help you?"

"Hi, Miss Allison, this is Mrs Baros. She's come to visit and insisted I bring her next door to meet you."

Miss Allison smiles, actually smiles. Who knew that was possible? She holds out her hand.

"Mrs Baros, I'm Jennifer Allison. It's a pleasure to meet you. You have a wonderful son. You must be very proud."

"Of course, of course." Mrs B hands me her bag, steps forward, and pulls Miss Allison into a hug, who stares at me over Mrs B's shoulder. I'm not sure which of us is more shocked. Mrs B releases her and turns her to face the other direction. "Now, I must meet your sister. You must tell us what we can do to help." With a little shove, she follows Miss Allison into the hall and turns to me. "Come on. Hurry."

I follow like a lamb to the slaughter.

An hour later, Mrs B has become a bosom buddy. The witches have agreed it would be wonderful to have her cook a traditional Greek meal for them, and I'm pushing a shopping trolley around Sainsbury's with Mrs B. She'd do well in the army. No one would dare ignore her commands.

No sooner do we reach home than I'm in the kitchen, peeling and chopping on her command. And I'm enjoying myself. Although I have to confess, I'm not looking forward to joining them all for dinner next door. That's going to be awkward with a capital A, but the food smells fabulous, and it will be interesting to see H interacting with his mother. I know I should warn him about what's happening, but I haven't had a free moment. With everything baking or simmering, Mrs B finally slows down. Her cheeks are rosy, and a smile plays on her lips as she flops onto the couch.

"I'll take a little rest. It's almost five. I hope Christos won't be too much longer." Slipping off her shoes, she puts her feet on the coffee table and rests her hands on her tummy.

"Shall I call him?" I ask. At last. I can get to my phone, which is now next to her feet on the table.

"Oh no. You should never interrupt a man at work unless it's an emergency. Especially now he's an Executive Director. How would it look if his mother, or..." She looks me with raised brows, "his friend should interrupt him? No, no. He has made promises. He's a good boy, so he'll be here as soon as he can."

"Yes, of course. I'll just get these pots washed while you take a rest. You haven't stopped, you're a dynamo." I send a silent apology to H. I tried.

She nods as her eyes close, and I pull on some rubber gloves. She's probably right. What do I know? And H is an Exec? He never said he was a bigwig. Washing up completed, I sit at the end of the kitchen table so I can cut him off in the hall when he arrives.

Chapter 13

Christos

I SING ALONG TO the radio on the drive home. At last a positive day, both the electricians and the IT guys came in, and miracle of miracles, they are working together logically. There is now a light at the end of the tunnel. It's faint, but it's there. And Cassie. I can't wait to get home. She sent me a cheeky text, which I didn't respond to because I've been flat out. She has her money and might be waiting in bed for me. If she is, I'm going to be late for Miss Allison.

I park the car and trot to the house. Yes, I'm keen. The key is still in the lock when I call to her.

"Hi, honey, I'm home. You'd better be ready for me." I laugh as she comes flying out of the living area, looking really cute in a floral dress. She opens her mouth to greet me, but I cover it with mine and pull her to me. "I've been thinking about this all day," I tell her as I kiss my way down her neck.

"H. Wait. I have to talk to you."

She tries to push me off, but I hike up her skirt and grab her arse, pulling her back against me. Definitely going to be late, because she's naked under this dress. "No knickers? You're living dangerously. I haven't got long. And you said the talking comes after. God, I want to get you up those stairs." The aroma coming from the kitchen is sublime and I breathe it in. "You can cook too? Jesus. I'm never letting you go."

"Christos, is that you?"

I freeze for several seconds before releasing Cassie, straightening her dress, and rearranging my tackle. "Mama?" I call back.

"I was trying to tell you!" hisses Cassie. "She's been here nearly all day. We're having dinner with the witches, and she's done the cooking."

"Shit!" I walk toward the living room.

"Quite. And she found me in your shirt, and my knickers under your pillow," Cassie whispers.

I groan. I stop walking and turn to look at Cassie, who is grinning through her blush.

"Double shit!" I whisper back.

"Again, quite. Here he is, Mrs B." Cassie turns me to look at my mother.

Cassie's calling my mother Mrs B and my mother is smiling at her. I relax a little as I open my arms and pull my mother into a hug, kissing her forehead.

"What are you doing here? It's wonderful to see you, but a surprise, I have things to do tonight. You should have warned—"

"No warning needed. Or is there something I don't know? I know what you're doing tonight. Cassie told me all about it. Jennifer and Elizabeth are expecting us. Poor ladies, so much to cope with at their age. If you go to help them now, you might be done by the time dinner is ready."

"You've taken over again, haven't you?" I accuse, and keeping hold of her shoulders I push her back so I can look her in the eye. "Have you been bullying innocent girls and old ladies?"

"Cassie. Cassie, come here! Come here and listen to how he speaks to me. Have I bullied you? No. Did I make a fuss about finding those...large panties under his pillow, or you in his shirt? No. Tell him."

Cassie is now almost beetroot, but her amusement shows in her eyes.

"No, Mrs B, you did not. But as I've tried to explain, it is—"

My mother throws her hand into the air. "Enough, or dinner will be ruined." She prods me in the chest. "Get changed. You cannot do sweaty work in those clothes. You have some explaining to do, my boy, but now is not the time." She slaps my arm. "Go."

I nod and, turning back towards the stairs, I grimace at Cassie, who looks straight through me. As I pass her, I can see how much it's taking for her to control herself. She's positively vibrating. I throw her a wink and take the stairs two at a time, listening to my mother issue her next instruction.

"Cassie, we need some trays. Do you have trays?"

"Coming, Mrs B. They live on top of the fridge. You'll never reach them with those short little legs."

"Ha! They might be short, but they can still kick ass, as you youngsters like to say. I'm just not sure who to start with. You or Christos."

Cassie giggles and disappears. She's bantering with my mother? That's my job. Only I'm allowed to tease my mother. Cassie has bewitched her, too.

I change quickly, ignoring the fact my mother has taken over my bedroom, and run back downstairs. Stopping just short of the doorway to the living area, I catch Cassie's eye and beckon her out into the hall. When she reaches me, I place my hands on her hips and rest my forehead on hers.

"Are you okay? She tends to take over."

Cassie rubs my upper arms. "It's fine, H. It's been an education. A whirlwind of an education, but I can now roll dolmades. Properly. Only one slap."

Her eyes twinkle at me and I want to kiss her, but know that as soon as I do, my mother will appear.

"You really are something else. I'm sorry, Cass. Really, I didn't know she was coming."

"Never apologise for your mother, H. She's bloody marvellous and you're lucky to have her."

"Will you kiss the girl and go? I have need of her in here." My ninja mother appears in the doorway.

"Mama!" I scold, letting go of Cassie's hips.

"Don't you mama me. You should be next door. Those poor ladies are waiting for you, and Cassie has work to do. Shall I close my eyes? Will that help?"

My mother has both hands on her hips. I don't look down, but I know her foot is tapping.

"No, Mama. What would help is if you would go about your own business and leave me to mine." I wink at Cassie. "I'll see you later."

"Oh my god. So dramatic. I come all this way to see you and help your elderly neighbours and I get this. Cassie either kiss him or come with me. Make it quick."

"Coming, Mrs B." Cassie blows me a kiss and turns away.

I ring the bell next door and Miss Allison opens it. I have no idea what to expect. My mother probably trampled her underfoot.

"Mr Baros, come in. Were you surprised to see your mother? What a lovely woman. She's making dinner, but I'm sure you know that. We rarely have foreign food and Elizabeth is quite excited."

"It was a surprise, but a nice one," I reply, following her through the house and into the kitchen.

"Hello, doctor. You're having dinner with us. It's foreign." Elizabeth looks at her sister. "He's dressed today, Jennifer."

"Yes, dear, I can see that. I'll just show Mr Baros what we've achieved."

Miss Allison takes me into the living room. The sofa and chairs have been lined up against one wall. A commode sits in the alcove next to the chimney breast, and judging by the pattern on the carpet, it's been vacuumed recently. I turn to face her, my hands on my hips.

"Did you move that furniture? I told you I'd do it when I got here. I'm not happy, Miss Allison. That's very naughty."

"Not me. I wouldn't have been able. Your mother did it with the woman, Cassie. That's it, Cassie. Then she made her vacuum. I'm still not sure about her, but she listens to your mother, so that's a start. I only did the dusting. Now let's get that bed down."

I was expecting a hollow divan, or perhaps a wooden framed bed. What I found was what felt like a three-tonne metal monstrosity. I swear it's made of lead, much like the mattress.

"I'll need some tools to dismantle this."

"Top drawer. Daddy got caught out once, so always made sure they were easily accessible." Miss Allison slides open the drawer. "Full set upstairs and down."

"Your father put this bed together?" I'm almost at a loss for words. "It's that old?"

"Of course. He was a capable man, and furniture was made to last in those days."

I hump the mattress down the stairs first. Miss Allison follows straightening the pictures that get bumped on the way down. Then I return to the bed. It takes a while to loosen the nuts and bolts, but once done, it doesn't take that long to get it all sorted. I position the bed and one of the chairs so that the sisters can watch the television together. The doorbell rings as I heave the mattress back onto the base.

Miss Allison opens the door.

"Hello again. Mrs B sent me over with the first load. I'll need to take the tray back because I think she's expecting double the numbers." Cassie steps into the hall.

"It's the Mediterranean genes I expect. We went to Spain once, and the dishes of food just kept arriving. We only popped in for refreshments. Do you know we didn't need to eat dinner that night? Go on through. Elizabeth will be pleased to see you. She likes you."

"Will do." Cassie laughs. "I'll make you like me, Miss Allison. I don't know how, but I will," Cassie says as she disappears towards the kitchen.

Miss Allison catches my eye and shakes her head. "You see. She's very cheeky. I didn't say I didn't like her. She simply takes some getting used to. At least she's fully dressed this evening. Very pretty." She lifts a pile of linen from a chair. "Now, I'll get this bed made up. I have the sherry out, so I doubt I'll want to make beds after a sherry."

I spin around as Cassie speaks. "I'll do that. Elizabeth is asking for you. H, you can take the tray back and help your mum."

"I'll help you. It'll be quicker with two." I wait until Miss Allison leaves the room and slide my hand up her dress, and she parts her legs a little for me. "You are not only very cheeky, as Miss Allison correctly pointed out, but you are also very naughty because she thinks you're fully clothed."

"It's a long story." Cassie gasps as my fingers hit the right spot. "H, pack it in. She's coming back."

I jump away from her, and she lifts a sheet, flipping it across the mattress. Miss Allison doesn't reappear.

"You lied," I accuse.

"Self-preservation, H. She might have come back. Take that tray back to your mum. This won't take me a minute."

My mother and Cassie transport the remainder of the food while I shower. By the time I get there, everyone is seated. My chair sits on the opposite side of the table to Cassie. I have Miss Allison on one side and my mother on the other. The chances of my getting a single sentence out tonight are slim. Still, I can sit here and look at Cassie. It's not all bad.

The food is predictably wonderful, but what's surprising is how much Miss Allison and Elizabeth are enjoying it. Each dish has to be described, and the recipe given, even though they will never attempt to make one of them. They may look like tiny little birds, but they have keen appetites. Cassie gets praised for her first attempt at making dolmades. She beams with pride, or perhaps it's the wine my mother keeps pouring into her glass.

When everyone has admitted defeat, except me because I'm a growing lad, as my mother tells them each time she puts more food on my plate, but I'm not complaining, because it's the best meal I've had for months, Miss Allison taps my hand.

"Another thing I wanted to ask, Mr B...Christos," she's still struggling with that, "is why Cassie calls you H? I've tried to work it out but can't even begin to guess."

Everyone turns to look at Cassie and the colour rises in her cheeks. Why is she blushing? I tilt my head and hold her gaze.

"I don't know. Perhaps she misheard my name and is too proud to correct it."

"Not true. It's because when we first met I didn't know your name, so—"

"It's true," my mother agrees. "When I arrived this morning, she didn't know who he was. Not by name." She elbows me and winks at Cassie.

"Didn't she? She only had to ask. So, why H, Cass?" I ask.

My mother elbows me again. "Cass? Who is that? Her name is Cassie, not Cass. Like you are Christos, not Chris." She looks at Cassie. "Are you not going to tell us?"

I laugh. "How can she? You keep interrupting her. Every time—"

"Christos! I know you've had a glass of wine, but you won't be rude to your mother at this table. Dear me." Miss Allison taps my hand sharply.

"Thank you, Jennifer. I tried so hard to teach him good manners. Sometimes he forgets himself." My mother throws her arms into the air.

I jerk upright as Cassie's foot slides up my leg and starts rubbing things that should lie dormant sitting at this table with these women.

"Christos, are you okay?" My mother asks, turning to face me. "Why are you jumping about?"

"Perfectly fine. Thank you. Cassie, you were going to tell us why H." I squirm in my seat as she increases the pressure and I slip my hand under the tablecloth to stop her, but she pulls her foot away before I can grab it.

"Well, when I first saw you, I was taken by your smile. You have a little dimple here." Cassie taps her cheek. "And I thought what a happy man, I said as much to my friend Joel. He agreed. So we named you H. I think it suits you."

My mother pinches my cheek and gives it a shake. "You are right. I agree. Such a happy baby, such a happy boy, and now I need a happy man. I also love his dimple."

My cheek gets another shake for good measure before I push her hand away. The foot is back. I'm being attacked on two fronts.

"Joel? The homosexual?" Miss Allison asks, causing Elizabeth to have a fit of giggles.

"We saw him kissing a man. Right outside. Jennifer nearly had a fit. She doesn't like public shows of affection, do you, Jennifer? I don't like men at all. Well, only the professional ones like Dr Christos." Elizabeth smiles at me. "Dr Christos was naked when he carried me, but he's dressed today, so we're safe."

Cassie's foot stops moving, and she lifts her fist to her mouth. Her eyes are glassy with the laughter she's holding in.

"Naked! A doctor? Christos, what have you been up to?"

My mother is patting her chest, and I don't know what to say without offending Elizabeth. So I look at Cassie.

"Joel is gay? I didn't know that."

She can't speak, so she simply nods. I'm confused. What the hell was going on in her room? Is she trying to convert him? Did he want to try sex with a woman? I have so many questions I can't ask.

"Don't change the subject. What did Elizabeth mean?" My mother asks again.

Miss Allison comes to the rescue. "It was all very simple, and all very innocent. Christos did nothing wrong, quite the opposite. I don't know what we would have done without him. Now, would you like me to wrap this food up for you? Much as I'd like you to stay longer, and will be forever grateful for your kindness, it is going to take us longer than usual to get ready for bed, and I have to clear up."

"I'll wash, you can wipe, H." Cassie gets to her feet and starts stacking the dirty crockery, whilst my mother convinces Miss Allison she must keep some of the food.

Twenty minutes later, a shocked Miss Allison gets a hug from my mother, who promises to visit the next day. Cassie has stacked the clean crockery on the table so Miss Allison can put it where it belongs, and I help Elizabeth into her makeshift bedroom.

When we get back to the house, my mother yawns.

"I'm very tired. What a long day. Christos, I am in your room. You will sleep on the couch. But first I would like to speak to you."

Cassie announces she has to sort out her laundry and disappears into the utility room after pecking my mother on the cheek and wishing her a good night.

"Christos, sit."

I look at my mother's hand patting the seat next to her on the couch. "Mama. Do I want to speak to you?" There's a warning in my tone.

"Sit with me."

I sigh and take hold of her hand as I sit. "I'm a grown man. Think I'm past needing to be spoken to."

"But you do, Christos. Tell me, where will you be sleeping tonight?" she asks.

I pat the couch beneath me. "Right here."

"Now tell me the truth," she says, squeezing my hand.

"Mama, I'm not having this conversation. I love you, and I would do anything for you, but my personal life is just that, personal."

"You have a wife."

"Not for much longer. Ana also agrees the sooner the divorce is final, the better."

"What if she changes her mind? What then?"

"She won't." I'm getting cross and I pull my hand free. "Where are you going with this?"

"I'll tell you where. You swore an oath before God."

"So did she. I didn't break it. Your point, Mama? I don't want an argument. We've had a—"

"And yet you walk away without a thought."

Oh boy. I'm going to be here all night. "Is that what you think? You really think so little of me?"

"At the moment, I don't know what to think. Ana isn't happy. Stella tells me—"

It's my turn to interrupt her. "Stella needs to put her own house in order. Stav has a child with his mistress, and all she worries about is other people's business. Stop gossiping with Stella, and if you can't, don't share it with me. I'm not interested."

Mama's hands cover her mouth. "Stavros! A love child? Are you sure?"

"Am I a liar now too? She knows about the child. There have been showdowns. Shouting matches in the street. It doesn't matter, not to me, it shouldn't to you, because it's not our business. Stella is a bitter woman, probably understandably so, but her life is not our business. Just like mine is not hers." I make to get up. "Now, you're tired, I'm tired. Let's call it a night."

She grabs my arm and pulls me back down. "Not so fast. What about Cassie?"

"What do you mean, what about her? She's a nice girl, I like her, a lot. She's my new housemate, and we're getting to know each other. It's time for bed."

"She is a nice girl, a very nice girl. I like her. But she likes you too much."

I smile. "She does?"

I get a slap for that. "You know it, or why would you take advantage of her? You are a married man, and I expected better of you. Leave her alone. Don't hurt her, do not break her heart."

"I have no intention of doing any such thing. And I am not taking advantage of her. We are both consenting adults and you are out of order. I'm sorry but this conversation is over."

"How long have you known her? Does she know you are married?"

"I am not married!" I soften my tone. "Not really. But, yes, she does. Enough, Mama. I'm getting angry."

"Does she know you still love your wife?"

"No. Wrong," I snap, and I'm on my feet, stepping away from her.

"Ha! You deny it?"

"Yes, no. Look..." I sigh and run my fingers through my hair. "I'll always love Ana. She's my best friend. But we were forced into marriage. You know that, Mama, we talked for hours about it. But we were good, obedient children who loved our parents. And believed that it was for the best because we got on so well. Our parents wanted it. But it wasn't for the best. We tried, and we did our utmost to make it work but we knew within a couple of years that we shouldn't have done it."

I jab my finger at my mother, knowing as I do it, it's wrong, but I've lost it. "Do you know why you don't have grandchildren? Do you? Do I have to spell it out? We didn't want children, because we knew we weren't going to last, and we only stayed together as long as we did out of habit. Come the end, we weren't even sleeping together. Ana found love elsewhere. I'm happy for her. Anyone who loves her should be happy for her. I don't think Yorgos is the right man, but it's not my place to tell her. And no, I didn't cheat on her before I get any more accusations thrown my way. Enough." I cut the air with the flat of my hand.

My lovely mama is blinking away tears. "I didn't know."

"Yes, you did. But I won't argue about it. We didn't hate each other, but it wasn't love, not proper love, not as it should have been. That girl," I point to the utility door, "that lovely, funny girl has made me realise how I should have felt." I roll my eyes as her hands fly to her mouth again. "What? What did I say?"

"You love her? You love Cassie?" I'm not sure if it's a statement or a question.

"No. Yes. I don't know. Probably. It's all very new, and all very personal. She makes me feel alive, Mama. Now, enough. Do you want a glass of water? I'll take you up to bed."

She nods and gives me her hand. I pull her to her feet and walk upstairs with her. Before I leave her, she takes hold of my hand again.

"Go to Cassie. She needs you."

I laugh, but there's no humour in it. "You have just been saying the opposite. Why are you now telling me to go to her? I think you drank too much sherry."

"Because I saw the way you look at each other. You're not very good at hiding your feelings, either of you. I wanted to protect her, to be sure."

"That's kind of you. Weird, but kind, because I thought you would always take my side? I'm your only son. But accepting I've been mistaken my whole life, how did your interrogation do that?" I'm laughing, and she waves a finger at me.

"Because she was listening. She heard the truth as I intended. Whichever way it went. If there was any doubt in your mind, she needed to know. To stop this...whatever it is, before she got hurt. Now she knows, and I think, so do you?"

My mouth drops open. "You set that up with her? Cassie was in on this?"

"No, of course not. You are my son, I would never do that. But I needed to know. You needed to know, and Cassie deserved to know. Whatever you said, I would accept. I had my advice ready whichever way it turned out. But I guessed she would listen, because who wouldn't? She is in love with you, but I wasn't sure about you. I believe she deserved the truth."

I pull my mother into my arms and hug her. "That was a dangerous game to play. I can't believe you were protecting her by making me angry. I don't think I know my mother! How long are you staying, Mama? How much more meddling do I have to put up with?" I smile at her, so she knows I'm joking, although I am shocked, because I never realised how devious my mother could be.

"Only tonight. I wanted to see what you really thought about Ana. I had to know you were doing the right thing."

"But why? You didn't even know about Cassie when you arrived. I'm so confused because I'd already told you I wasn't coming back. You needed to come down here and look me in the eye? Why?"

"Because I was telling the truth about Ana. Stella may be a gossip, but her gossip is accurate. Ana is unhappy. If you'd told me you loved her, I would have told you to come home and take her back. But now? Now I'm telling you to go to Cassie. Ana made her bed. I need my beauty sleep." She pulls my head down and kisses my forehead. "I love you. Go." I kiss her cheek and leave her looking over the banister at me. "And, Christos," she calls, and I pause and look up at her. "No headboards banging. I need my sleep." With that, she laughs and goes into the bedroom.

I know I'm blushing. Why can mothers embarrass you even when you're an adult? I run down the remaining stairs in search of Cassie. I need to know how much she heard.

Chapter 14

Cassie

As I fold my laundry, I hear Mrs. B tell H to sit down, and I know I shouldn't be listening to this. It's too personal. But I can't stop myself. This is what I wanted to know, after all. H promised to talk to me today, but perhaps it's better this way. Less embarrassing for him, and he'll be more honest with his mother, won't he? All these thoughts and more are swirling around as I step closer to the door I should have closed.

Well, eavesdropping is backfiring. I like Mrs B, not sure how long that will last. She's telling him to go back to his wife, and I don't understand why. It sounds like this Ana did the dirty on H, so why tell him to go back? Now I know why he says he's not really married, but what about the ring?

Relief floods through me when he says he doesn't love her, only to dash back out when he says he always will, but not in the right way.

Shit! I stub my toe on the corner of the machine as I dash away from the door. But it's not that that's making me jump about, it's not that causing the blood to rush up and down my body like some liquid Mexican wave. H thinks he might love me. H! Me! I'm going to faint. I need a drink. Bloody hell, I need something. I can't keep still. He's only known me four days, and only bits of them. How can he say that? This is me he's talking about. Perhaps he's making it up to stop his mother from going on about Ana.

I dash back to the door, but it's all silent. They've gone. Bugger. I didn't get to hear the end. My chest rises as I draw in a breath and pick up the pile of folded laundry. I need to act normally when I go out there. Act like I didn't just hear all that.

Good. No one is about, so I blow out the breath that I'd trapped, and I head towards the kitchen. I really need a drink, so I place the laundry on the table. Will H want one? I get two glasses out just in case and grab the red wine next to the hob. Mrs B says it's only good for cooking, but what does she know? I pour a couple of inches into a glass and knock it back. Tastes okay to me. Now that's established, I can have a proper glass.

"Drinking alone, little bee?"

If Mrs B was asleep, she's not now. My scream could wake the dead, and I slosh red wine over my clean laundry, and round on H.

"What the hell are you playing at? Look at my sheets. I'll have to wash them again now. Why are you creeping about? And what's the bloody smirk for? I hate that dimple." My hand pats my chest. H steps closer, and I can't help it, I return the grin. "What? Speak to me, H. Why are you creeping about with a creepy smile on your face?"

H takes the bottle of wine and places it on the table with one hand and wraps the other one around my back.

"Why are you listening to other people's conversations?" His cheek is pressed to mine, his lips are next to my ear, which is just as well because I must look like an overripe tomato.

"What people?" I ask and feel his cheek rise as he smiles.

"How much did you hear?" he asks as he blows on my ear.

Tingles and a major shudder from me, and a chuckle from him. I can't lie to him. One look into those eyes and I'll be admitting my guilt. I'm almost confessing now, and he's not even looking at me.

"Are you not talking to me?"

I can hear the amusement in his voice, and I so want to look at him because I know his eyes will have that twinkle. But if I look at him, I'll be lost. There won't be any talking.

Talking! I have a plan.

"Of course I'm talking to you. Talking of which – see what I did there – we're supposed to be having a conversation. I think now would be a good time, don't you?"

I can resist him!

"Honestly? No. I can think of much better things to be doing." Now he's nibbling along my neckline, and I don't know whether to push for the conversation or just go for the sex.

"I'm very talented you know, I can do more than one thing at a time. Perhaps it's because I'm a woman. Shall we give it a go?" I groan as he lowers his head and takes a nibble at my boob through my dress. He mumbles against my nipple. "What? I didn't understand a word of that."

And there they are. His eyes. His beautiful, beautiful eyes. And his hands. What are his hands doing? Oh. He grabs my dress and yanks it up. Being an idiot, I lift my arms and allow him to take it off and drop it onto the wine splashed laundry. His eyes travel down to my feet and back up again, and he clears his throat.

"I said, and I sort of proved my point, I was taught not to speak with my mouthful, and I'm planning on my mouth being otherwise occupied. Your thoughts?"

My thoughts are: Why are you fully clothed? Put your plan into action. What are you waiting for?

But what I say is, "So, you don't think we need to clear the air? You don't have any questions for me?"

Oh bloody hell, he's dropped to his knees. My legs part like he's some sort of Cypriot Moses. His tongue and that magnificent nose start doing their thing, pausing at quite a crucial moment.

"Do you still want to talk, little bee?" he asks, before blowing a steady stream of cool air in little circles.

Of course I don't want to talk! Is the man mad? I run my fingers through his hair, and then grab it, pulling his head back so he's looking up at me.

"I think you're losing the plot, H. I think you have too many clothes on, and you're wasting time asking stupid questions, but I also think that we should take this elsewhere. Your mother is in the house. The one who took three days to birth you and wants you to go back to your wife."

He jumps to his feet and slaps my arse. "So you were listening?" His brows come together. "Or were you? We didn't talk about my reluctance to come into the world. Has she told you she thinks I should go back to Ana?"

Ha! I have him flummoxed and I should take advantage.

"Oh, so now you want to talk?" My shrug is nonchalant. "Okay, but you have me at a disadvantage. You need to get naked, too. Then we should go over to the couch and sit down, because if we sit on those chairs, we'll stick to them, what with being naked. Ooor, we could just go to bed and talk later. Your choice. What do you think?"

"Hmm." He taps his lip. "Does your bed have a headboard?"

"Why? Would you want to tie me to it?"

"Oh yes. But you didn't answer the question. Do you have one?"

It's really hard to concentrate on the detail of a question when someone is tweaking your nipples. So I ask again, "Why?"

H kisses the end of my nose. "Because my mother said she was tired and didn't want the headboard banging all night."

"She said what?" I pull my body out of his reach. Instantly missing his touch.

"I don't think you're going deaf. That's what she said. Shall we just talk?"

Yep, that's what he asks, but he's unbuttoning his shirt as he's speaking. Now he's unzipping his jeans. I've forgotten the question again.

"Cassie, talk to me. What do you want to do?" His boxers hit the floor with his jeans. I can ignore the fact he still has socks on because what he wants to do is pretty obvious. Pleasingly so. I really want to follow his lead and drop to my knees, but he asked me a question. Didn't he?

"What?"

And now he's laughing again. He steps away from his jeans, still wearing his socks, and takes my hold of my hands.

"Talking comes later. Where would you like me to start? I'm happy to work my way through the house. I've got so many things I want to do with you, you might need a change of scenery."

My tingles are in overdrive.

"Okay then, let's get on with it. But I think we should leave your room until your mum goes home."

His nod is solemn, and he pulls out a chair and sits down, slapping the table.

"Get on the table."

"We cannot have sex on the kitchen table with your mum able to walk in at any moment." My protest is pointless because H slaps the table again.

"Now."

H can be very convincing when I've got the tingles, I'll have to watch that. So I do as he says, and sit there, my knees pulled up to my chest, facing him. "Take your socks off. You look ridiculous," says the naked woman sitting in the middle of the kitchen table, laundry to the left, fruit bowl to the right. He's laughing, but his socks are coming off. I nod approval. "Well done. What now?"

"Now you lay down." He's still sitting on the chair when he grabs my hips and pulls me forward. "Hold my hands." I take hold and he lowers me to the table. Releasing my hands, he untangles my legs, which are still crossed at the ankles, bent at the knees, and clamped together. Now untangled, he pushes them apart and gives a little growl. "Are you ready? You look ready."

I lift my head from the table to look at him, looking at me. "H, has anyone ever told you that you talk too much and ask too many questions?"

He's still laughing as he lowers his head. My head returns to the table with a thud, but it doesn't hurt because all I can feel is the vibration of his laughter.

I open my eyes and watch H reach across me for his phone. He looks surprisingly good for someone who took me at my word – almost, and led me naked through the house. The sex was...I don't have a suitable word, so I'll settle on amazing, which doesn't even come close. But despite all the amazing sex, my favourite bit was when we went to bed. When he wrapped his arms around me and rubbed that marvellous nose against mine before kissing me goodnight. Oh, and when he turned me over, pulled me close and gave a contented sigh as he told me to sleep tight. And I mustn't forget when he...He looks at the screen and groans.

"I have to go to work."

"Really?" I thump the headboard. "I don't think we did it in here. Isn't there a time limit? You didn't fulfil your side of the promise."

His kisses are soft as he peppers my face with them. "You told me if I touched you again, you'd get into bed with my mum."

My eyes widen. "I'd forgotten that. But I lied. I slept well, though. My dreams were more detailed than before." I grin as he gasps.

"You dream about me?" He rolls on top of me, holding his weight on his elbows, and I thrust my hips up to greet him.

"I do. I dream about teaching you how to pleasure me."

Rocking his hips, he shakes his head. "I thought I did. You sounded like you were enjoying it."

"Oh, I was," I assure him before tutting. "But I still think we need to practise."

"Anything in particular?" he asks.

I close my eyes and smile. "Everything please."

"You make—"

H stops speaking as someone, his mother, bangs on the door.

"Christos, are you up? Have you seen the time? I have breakfast cooking. Bring Cassie." There's a pause, and she adds, "Good morning, Cassie."

H collapses with a groan, and I can barely breathe. I'm laughing as I try to push him off, but I'm not kidding.

"Get off me. I can't breathe. H. I'm not joking. If I have to have breakfast with your mother, I need to shower. I smell of sex."

H sniffs me. "You do, and strawberries, and do I smell a trace of eucalyptus, no, mint?" He pushes up on his hands and looks down at me. "Only if I can join you."

"Stop messing about, we haven't—"

"Cassie, are you awake? Christos needs to get out of that bed. Kick him out. I want breakfast with you before I leave," Mrs. B shouts. "I've left your clothes outside the door. I will expect you in ten minutes. No longer. My taxi is booked."

H rolls off me. "Cancel the taxi, Mum. I'll take you."

"How. Does that bed have an engine?" I can hear the laughter in her voice. "Ten minutes."

I take advantage of his distraction and jump out of bed. Grabbing my dressing gown, I put it on and pull my shoulders back as I open the door. Mrs B smiles at me.

"Good morning, Mrs B. I'm up. Quick shower and I'll be down," I tell her, looking at the bathroom door because I can't look her in the eye. I march forward and trip over the pile of clothes we'd left strewn around the kitchen and yelp. Bugger.

"Cassie, are you okay?" H calls, and I hear the bed squeak as his weight shifts.

"Christos! Put that thing away. I'm your mother. Get dressed right now."

I'm so glad I couldn't see the condition of 'that thing', but I can feel my cheeks flaming on his behalf. I dash into the bathroom and lock the door.

When I arrive downstairs, dressed in leggings, a baggy shirt and a full complement of underwear, H smiles at me.

"You're late for breakfast. Coffee?"

My eyes dart around the room. Mrs B is nowhere to be seen. "My housemate kept me up late, and I prefer tea."

He stands, walks over to the kettle, and switches it on. He's wearing jeans.

"Did you decide not to go to work?" I ask, hopefully.

"Unfortunately, I have no choice. We have visitors later, so I need to make sure it's as ready as it can be. I'll dress before I leave. I didn't want to risk getting buttery fingers on my clothes." He pushes a plate towards me. "Sausage?"

I ignore the innuendo. "Buttery fingers? Does your mother still do your tie for you?"

He reaches me in a few strides and pulls me into his arms. "Your bum print is still on the table, but don't worry, she didn't see it. She would have cleaned it if she had. I've hidden it. You have the most prefect—"

"Christos! Put her down. Let the poor girl eat." Mrs B is back in the room.

My eyes sweep the kitchen table as I turn to face her. Sure enough, the fruit bowl is now sitting where I had been last night.

"Mrs B, thank you so much. You didn't need to do this. I'm usually a yoghurt and an apple kind of girl." I turn away and pick up a sausage as I take a seat. "Lovely sausage. What time do you leave?" I ask as she busies herself with her handbag. Looking at H, I put the sausage in my mouth and slowly ease it in and out. He grins and lifts the fruit bowl.

"You can still have an apple, here help yourself. The plums look good too."

My eyes dart to the table. Bloody hell, he wasn't lying. He's revealed two perfect butt cheeks. I grab for the bowl, and he pulls it back out of reach.

His mother turns and places her bag on one half of the bum print and slaps the back of his head.

"Don't tease. Let her have an apple."

I grasp the bowl and place it next to her bag, thus hiding the remaining evidence.

Mrs B waves her train ticket at me. "My train is at ten. Christos tells me he can take me. We don't have long. He needs to get a move on. At least you're dressed."

"It's only eight thirty. Stop panicking," Christos tells her.

Mrs B rolls her eyes, then wags her finger back and forward. "So, did you two do some talking in between throwing your clothes around the kitchen?"

Oh no. Here we go. A hot flush takes over, I reckon even my toes are blushing and I'm willing H to speak, because I can't look at her. I know he's smiling, but I can't look, and I bet she is, too. The silence continues. I break first and flap my hand in front of my face. "Phew, it's hot in here. It was last night, too."

I don't know who laughed first, Mrs B, who cackles away, dabbing a tissue to her eyes, or H, whose shoulders are bouncing around before he folds his arms on the table and buries his face. It's not funny. Well, it is, but it's at my expense. I decide I'll be the bigger person.

"We didn't talk no. H...I mean Christos didn't want to."

H receives another slap, and he calls out in protest.

"I tried, Mrs B. I promise I'll try again tonight. I'm sorry your visit is so short, I was hoping for more cooking tips, although I think it will take us a week to get through the leftovers. It's a shame I haven't got a car or I could take you."

Mrs B's hands fly to her face. "The ladies, I promised I'd go over. Christos, get dressed. I'll be back shortly."

Mrs B leaves the room.

H points a finger at me as the front door slams. "You told me I was talking too much."

"You told me it was rude to talk with your mouthful, it's also rude to point," I retort. "Seriously though, I'm glad we put the talking on hold, but we need to do it."

H scoots his chair back and slaps his legs. "Come here."

I walk around the table and straddle him. "You said we haven't got time."

He runs his hands up and down my thighs. "We haven't. I just needed one more cuddle. My mum likes you. She only teases people she likes."

"I'm a very likable person, and I like her too. Mrs B's good fun."

"You are, and she can be. She can also be cantankerous and interfering, but she always means well, even if it doesn't feel like it. Don't invite her back, she'll be back anyway, but if you invite her, it will be at the end of the week, and I want more time on my own with you." He kisses me and I rotate my hips. "Enough." He stands and sits me on the table. "You, young lady, are temptation. I haven't got time to be tempted because I need to get dressed. What are you up to today?"

"Well, my lover is leaving me alone for the day, my playmate has gone away to work, so I think I'll go down to the agency, remind them I'm a client, and that they are supposed to find me work. And make sure they've got over the bee fiasco."

H looks angry for a moment.

"What? What did I say?"

He considers his words, but his hands are on his hips. "When you say playmate, you mean Joel, yes?" I nod and he joins me, but his head keeps moving. "What sort of playmate? What were you up to in your bedroom on Sunday?" he asks.

It must be catching, because my hands fly to my face a la Mrs B. "You heard?"

"I heard enough. Want to share?"

He's trying to look casual, but his tone tells me otherwise.

I go for a joke. "What did you think we were doing? You know a lady never tells."

He steps forward quickly and takes hold of my chin. "I don't want to think about it, but I want you to promise me it won't happen again."

I flap my hand. "Don't worry, I doubt I'll get it anyway, because I couldn't stop giggling."

"Get? Get what?" Releasing my chin, he scratches his head.

"The porno audiobook. It was bloody awful. Hearing Joel tell me how much he loved a wet pussy was too much. And I'm good. I had a passionate snog with Jeremy Franks in front of hundreds of people ten nights in a row. He smelt like a horse and kept sniffing. I even managed tears when he left me. Although they were probably tears of relief, but the audience lapped it up. Longest applause we had for the end of any scene."

"You're talking about acting, aren't you?"

"Yes. Joel promised me doing verbal porn would be easier than physical. After last night's performance I'd have to argue with him, but seriously, it was cringeworthy."

"And Joel's gay?"

"Yes. You've met him. Ooh, does your gaydar not work?" I ask with a giggle. Then I realise what the matter was. "You thought that me and Joel...that we. Oh my god, that's hilarious, H. I can't wait to tell him."

His smile is back. "You will not tell him. And whether or not you get the job, practise that voice. You can use it on me."

"You were jealous," I accuse. "And snooping."

"Of course I wasn't snooping. I could hear everything as I walked past your door, and I didn't know it was you at first. Didn't know until he told you off for not being serious. Then I was jealous. Fucking jealous, with no right to be. That made me even more angry. So, now we've cleared that up, I can get ready for work."

I have no words, so I just grin at him. I like him being all possessive. He thought I was banging Joel, and he still wanted me. I keep smiling as he runs upstairs.

Both H and Mrs B return at the same time, and I grin over her shoulder as she pretends to straighten his tie. When she steps back, I whistle. He looks hot in a suit. A man who can wear a suit that well deserves a whistle.

"Do you approve?" he asks.

"You know how men ogle women in sexy undies? That's what women do to men in a good suit. Turn around and lift your jacket."

He does, and his muscular arse allows the trousers to fall perfectly.

"Yep, I'm whistling again. Only silently, Mrs B is here."

Mrs B slaps his arse. "Put it away, get my bag, and put it in the car. We must go. Cassie, look after him for me."

She holds out her arms, and I walk forward.

As I hug her, I have a brainwave. "I will. Actually, H, can I come too? I can walk to the agency from your office. It's not far."

So I do. Mrs B gets tearful as we wave her off, and H teases me on the way back to his office. It's nice. It's natural, and for the first time in as long as I can remember, I feel comfortable and safe. He parks his car, and we walk hand in hand to his office. H threatens to buy me a bee outfit for my birthday just so he can cut me out of it and take me in the shower again. I tell him to behave because I'm getting the tingles back and he grabs me, wrapping his arms around me. He kisses me in a way one shouldn't kiss in the street and pulls away as the door opens behind him.

A suited man exits, and I feel H still for a moment before he steps forward, his hand held out.

"Jackson? Chris Baros, apologies. I was expecting you later."

The man looks distinguished. He's about sixty with neat greying hair. His suit is expensive, his shoes shiny. He pumps H's hand up and down, telling H it was he who's in the wrong because when they spoke before he was jetlagged and thinking in the wrong time zone. The suit is American. He suggests they grab a coffee before going back in. He then looks at me and holds out his hand.

"Where are my manners? I'm sorry, ma'am. Jackson Courtney at your service. I'm looking forward to working with Chris, I can tell you, he's worked miracles in there."

I smile and shake his hand. "Cassie. Nice to meet you. I'm—"

H jumps in, wrapping an arm around my shoulder. "It's me who should apologise. My mind was elsewhere. Cassie, this is Jackson, Gemini's communications director, Jackson, this is Cassie, my beautiful wife."

H pulls me closer and kisses the top of my head. My hand is still up in his jacket and I pinch him, hard. He doesn't even flinch.

"I can see why your mind was elsewhere. Say, I'm in town alone, why don't you two join me for dinner tonight? I hate eating alone. Are you free?"

"Not really," H says, quickly.

But I'm not having that. His wife! "Don't be silly, darling. We can put that off. We can't have Jackson eating alone. What time and where? Actually, I'll leave that with you two or I'll be late for my appointment. See you later, Jackson. Looking forward to it." I blow H a loving kiss, my eyes telling him I'm going to kill him, and walk away.

I'm seething because just when you think you know someone. Poof. It's a wonder he didn't call me Ana.

Chapter 15

Christos

FUCK, FUCK, FUCK! WHAT did I just do? I must have a death wish or a self-destruct button or something. First, I tell them I can get this office up and running by July, then I introduce Cassie as my wife. What was I thinking? I wasn't thinking; I was panicking. And what was Cassie doing offering to have dinner with Jackson? She didn't look happy, so why agree? What's she going to do, stand him up?

We're tied up for most of the day, and I don't have time to speak to Cassie, because when we're not working, he's asking what feels like a million questions. I almost hug him when at four o'clock he tells me he's calling it a day so he could get a nap before dinner. We agreed that Cassie and I would meet him at his hotel at seven thirty.

I leave shortly after Jackson does and call Cassie from the car.

"Hello, hubby." Her voice is flat. She's pissed off with me.

"Cassie, I can explain."

"Oh really. You keep promising to explain a lot of things. You'll explain them tonight. What time will you be home?" She's actually sounding like a wife now.

"I'm on my way."

"I'll be ready," she snaps and hangs up.

Before Jackson appeared, Cassie telling me she'd be ready for me would have made my heart sing. Now it sinks into my boots. When I get home, I step inside with trepidation.

"In here," she calls from the kitchen.

I go to join her. Cassie sits at the end of the kitchen table, a pen and a notebook in front of her. All the other chairs are leaning against the table except one. The one furthest away from Cassie. She points at it with her pen.

"Sit."

I pull off my tie, and turning the chair, straddle it, my arms across the backrest. "Can I start by apologising?" I ask rolling my tie up neatly and placing it on the table.

"No, save it. Why do you still wear your wedding ring?" she says, holding my gaze.

"Because I'm stupid. Initially it was habit, now it's necessity."

"Explain."

"This is a new job for me. A great job. I was head to head with another candidate, and do you know why I got the job?" I pause for comment, but Cassie winds the pen in circles for me to continue. "Because I was married. Gemini is a family-friendly company, over the top family friendly. No scandals, no skeletons in the closet. I have to be married, or at least not divorced. Ana left me on the day I found out I'd got the job."

"That's ridiculous. What a load of crap! Your marital status does not prove whether you can do the job. Sorry, not buying it."

"Do you think I don't know that? But I get it, sort of. My boss, the one who sold to Gemini, he built his business on families. It sounds corny, I know. But he always found the best product for that particular family: be it endowments, saving plans, pensions. He was upfront with what he would make. That's all there was to it. Didn't matter if he was offered more by someone else to sell their product. If it didn't suit that family, he'd look elsewhere. When he invested funds for clients, he invested in companies which were ethical in whatever they did. He never set the world on fire, but he made a good living and set up a comfortable future for him and his family, which is what he wanted for our clients. He was already considering retirement when Gemini made him an offer, and he wouldn't have sold to them if they weren't the right fit. We investigated them. They did pretty much the same as we did, but with knobs on. We were worried that there would be religious nonsense behind it all, but there wasn't. Just honest Joes, doing their bit and still making money. Good money, but not by ripping anyone off, not by exploitation, not by lying. But, and here's the big but, they make a big deal about who they employ. So when Ana left, the timing couldn't have been worse. I kept the ring, to keep up the pretence that I was a happily married man. I figured that no one has total control over their personal situation, and once I had established I was sound, my marriage would fail, with no drama etcetera. Had I explained all this to Ana, she would have pretended for me, but I didn't want her to. She'd found someone else. She was free. And now here we are. I'm sorry."

Cassie looks concerned, worried maybe? Why? Is she going to bail on me? "That's ridiculous. Crazy even. If this is so important to you, that you'd announce me as your wife, me, who you've only known for the blink of an eye. Why didn't you ask your wife to pretend?"

"First she's not my wife anymore, not really, and—"

"Nor am I, yet here I am wondering what I'm going to say to explain away the lack of a ring." Cassie holds up her hand and wiggles her fingers. "I come from a broken home. Do I lie if he asks me about my family?"

"No, of course not."

"So why lie about yours? Why not just say my wife left me? Surely, with all these *values*, honesty should come at the top of the list? Did you think Ana would come back to you?"

"No. It was all pretty final."

"Yet you think she would have pretended for you."

"I know she would. I didn't ask because she deserved to do what she wanted to with her life. Asking her might have ruined that for her."

"Do you still love her?"

"Not in the way you mean. Never have."

Cassie's brow furrows. "What does that mean? You married her. Are you expecting me to believe that you had an arranged marriage?"

"As good as. Look, Cassie, I—"

"Keep talking. Explain." Cassie is taking no prisoners.

"It's complicated if you're not from a close community, I'll do my best," I tell her.

"Talk, H. Stop procrastinating. You're making me even more irritated."

"Bloody hell, this is worse than the interviews I had to go through."

Cassie doesn't reply, just winds the pen around again.

"Our parents were close. Our fathers were cousins, sort of. We were best friends growing up. Ana is clever, funny, and good company. As we grew older, we were close. We told each other everything. I saw off blokes who were bothering her. She told me which girls I should avoid. I suppose we were always together when not at school. Christmases, holidays, family parties. When I approached eighteen, the hints started that I needed to think about getting married. That I needed a good Cypriot girl who would know how to look after me, how to raise our children properly. I shrugged it off and said sure, because I had no intention of getting married, as I still had things to do. There weren't that many eligible girls in York. Not that fit their perfect criteria, anyway. We'd all moved there when I was fifteen. Our fathers opened a restaurant there. There's a big Cypriot community in the UK, and everyone knows someone wherever you come from, and if they know them, you know them. I thought they'd start making me visit families with suitable girls. I'd seen that happen to friends."

"And you didn't protest?" Cassie asks.

"No. They couldn't force me to marry. They wouldn't force me, especially my mother. It either would or wouldn't happen. So I threw myself into life. Parties, night clubs, stag dos abroad. The usual teenage stuff. Then, when I was nineteen, my father had his first heart attack. When he came home, he piled on the pressure. I needed to stop partying and step up and be a man. I needed to marry, and I needed to be ready to take over the restaurant."

"So you agreed?" Cassie asks.

"Not immediately. I told him I would do all that, but I hadn't met the right girl. And he laughed at me. He said Ana was the right girl, and she wanted me. It was the first I'd heard of it, but Ana texted me the next day and asked to meet. Her father had given her the same story. Only he'd asked what non-Cypriot did she think would look after her like I would. Could she guarantee they wouldn't run off and leave her holding the baby? Christos would never do that. Who would look after her better than me? She told me she agreed with him."

"So you married her?"

"Not just like that, no. But yes, eventually. We loved each other, but not romantically. I had some experience. She was a virgin. We'd never been intimate together, nothing more than a kiss on the cheek. It took five weeks for us to...you know."

"Have sex?" Cassie suggests sarcastically.

"Yes. Have sex."

"So you married some ugly Cypriot girl just because your families wanted it."

"She's not ugly. She's pretty."

"Ah, so you fancied her. Thought she'll do, and it will keep the parents quiet."

"No...sort of...I didn't fancy her. She was my friend, my best friend. But, yes, I did think why not? There are no guarantees, and Ana was a good choice for any man. She was a lovely girl. Ana thought the same about me. So we said, sod it. If nothing else, we'll escape the parents and the nagging, have our own little house. We agreed that if at the end of five years we didn't feel any differently, we'd separate. When we hit the five-year anniversary, we went out for a meal and agreed we'd done our best. We'd never be love's young dream, but we'd stay together because it was easier, until one of us wanted to move on. There would be no children because that would be a disaster waiting to happen, something that would tie us together because we'd never leave our children. The sex became less and less until it petered out. I'll be honest, I was beginning to think we'd go on like that forever. I was so busy at work. She was working in the restaurant. We were ships that passed in the night, and both too knackered to look for love elsewhere. Sad but true."

"You expect me to believe you were happy to live with your pretty best friend and not have sex?"

"I do. Just like you expect me to believe that your tall, dark, and handsome friend is of no interest to you."

"He's gay!"

"And if he wasn't? Would he still be your friend?"

"Yes. We're mates, but okay, I'll give you that." Cassie shrugs. "Then what happened?"

"I left work early to tell her we were moving to Bristol, but she got in first and told me she was leaving me. Setting me free. And I was glad, Cassie, fucking glad. I'd rather she'd have chosen someone else, but she's not my responsibility anymore, whatever anyone else thinks. She was happy, and I was free. Free to come to Bristol and meet someone special. Someone who makes me feel all the things I've never felt. Is that enough now?"

Cassie runs the pen down the notepad.

"You made a list?" I laugh.

"Yes, I made a bloody list. You distract me. I didn't want distractions. So, one last question. Why the hell did you tell Jackson I was your wife?"

I run my hands over my face. "Because I'm a fucking idiot. But because he caught us kissing. I'm a married man. I shouldn't be kissing anyone but my wife in the street. Do you remember the bit about what swung the job for me? Why are you smirking?"

"How did you know I'd go along with it?" Cassie asks, her smirk going nowhere.

"I didn't. But I know you're a decent person. You like my mother. I was hoping you would. No, that's a lie. I wasn't hoping anything. I really didn't think it through."

"You need to work on that. What happens now?"

"Now, you forgive me, hug me, maybe a little jiggy-jiggy if we stop talking, and then we go to dinner with Jackson, and you will be my perfect wife. Beautiful, witty, and you. Then Jackson will get on a plane tomorrow, and you can revert to being my very perfect lover. Deal?"

"Only it's not that simple, is it?" Cassie looks at me as though I'm stupid. She's been taking lessons from Miss Allison. "Not simple at all. It's more complicated than that."

"Why?" Cassie seems very confident about this. I've missed something. What did I miss?

"Because, my lovely, H, what happens when the next VIP comes here? I'm assuming there will be a launch, dinners, parties, Christmas dos. You know stuff where you drag the wife along. Am I to be delicate and take to my bed regularly, like a Victorian lady?"

"Shit!" I hadn't thought further than explaining why I was feeling up a woman in the street. Cassie is right, although ... "Cassie, I know this is all pretty new. It's not been a week yet, but the sex is fantastic, and we're already living in the same house, you like my mother and she you, how do you fancy being my wife long term?"

Cassie colours but recovers quickly. "Why sir, I do believe that was a proposal, although not a very romantic one. How do I know you'll be honourable? That you will treat me kindly and provide a good future for me and my cats? Not run off sowing your oats all over town?" She's become a Southern Belle.

I stand and walk to her slowly. "Because I'm not stupid. Why would I do that when I have you? Was that a yes?"

"It was my best pretend yes. I'll have fun playing this role, H. But you need to think seriously before we take this any further. It will come back and smack you in the face. It's the most ridiculous thing I've ever heard. If you want my advice, I think it's best you go alone. I'll be ill or at the whatever it was we had booked, and I'll never be seen again. That way, you won't get caught out. Then, when you've cemented your position within the company, you can split with your wife. Eventually you'll find a real wife, the one you actually want to be married to with no pretence and no pressure from the parents, and you'll be able to present her. She'll need a bit of coaching on the backstory, or. . ." Cassie gets to her feet and runs her nail down my chest, "I know this is a bit out there, but you could just tell the truth. Come clean. The wife ran off. You've taken to shagging your housemate and snogging her in the street. None of it is your fault. They can't blame you, H. Tell the truth."

"No."

"Why?"

"Because."

"Because has never been a good reason."

"It's good enough for me. What have you got to lose?" I'm sliding my hands down into her leggings and she pushes against me.

"Everything," she whispers, as she kisses me.

I push her away. "What do you mean?"

"Um. I mean, you have everything to lose."

"Would I lose you?"

"No, I meant the job."

"Then I'll risk it."

"You're playing with fire," Cassie warns.

"I know." I slide my hand into her very un-granny like knickers, and she pushes me away.

"In which case in true wife-like fashion, I haven't got time for all that. I need to get ready. Oh, by the way, you owe me sixty pounds."

"I do?"

"Yep. You bought me a dress. I have three dresses, two are not appropriate, the other is too boring. I had to buy a new one."

"Not appropriate? I think I'd like to see them."

"You've already seen the black one."

"Almost. There's not a lot to it. Now I want to see the other inappropriate one."

"You will, but not tonight. What time do we have to leave?"

"Seven. I don't like to be late. We can always have a drink in the bar."

"What? If I'm not presentable, you only have yourself to blame. I've told you about talking too much."

When Cassie returns, with five minutes to spare, she looks absolutely perfect. She's wearing a deep blue dress with a tiny white floral print, and she tells me it has a sweetheart neckline. It has a flowing skirt which swishes around her legs as she walks, and pale pink toenails peep out of white sandals.

"Wow! Little bee, I don't know about sixty pounds, you look like a million dollars. Come here." I hold out my arms.

"Don't you dare. You'll smudge my lipstick. I'm a very thrifty shopper. This was in the sale."

I don't know how I keep my hands off her. I've never seen her with makeup before. It's not much, just enough to emphasise her eyes, and those gorgeous lips. I'm almost lost for words when she takes my hand, and I wish it was real. Truly wish I was taking my wife out to show everyone what a lucky bastard I was. I'll still be proud, smug even, but it's just pretend. So I settle for saying, "Thank you." And I walk her to the car.

Chapter 16

Cassie

WHEN I SEE H waiting for me in the hall, I wish we weren't going to dinner with someone else. I want him all to myself. But we have a job to do, and I refuse his advances. It's tough, because he keeps looking at me with those eyes. I won't need to employ my acting skills to be affectionate. He keeps glancing at me as we drive to Jackson's hotel, a little smirk on his face. It's not doing anything to dispel the tingles, but a lot for my ego.

H leads me into the bar, wrapping his arm around my waist when two men take a little too long to look at us as we approach the bar.

"They're jealous," he whispers. "They want to be me."

"Ego much?" I reply, knowing exactly what he meant, and giggle as he tries to explain. He catches on eventually and pulls me in close.

"Behave, or you'll be in trouble once I get you home." And those eyes tell me all I need to know about what sort of trouble that will be.

"Is this man giving you trouble, ma'am?" Jackson booms out a laugh and slaps H on the back. "May I say you look stunning, Mrs Baros."

I shake his hand. "He's always giving me trouble. You arrived just in time to save me. Please call me Cassie."

Jackson holds out his elbow. "Our table is ready. Let me escort you to the restaurant."

Jackson pulls out my chair, orders some wine, and we discuss the menu before placing our orders. Once done, he turns to H.

"I've just been speaking to MB. He's delighted with the progress, and asked you to send some photographs tomorrow. He's frustrated that he can't get away but says he's going to try to do a flying visit on his way to

Germany next week. He agrees with you and thinks you should go ahead with the new recruits. Do you need Bernice over to assist?"

They then get into a boring conversation about recruitment and training, but I plaster a serene smile on my face and sip my wine slowly as I wonder whether Glen was being genuine about the bee issue not being a problem. I resolve to call Jan and find out, and I almost jump off my chair when H squeezes my knee unexpectedly.

"I'm sorry, Cassie. I told you it would probably be boring. Where were you then?"

I smile at him. "What do you mean?"

"You were frowning and didn't hear me speak to you," H explains.

I flip my hand. "Oh, just thinking about work. I'm sorry, what did you say to me?"

"Chris was just asking if you were bored yet. Tell me about your work, Cassie. It will be far more interesting than us," Jackson answers.

"I'm an actor. Or would be if I could get enough work. My last job was a production by a local writer. It wasn't challenging, and my next job isn't until the end of July, and then it's only a two-week gig. I'm hoping my agency will find me something to help me keep...busy. H works such long hours." I was going to stay afloat, but then Jackson would question if H was keeping me short.

Jackson claps his hands. "An actor. That's wonderful. Have you been in anything I might have seen?"

"I doubt it. I do mainly theatre and have a few television series under my belt, but I'm guessing you're based in America, so highly unlikely." My resume sounds pathetic, and I wonder if H wishes I'd bumped it up a little to make his pretend wife sound more exciting. I wink at H. "H is very patient with me." H looks at me and, while assuring me that isn't the case, his eyes start doing that thing. Tingle! I'll have to have a word about that.

"H? You call Chris, H? Why?"

While we were in the middle of our quest to have sex in every room of the house, I admitted the H was for Hottie, because I felt he deserved to know. So H now leans back in his chair and grins at me.

"Tell him," H instructs me, and I don't know if I should go with the happy or the hot answer.

"Are you sure?" I ask, hoping he knows that my raised brow is a warning.

"Of course."

I sigh and twitch my shoulders. "I told his mother I named him H because when we met I didn't know his name and he was always happy, so H. But it was because I thought he was hot. Still do."

Jackson booms out a laugh, and H gets another hearty slap on the back. "You're a lucky son of a gun and no mistake."

H grabs my hand. "You don't need to tell me that."

Our starters arrive, and Jackson taps the table. "Do you do television advertising? I know some actors shy away from it."

"I always said I wouldn't so that when I was famous and being invited onto chat shows, they wouldn't be able to drag it out of the archives and embarrass me. But now I'm more realistic, I'm happily married, I don't need fame, so I'll do most things within reason."

"That's a refreshingly honest answer," Jackson says as he spears a prawn. "I've got little time for pretenders."

I hope he doesn't see the look I exchange with H.

"Thank you. But I pretend all the time. It's the nature of what I do." I go for a cheeky wink, and he booms again. I have never known a laugh like it. He's attracting attention from the other diners.

"Have you done any promotional work?" he asks, another prawn poised on his fork.

I've got a mouthful of goat's cheese so H answers for me.

"She dressed up as a bee once to promote how important they are to the world's survival. Didn't you? It was quite a sight. One I'll never forget. Mmm. These mussels are delicious."

"That's true. Well done, Cassie. We should all raise awareness of the need to protect the planet." Jackson nods his approval as he devours his last prawn.

"She's a remarkable woman," H says and the look in his eye gives me another instant thrill. I can't wait to get home.

I wave my fork at them. "That's what you should do. For promotion, I mean. Bees. I'm sure it won't cost you much, but given your company's ethos, it would be a nice little byline for your launch. Have you got a flat roof?"

H frowns. "Part of it is. Why?"

"The Bristol Bee project might be able to put hives up there. Even if they can't, I'll bet they can do some little wildflower boxes. Every little helps." I don't know where that came from, because I'll be happy if I never see a bee again, even though they brought H into my life. I've probably overstepped the mark, so I flip my hand. "Ignore me. I'm probably being silly."

Jackson tops up my wineglass. "No, no, you're not. I like it. Not just because it is good publicity, which it is, but because it's simply good. Do you know how I contact these people?"

"I can find out." I shoot a glance at H, who gives a nod of approval.

"Splendid. Christos has my contact details."

I relax back in my chair as the table is cleared. That's enough talking from me. I'll speak only when spoken to from now on. Who knows what will come out of my mouth next? I glance at Jackson. He's also relaxed back while we await the main course, but he's staring at me. I kick H under the table as I take his hand with a little jerk of my head towards Jackson. H looks from me to Jackson and back again. I'm not sure if he's amused or concerned. H clears his throat.

"Are you okay, Jackson?"

Jackson springs into action, and leaning forward, raps the table, before leaning back and covering his mouth with his hand while looking at the ceiling. After a few moments, he sits upright, gives his head a shake and looks from me to H.

"Would you mind if I ask a personal question?" His head is swivelling from one to the other of us.

Shit! Has he rumbled us? I look to H for guidance.

"Personal? What sort of personal?" H enquires.

"Now, you must tell me if I'm out of line. If I've jumped the gun. But are you two planning on having a family? Do you want kids?"

H is clearly flummoxed, and takes too long to reply, so based on what H has told me, I fill the silence, despite promising myself to keep my mouth shut. "Oh yes. The more the merrier. We're just waiting until we're settled, aren't we, H." I give his hand a squeeze in the hope he'll help me out.

H nods slowly as he turns to look at me. "I can't wait. You'll make a perfect mother." He's stroking the back of my hand with his thumb.

It's not tingles I'm getting now; it's something warm and fuzzy and comforting. And pretend! I snatch my hand away and turn back to Jackson.

"Why?"

It's more of a demand than a question, but our main courses arrive, and he holds up a finger asking me to wait. I don't want to wait. I want to get out of here. This all felt too real for a moment. I want it to be real, but it's not, and I hate H for knocking my guard down, for letting me feel what it could be like. I want to go home.

Jackson cuts into his steak. I'm ignoring H tapping my foot under the table, and I'm certainly not going to push for an answer to my question. I don't want to discuss having children with H, because that will never happen. We eat our meal in silence, other than compliments for the food. I relax a little but will start yawning the minute these plates disappear in the hope they'll get the hint and I can go home.

The table is cleared, and we all decline the offer of a dessert. Jackson offers a nightcap which H refuses on the pretext he's driving but I'm guessing it's because he thinks I'm being awkward and wants to get me out of here. Which is fine by me.

"Okay, I'll let you youngsters get going, but before I do, something to consider. We have a set of ads scripted to promote our UK operation. It's all based on family life, and as you would expect what a family needs, but I want you to do it. Both of you, preferably. But particularly Cassie. I want to get some new scripts drawn up."

H looks like someone's just threatened to cut his tackle off, so I jump in. Again. On his head be it. I hope he's better in the boardroom than he is at acting.

"What do you mean, you want us to do it?" The penny has dropped, and I know exactly what he means.

"It will be real, in the way it should be. Do you see?"

I see nothing of the sort, because this whole bloody thing is a pretence, and H, all he manages to do is raise his eyebrows.

"I think so, but elaborate, because I'm sure H would like to know what you have planned for him."

As Jackson booms this time, the server behind him visibly jumps.

"Ha. Yes, of course. The wording of our advertising is all true. Most of it is taken from the people we've dealt with. Think how much better it would be if you say those words. My husband and I are planning ahead. We want to ensure that our children's future is secure. Be that school fees or blah blah blah. Or, I'm delighted my husband is the Exec Director of Gemini UK. With the products they source, I know we can plan our family with confidence. That sort of thing. Not acting, not telling lies. We never usually use our staff because they all get tongue-tied or overact, but you're a professional, and I'm sure Chris will be able to deliver a line or two. It helps that you're a good-looking couple, and your chemistry is unmissable. Perfect. And Cassie, of course you will get paid as I know we'll be eating into the time you could be doing something else." He waves his hand. "Anyway, don't answer now. Have a think about it. I'll speak to MB tomorrow and see what our guys can come up with. Or would you rather not have him trying to convince you too?" He releases the boom again, before getting to his feet. "Mrs Baros, may I escort you to your car?"

I take his arm, and H follows us out. He's rewarded with a bear hug and another slap on the back, while I get a kiss on the back of my hand. Jackson stands in the carpark and waves us out of sight.

"Fuck!" H exclaims as soon as we're clear.

"I warned you to let me stay at home, husband darling. One day you'll come to realise I am always right. What are you going to do? Come clean?"

"No! I can't. After that bloody performance, how can I?"

"H you have to. I don't mind because he said he'll pay me, but your job is on the line. And you're speeding, slow down."

"Because I'm trying to keep up with my blood pressure. I thought only you did that to me. I'll think of something."

The car slows down and he holds out his hand, which I take.

"You were perfect tonight."

I want to tell him it was easy, but I can't, because it wasn't. "Thank you."

"You even convinced me," he says, taking my hand to his lips.

"I'm a talented actor. I told you that."

"You did. You should get a bloody Oscar, because I was choosing our kids' names at one point."

I giggle despite the warm flush washing over my body. "What did you come up with?"

"Stavros and Eleana good, strong Greek names," he tells me with a grin.

"So, we're only having two?" I joke.

"Initially, because I wouldn't want to be denied my marital rights for too long."

He sounds so serious, it's like we're actually having a real conversation. I can't cope with this, so I punch his arm.

"Stop. You're getting too serious about this. You have to tell them. Anyway, you're not having Stavros. I don't like it."

He parks the car around the corner from the house and turns to face me. "It wouldn't be too awful if it was real, would it?"

My heart is fluttering. Why did I have to meet him now when everything is so messy? I shake my head while I swallow back my real thoughts. "You'd never cope with me. Anyway, it can't be real. You already have a wife."

"Not for much longer." He clears his throat.

He won't stop looking at me, and he's giving me too much hope, so I poke him in the chest. "I'll tell you what, we'll carry on pretending we're married. You can fall into bed and snore and fart because I've got a headache. How does that sound?"

"Like the life I escaped. Why don't I remove that dress as soon as we're on the doorstep and you wiggle that pretty little arse up the stairs to my bed? I might have to take the granny knickers off first, though."

"Oh, didn't I say? I bought new undies. Sexy ones. I thought that's what your pretend wife should wear. Shall I race you to the doorstep?"

Chapter 17

Christos

I DON'T KNOW WHAT'S happening to me. On the one hand, I have to get myself out of this advert nonsense. What a nightmare, there's pretending I'm happily married, and then there's making a film about it. It can't happen. But more concerning at the moment are the feelings Cassie evoked while putting on her performance. I know she was acting, but I wasn't joking when I said she deserved an Oscar. I wanted to be her husband. Who wouldn't? Cassie had Jackson eating out of her hand. She was too good. She almost convinced me, and I know she was lying. Shit, if I wasn't already married, as she reminds me regularly, I'd have proposed to her before we got back in the car. Almost did once we were in it.

And now look at her. Standing there looking all coy, a flush on her cheeks as I walk towards her unbuttoning my shirt, frightened to speak in case I say the wrong thing, and burst this happy little bubble I'm bouncing around in. And the question looping in my head? *Why isn't this real?* I'd tell her that, but I don't want to frighten her off.

Stooping, I pick up her dress, take her hand, and lead her upstairs.

We've almost reached my bedroom when she squeezes my hand.

"You're very quiet, H. Should I be worried?"

"No." I clear the frog in my throat, and I twist the dress ring she's been wearing back to front around her ring finger. "May I make love to you, Mrs Baros?" Cassie looks down at her feet and shakes her head. I grab her chin and lift her face to look at me. "What is it?"

Her eyes are shining. Tears? That's why I was trying to keep my mouth shut. What did I say?

"H, we've established you're a gentleman. But you have to stop pretending. If you don't, I might start to believe you, and this ball of lies will snowball way out of control. Explode, and we're in enough trouble as it is."

I drop her dress and, taking her by the shoulders, walk her backwards into the bedroom until she hits the bed and sits in front of me. My kiss is gentle. "I'm not pretending, Cassie. You—"

"H, we've spoken about this. Stop talking and make love to me."Her voice was steady, but her fingers trembled against my chest.

"My pleasure."

I lower my mouth to her shoulder, tasting the salt of her skin as she arches beneath me. Her breath quickens with every kiss I leave down the curve of her stomach. When I finally press inside her, she gasps my name like it's been torn from her throat.

"Fuck, Cassie," I manage, my voice ragged, "what are you doing to me?"

"Ditto, H. Ditto."

Afterwards, she snuggles up against me. She fits perfectly. I think she's dozed off as I lie here wide-awake staring at the ceiling and wondering how we sort out this mess, and how I can keep her.

"Are you awake?" she whispers.

"How did you know?" I give her a squeeze.

"Because you're not snoring or farting. What are you thinking about?" She's dragging her nails along my forearm. "Your arms would look fabulous inked up," she tells me. "But back to your thoughts."

"I don't like tattoos much. Certainly not on me. Don't want to be covered in gargoyles when I'm old and wrinkled. Mind you, if we carry on like this, I don't think I'll reach old age. Perhaps I should get some."

"Don't change the subject. What were you thinking about?"

"You, of course?" I reply.

"What about me? I'm not after flattery. I'm genuinely interested."

"So am I. I know nothing about you. From the little I do know, I don't think you had a happy childhood, and that makes me sad. You deserve to be happy."

With a sudden burst of energy, she sits cross-legged in front of me. "I know! That's what I think. And although I keep telling myself that, I keep waiting, and waiting," she sighs. "I've worked out that some people aren't supposed to be happy. I'm probably one of them."

"Don't say that. That's awful. Why aren't you happy? I know you'd like more work and would probably rather not be sharing your home with a bloke who bribes you into ridiculous situations with sex. But seriously, it hurts to know you're unhappy. Why?"

She groans and huffs out a breath. "I'm okay. Probably being dramatic after the pretend love-in. I'm not unhappy, but...you know, it feels like I'm just treading water until I get pulled under some days. I get so fucking lonely, even when Joel's doing his best to drag me around with him. There are no flowers around the door, not even a dandelion wilting in a pot. Just life. And I don't have an awful life. I know it could be a lot worse, and I'm so much better off than so many people but it could be better. And don't start me on the money. I'd like a little more money coming in a little more often. Joel tells me to ask my dad, because he's always trying to buy his way back in, but I'm never going to do that. After what he did, I won't ease his conscience. Fuck him." She lifts her hand to scratch her face, but I see the tear she's wiping away.

"That sounds bad. What did he do?"

"Killed my mother."

I sit up to join her. "What?"

"Not in person. He left us. I was thirteen, all spots and hormones, and he phones me and tells me he's going to live somewhere else for a while. To be good for my mum, and he'd see me in the holidays. I asked him why, and he said people change and it was for the best. I hadn't changed, other than the acne. Mum hadn't changed, and if he had, I didn't know about it because he was always working away. When I asked my mum, she said it was for the best, too. She defended him, but I wasn't convinced. And I was right, it wasn't. Nothing was better. I missed him, but even when I tried to call him, he was always in a meeting, or on his way to one, or at dinner and on and on." Her sigh is heartfelt.

"Do you still miss him?"

"I'll never admit that."

But she doesn't deny it and I kiss the top of her head. "Why did you say he killed her?"

"For a little while I thought it would be okay. She got a boyfriend, Alan. I didn't like him much, and not because he wasn't my dad. It didn't last very long. But after that ended, she cried all the time. I told her to ring dad, and she said she couldn't, she wasn't good enough for him anymore. I went ballistic. So I called him. I told him Mum needed to speak to him and I held out the phone. Mum told him she loved him, and she wanted him to come home. She was weeping, and he told her no and hung up on her. She fell to her knees, and I couldn't make her get up. We slept in the hall that night because that's where she'd fallen asleep. A few weeks later, the divorce papers arrived, and she started drinking."

I rub her arms. "I'm sorry. That must have been tough."

"It was. All my mates were going out with boys, sneaking into clubs and pubs, and I was sitting at home hiding bottles and cleaning up behind her. I called him and told him how bad it was. Do you know what he said?"

I can guess, but I shake my head.

"He said he was sorry, he'd get her checked into rehab, and I should go and live with him where I'd be safe. I told him to fuck off. First time I'd ever sworn at him. He hated it, so on the few occasions I've spoken to him since I make sure I slip it in. Childish but true." Cassie draws in a breath and holds it. When she lets it out, she climbs on to my lap. "And then she died. No warning. I came home from uni for the weekend and there was nothing in the cupboards so I told her to clean the kitchen while I went shopping. She told me she was too ill, I told her she was too drunk. When I got back, she was lying on the kitchen floor. Dead. And not from the drink. She had cancer. She must have been in terrible pain, but she never mentioned it, and never went to the doctor."

Cassie's tears are flowing freely, and I lift the sheet and wipe them for her.

"Cassie, I'm so sorry. I shouldn't have asked." I kiss her head and hug her tight.

"It's fine. He came home for the funeral. Mum hadn't left a will, so everything went to him. He asked if I wanted to keep the house and I said no. I really didn't. It made me miserable just walking through the front door. So he said he'd buy me a flat nearer uni, and I told him I was happy in my student digs. Everything was sold off or given to charity. He asked for my bank details because the money should come to me. But I told him to fuck off, and after asking me not to swear at him, he told me he'd open an account and I was to let him know when I wanted access. Guess what?"

"I'm guessing fuck off came into it somewhere." I kiss her cheek.

"Correct. There's an endowment due to me when I hit thirty too. He can shove that as well. I'll never take anything from that man."

"How do you afford this place? It's not cheap and you're broke?"

"Ah, well, and you mustn't tell Steve, I know you won't be around long enough to worry, Mr Bigshot. One of my mum's friends called and said if I was coming back to Bristol, she had a house and was looking for sharers. As long as I oversaw the cleaner, gardener and any maintenance men, she'd let me have it cheap. I nearly fainted when I saw this place."

"We have a cleaner? I wondered who did it and assumed there was a rota." I lie back down and keep hugging her close to me. "Do you want my opinion? No, forget it, you won't."

"Go on. Tell me. I won't comment if the comment is going to be nasty."

"No. Let's get some sleep. I have a long day ahead of me tomorrow."

Cassie clamps her teeth on my nipple. "Tell me or bite," she mumbles.

"Ow. Ow. Get off. Why do you like me doing that?" I push her away and pull her back one handed, my other arm covering my chest.

"Because it sends a signal, or tingle if you will, from here to here." She drags her nail from my nipple down to my cock and takes hold. "You see!"

"I do. How am I supposed to get any sleep now?" I ask as it twitches in her hand.

"Would you like me to wear you out?"

"Very much."

When my alarm sounds the next morning, I groan. As I grope for my phone, I realise Cassie isn't there, so I switch it off and go in search of her. The smell of coffee greets me as I reach the hall.

"There you are. I missed you, and I thought you liked tea first thing?" I smile as I see she's wearing the shirt I had on last night.

She points at the mug next to her with a spoonful of yoghurt. "I do. Already drinking it, but as a newly pretend bride, and an unemployed one, I thought I should do something wifely, so I put the coffee on. What would you like for breakfast?"

"Toast, and don't remind me. I've got to face Jackson in an hour or so."

Cassie puts the bread in the toaster and points to a chair. "Sit."

"Oh no. You haven't got another list, have you?" I'm only half joking.

"Just the one question. What was your opinion? You distracted me."

I think about fobbing her off again, but I can see it's important to her. "Just something you should consider." I shrug.

"Go on, I'm all ears." She folds her arms across her chest.

"I think you should ask your dad why he left. 'It's for the best' is something you would tell a child. Most parents would avoid dragging their kids into the murky world of marriage failure. As someone who has just come out the other side of an unfortunate marriage, I know it's never black and white."

"But you would have stayed if she hadn't left you." Cassie throws out her arms, then brings them back across her chest.

"Only because I was lazy. Not because I was happy."

"Not sure I agree, but in your situation, by your telling of it, you're both happier now. My mum wasn't." Cassie turns away to butter the toast.

I think about what my mother said about Ana being unhappy, but I nod. "Okay, point taken. But that means what you're saying is that he should have stayed and ignored his own feelings because your mother's were more important. However, from someone who wasn't there, I would suggest that it wouldn't have made either of them happy."

Cassie spins round, the butter knife her choice of weapon. She swishes it about. "Okay, a scenario for you. You're coerced into a marriage you don't really want, but it's your best friend. She's pretty, and funny and all that other wonderful stuff you said about her, but she falls for you properly. Loves you, and you know it." Cassie bangs the knife on the table. "Then you get the opportunity to be free. What do you do?"

Well, I walked into that one. Whatever I say is going to be wrong. I point at her. "Good point, well made. Honest answer? I don't know. All I know is how it was. You don't know with your dad because you won't talk to him." I hold up my hands. "Ignore me. Give me my toast and sit on my lap so I can cover you in crumbs."

"Why would you want to do that? Disgusting." Cassie's nose wrinkles.

"Because then I'd have to eat them off you. On that note, that shirt should come off."

"Another good point well made. Well done, H. You're learning. Have you got time to be eating crumbs?"

I check the time and groan. "No. I can't be late again today." I swig down my coffee and kiss her. "To be continued."

"That's what you keep saying."

"And do I deliver? Yes, I do. Hold that thought. I have to get ready."

When I come back down, she whistles, and I take a bow.

"H, I really like you in a suit. The tingles are off." She jokes as she pulls me closer with my tie. "Have a good day, darling."

"Thank you. I doubt that very much, but I shall try. What are you up to?"

"I'm going to go back to bed! Do you know what time I had to get up to see you off?" She slaps my shoulder.

"And it was appreciated. Only you and my mother have ever done that for me. Thank you." I pull her tight against me. "For everything. I l...I like living with you." Shit! What was I going to say? I need to get out of here. "Let's have a quiet night in."

Cassie sighs and allows her head to fall against my chest. "No more talking, H. You've given me enough to think about."

"You were listening?" I tease.

"Out now. Or you'll be in big trouble, buster."

I kiss her and escape. If I hadn't been so stupid as to introduce her as my wife, I wouldn't have this sinking feeling in my stomach and would instead be skipping to the bloody car.

Jackson arrives thirty minutes after me. I buzz him in and walk over to greet him.

“Morning, Jackson. How’s the jet lag?” I ask and steer him out of the way of a mini forklift.

“Dealt with until tomorrow when I arrive home. You’re looking cheerful.”

I walk him further into the reception area and flick out my hand. “The reclaimed marble has arrived. They’ll start on it tomorrow...and the hub desks will be in by lunchtime, so the IT guys can start getting them wired up. There’s been little movement for days, and then it all happens at once. I don’t know how George copes. Give me a spreadsheet or a complicated investment any day.”

“That is good news. How’s the lovely Cassie this morning? I was telling MB about her. He thinks having you two as genuine stars is a great idea. Don’t forget those photographs.”

I ignore the question about Cassie, and the mention of using us for the adverts, and say, “Already sent the photographs and updated him on the progress today.”

“Cassie and the other matter? I can see I won’t like the answer,” he says as I grimace.

Turns out Jackson is no pushover, but I knew that.

“Cassie is fine. She’s having a lazy day at home. Regarding the other matter, I don’t mind doing a promo thing, you know explaining the why, what and how. But talking with Cassie last night about what you want, I realised it might sound a little insincere. You know, ‘well they would say that wouldn’t they’, or ‘self-praise is no recommendation’ That was one of Brad Thomas’s favourites.” My hands are behind my back, and I cross my fingers. He’s nodding as I speak.

“And Cassie agrees?” Jackson asks.

“Yes. Pretty much.” Or she will once I tell her.

“Okay, and what about just Cassie doing the advertisement? None of the ‘I’m married to a big cheese’, just following the original script? She has a remarkable presence. Memorable, genuine, trustworthy. I’d really like her to think about it.”

“I’ll speak to her tonight. What time is your flight?”

"Four this afternoon, Heathrow. I'm only here for a couple more hours, so let's have a look through the files on the new recruits, and I'll have a chat with Bernice when I get back."

We spend the morning discussing and then contacting the new recruits where possible, and I'm optimistic again. By the end of July, I'll have a full team, and I can't wait to get going. As we approach lunchtime, I ask Jackson if he wants to grab some lunch.

"No, thank you, because with your permission, I have one more errand to run before I head to Heathrow."

"My permission?" I ask.

"Yes, I want to pop in and speak to Cassie. I really want her to do this, and I can be very persuasive, but I'm getting the impression that you'd rather she didn't get involved."

Fuckety fuck. I'm going to have to warn her. I shake my head. "Not at all. Cassie is very much her own woman. If she wants to do it, she will. But be warned she's a straight talker. She'll give an honest opinion and probably haggle her fee up."

Jackson slaps my back as his laugh echoes around us. "Like I said, I don't like pretenders. What's your address? I know it's not far, so I'll grab my bags and jump in a cab."

"My car's around the corner. I can take you." I offer because I don't want Cassie to be confronted by Jackson and cope alone. Not that she couldn't cope, but I got her into this mess.

"No, no. You've got enough on your plate. I've got broad shoulders, I'll handle whatever she throws at me."

"Here's hoping," I say as I text him the address. My back receives another slap, and I walk him to the door.

My phone is back in my hand the minute the door closes. I call Cassie. It goes to her message service, and the next time, and the next. Where the hell is she? I leave a message, and then text her too, just to be on the safe side.

Where are you? Jackson is on his way to the house. I've told him that us doing the ads and promoting Gemini would sound insincere and he wants you to go solo but with the original script. I'm sorry.
Guess how I'll make it up to you? H xx

Then I cross my fingers and wait for the shit to hit the fan.

Chapter 18

Cassie

IT'S BEEN A FRUSTRATING morning. I couldn't get back to sleep when H left, because all I could think about was H liked living with me. That's not what he was going to say. It was an L word, but it wasn't like. His face when he realised he'd almost said it! I'd have laughed if I wasn't in shock. He couldn't wait to get out of the house. So many questions were spinning around in my head, and most I couldn't answer.

What the actual fuck? Did I imagine that? Did he mean it? Was it habit? Did he say that to Ana every time he went to work? Do I want to hear the other L word?

Finally, I come up with an answer. Yes, I do. And having reached that conclusion, I give up all thoughts of sleep and try to keep myself busy. You name any mindless task and I've been doing it. But they're not called mindless for nothing. My hands are busy, but my mind has stayed fully occupied with the questions around the L word.

Is that what he was going to say? If it was, what would have been my response? I settled on fuck off for that one, as he would have been lying. Wouldn't he? What if he wasn't? And on. And on. And on.

I'm driving myself mad.

To stave off insanity. I call the agency. Glen has the cheek to offer me another job dressing up as a character, but promises he's chasing a few other leads. Joel rings to tell me that his leading lady is a bitch, but more importantly, the producers love our audition. Looks like I'm going to be a porn star. I need to think up an appropriate porn narrator name, because there ain't no way I'm using mine. The cleaning lady arrives. Emily is lovely, but far too talkative and cheerful, which I usually look forward to, but not today, not with the L situation on my mind.

The big news is that in amongst all this, I've decided that today I'm going to take H's considered advice and give my dad a call. Not to ask for money, just see how he is. To give him the chance to explain. It's my next task as soon as I get rid of Emily. But just as Emily's leaving, Miss Allison appears on the doorstep.

"'Bye, Em," I call as I channel happy Cassie. "Miss Allison, how are you? How's Elizabeth doing?"

"Very well, thank you, Cassie. And how are you?"

She wants something. She's making small talk, and nobody changes that much. Even if they have seen H almost naked.

"I'm well, thank you. Do you want to come in for a cup of tea?" I ask, with my most charming smile.

What the hell? I am not a happy stay-at-home housewife. I don't have coffee mornings, or 'do' lunch. Even if I did, I would not be offering to share tea with Miss Allison. H has addled my brain.

"Oh no, thank you. I can't leave Elizabeth, which is why I'm here."

"Of course not. Silly me. So what can I do for you?" I ask, trying to come up with what could possibly be the answer to that question.

"I wondered if you'd sit with Elizabeth. Only for thirty minutes, at the most, because I must go to the shops and to the chemist. I shouldn't put it off any longer."

"I can go to the shops for you. Two minutes, let me—"

"Oh no. Elizabeth is quite excited at the thought of having you visit. I was dreading you being out. There's no one else she'd be happy to stay with. Not even Doctor Christos." Miss Allison gives a giggle. Straight up. She giggled. Wait until I tell Steve.

"Of course, I'll just—"

"Splendid. Don't forget your keys. I already have what I need." She first points to the keys on the hall table, then pats the bag for life swinging from her arm. She knew I'd be a pushover.

I pick up my keys and follow her next door. When we get there, Elizabeth has nodded off. I hope, because she's motionless. At least I think she's asleep.

"Is she okay?" I ask, too concerned to go further into the room.

"Bored, I think. She rarely naps until after lunch. Don't wake her. She had a very disturbed night. I won't be long."

Miss Allison leaves and I rush over to Elizabeth and peer at her chest. Phew, it's moving. I pull my phone from my pocket and put it on silent. I check my emails and socials and find nothing of interest, so I wander around the room looking at the various photographs. The sisters were certainly good-looking girls back in the day. I wonder why neither of them married. I can guess with Miss Allison, and perhaps Elizabeth has always been a nervous wreck.

"Hello, dear. That's one of my favourites. We were taking the sea air at Burnham-on-Sea. Such a jolly day."

A small yelp escapes, and I spin around to face Elizabeth, who waves. After I've regulated my heartbeat, I smile at her. She really is a sweetie.

"Hello, Elizabeth, how's the recovery going?"

"Too slowly, because I want to get back out into the garden, but Jennifer won't let me until I can walk properly. I get so bored. I like my garden."

"I'm not surprised it's beautiful. Let's find something to entertain you. What do you fancy, a game of cards, monopoly, twenty questions? You choose; your wish is my command. But it mustn't be something Miss Allison doesn't approve of. I don't think she likes me." I roll my eyes and Elizabeth looks shocked.

"She does, you know. Said so to Mrs Baros, who's a wonderful woman. I'd be as fat as a house if I lived with her."

"What did she say?" My ego wants to hear this, but Elizabeth is stroking her cast like a pet dog and has a contented smile on her face. Come on, Elizabeth, don't wander away. I pat her good hand in encouragement.

"Who, dear?"

"Miss Allison. What did she say to Mrs B about me?" Here's hoping.

"Who's Mrs B?"

And I've lost her again. I let it go. I'm sure Elizabeth probably got hold of the wrong end of the stick anyway. "It doesn't matter. What do you want to do?"

Elizabeth flaps her hand towards the table. "Would you read to me, dear? I can't get two pages in without falling asleep."

I pick up the book. "Ooh. *Mary Poppins*. I played her at uni, you know. Do you want a full production, or just me?"

"I don't know what you mean." Elizabeth looks startled.

I open the book at a random page and grin. "Okay, here's me reading the book." I read a couple of passages, going into character for Mary and Bert, of course. Van Dyke has nothing on me.

Elizabeth's eyes light up. "Oh yes, dear. So much better than Jennifer."

"Or what about this?" I know these scenes inside out, and rather than reading from the book, I act them out, stepping from one side to the other as I become first Mary and then Bert.

"Marvellous," Elizabeth calls. "Do the chimney song."

So I do.

"Now 'A Spoonful of Sugar'."

Elizabeth joins me, and even mimes taking the spoon in her mouth as I present my invisible one to her.

"What about the other one, um. The one with the long name." Elizabeth clicks her fingers.

I'm halfway through a very rousing, knee raising, elbow pumping, rendition of supercalifragilisticexpialidocious when I catch a movement behind me from the corner of my eye. I guess that Miss Allison is back, and as Elizabeth is currently thumping the floor with her stick, and has the biggest smile on her face, I carry on. Then I'm down on one knee, holding the last note with my arms flung wide.

"Bravo, Cassie, Bravo. What a performance," says a male voice behind me.

I close my eyes. That sounded like Jackson. Only he could clap that loud. I get to my feet and turn to face him.

"Jackson. I wasn't expecting to see you today. Is H with you?" I try to look around him into the hall.

"No, no. I left him to it. I wanted a quick word with you."

Jackson is looking concerned, and I glance at Elizabeth, who is holding up crossed arms in front of her face as though warding off a vampire.

Miss Allison tilts her head, her eyes wide. "Shall I put the kettle on? Elizabeth, dear, calm down. Jackson is a friend of Doctor Christos."

What? After letting no one cross the threshold in a million years, she's now making tea for strangers! Strange men at that. I shake my head.

"No, that's fine. We'll go next door, I wouldn't want to—"

"Is he a doctor?" Elizabeth asks, good hand on chest.

"No, dear. Mr Courtney works with Christos. I'm sure he's quite trustworthy."

The way she's looking at me lets me know she doesn't think that I am.

"But Doctor Christos is a doctor. What is he then?" Elizabeth won't let this drop.

"I'm sure it's something similar. But perhaps Mrs Baros is right, they'll never get to the end of a conversation with us interrupting them, and Mr Courtney has a plane to catch."

She knows. I don't know how long she's been speaking to him, or what she's said. Damage limitation might be necessary. I'm nodding like my neck is on a spring as I hurry out of the room, flapping my hands to encourage Jackson out of the house.

"And I'm sure it will be boring. Lovely to see you, ladies." I've got Jackson out onto the pavement when I realise I've forgotten my phone. I hand him the house keys and point next door. "Forgotten my phone. Let yourself in, won't be two seconds."

He booms out his laugh and walks away.

Miss Allison steps back and allows me to enter. I run into the living room and snatch my phone from the mantel. Miss Allison blocks the door.

"Two secs." I hold up two fingers.

Bugger! Five missed calls, one message and a text from H. I open the text. My shoulders slump and my chin hits my chest. I turn to Miss Allison.

"You called me Mrs Baros."

"Oh splendid. You married him. Congratulations. Isn't that splendid, Jennifer?" Elizabeth calls.

"I'm not sure. It was all so quick." Miss Allison's head is tilted so far, it's almost resting on her shoulder.

I resist the urge to roll my eyes. "It's too long a story, Miss Allison, but I promise to come back and explain all once I've dealt with Jackson. What did you say to him?"

"Very little. He likes to talk."

"So you didn't tell him I wasn't Mrs Baros?" I'm holding up crossed fingers.

"Not in words, no."

"What the hell does that mean?"

Miss Allison's back stiffens, and she wags a finger at me. "Don't curse, Cassie. Cursing will not make this situation any better. Why are you masquerading as Mrs Baros?"

"Long story short? H asked me to. It wasn't my idea, far from it." I manage another step towards the door.

"Why? I understand he already has one."

Elizabeth gasps and Miss Allison pulls me into the hall.

"So, I understand. Look, I promise to come back and explain the best I can, but please tell me what I might be walking into next door."

Miss Allison gives a curt nod. "I might have gasped when he told me he was looking for Mrs Baros, Cassie Baros, and I'm told my face can hold many expressions. But I did not tell on you."

"Miss Allison, you are a star." Before I know what I'm doing, I grab her shoulders and kiss her on the cheek. A quick exit is required. "I'll see you later," I shout, making a dash for freedom.

When I get home, I find Jackson sitting at the kitchen table eating an apple. He jumps to his feet.

"Cassie, apologies for gatecrashing your performance. You didn't say you could sing. What a remarkable woman you truly are."

"Thank you, Jackson. Just doing my bit for the old girls. Would you like a drink?"

"No, thank you, I've already stolen an apple. Did Chris tell you I'd be popping in?"

"No. Had he done so, you wouldn't have found me putting on a one-woman production for an easily pleased old lady. Shall I check my phone?" My hand goes to my back pocket.

"Oh no. So, quickly, because I don't want to take up too much of your time, I know you and Chris have decided not to do the ad together because of your concerns about sincerity. Can't say I agree, but I accept that. So I want you to be the star of our other ads. It will mean working with children, or possibly a child, but there will be no animals. What do you say?"

Having read H's text, I'm ready for this.

"When?" I smile at him. "I've given my agent a kick, and they've found me several jobs. One I know is next week, and I'm just waiting for the timing of the others. I don't want to say no, but I absolutely can't let my agent down, having been nagging him for so long. I won't mess him about."

Jackson holds up his hands and gets to his feet. "Understandable. Let me know your schedule, and we'll try to work around you. I knew you'd do it. Now, I'll get out of your hair." He drops his apple core onto an empty plate and holds out his hand. "Thank you for your time."

I give it a firm shake. Bloody hell. I nearly had a heart attack over nothing. I sweep a gracious hand towards the hall. "All two minutes of it. Come, I'll see you out."

"Oh, one more thing, I'm sure I'll be back and forth to the UK over the next year, is it worth me going to York? The guys over here say it's incredible. All olde-worlde, like stepping back in time. I've no need to go, but as you've lived there, is it worth me taking the time out?"

I have never been to York. I've seen photographs and watched Emmerdale, which is as close as I've been, so I blink and shrug. "It looks olde-worlde and some of the architecture is fabulous. The cathedral is worth a visit, so on balance, as you're American, I'd say yes. But don't quote me, I think the inhabitants are normal humans."

"Ha! Thank you, Cassie, now I must dash."

He skips down the steps to the pavement, and I kid you not a car appears. He's not touched his phone. How? I don't ask, I've got other things that need sorting. But he's seen my face and booms before explaining.

"I've had him circling, as I knew I wouldn't be long. I wasn't expecting a show. See ya, Cassie, it's been a pleasure."

I wave, and as soon as the car is out of sight, I'm on the phone to H.

"How are you?" H is treading carefully.

"Bloody dandy. Thank you. Babysat Elizabeth and put on a production of *Mary Poppins*, had a special guest who I wasn't expecting to be in the audience. He must have liked it because he's offered me a job, one that he will schedule around my very empty diary. But guess who invited him to the show? Yes, you've guessed it, Miss Allison. When she found him on the doorstep, and he told her he was looking for Mrs Cassie Baros, she invited him in." I pause for breath. "H?"

"I wasn't sure if you'd finished. Cassie, I'm so sorry, he dropped it on me as he left. I tried to warn you." His amusement is clear.

"Glad I'm entertaining you, H. Now, I must dash, because Miss Allison is waiting for me, and I'm too scared to leave it much longer. She will have seen the car leave."

"I told you she likes you," H says smugly.

"Probably not anymore. I'm going over to explain why I am masquerading as your wife when you already have one."

"Shit!"

"And now the penny drops. For a bloke with a posh job, H, you can be really slow on the uptake. What would you like me to say?" I ask.

"Don't know. I hate lying, and now we're compounding it. Damn!"

"Can I remind you I told you this wouldn't work? Not that I'm expecting many of your colleagues to meet Miss Allison, but she's the first, and she won't be the last, who gets dragged into this mess."

"I know, I know. I am sorry." H groans.

"You keep saying that. So, any ideas?"

"Not one. I'm sorry, Cassie, I have to go. There's someone here to see me. Maybe just avoid her until we have a plan. I'll make it up to you."

"You will. I'll tell her you'll pop over later." I hang up as he gasps, and before he can argue.

I decide to avoid her. We'll go together, he can explain, and I'll enjoy watching him squirm. After all, this is his fault.

I go back to bed. Whatever else happens tonight, I'm betting I'm going to need some energy. I hope. Perhaps just a couple of hours. H won't be home before five. But sleep is elusive as I think about the last few days, and despite all the tears, I'm smiling.

Such a short time ago I was wallowing in misery, now I'm wallowing in the memories of tingle overload. I'm never going to get any sleep. A sandwich is in order. Cream cheese and pickled beetroot is my current favourite, and as I eat it, I get a message from Joel. Porno signed, sealed and full script delivered. I find it in my emails and hit print. My life has come to this.

It's too hot to sit in the garden, so I stretch out on the sofa with the script and start reading. The opening paragraph gets straight to the point. Kelly is a virgin, her father is away for the weekend, and she's going to...I was going to phone my dad and got sidetracked. Should I bother? H thinks I should. So, I set the script to one side and find his number. I don't know where he lives, and if he's abroad what the time difference may be, but then, he never answers. I'll just leave a message.

As I listen to it ring, my foot is tapping repeatedly. Should have planned what to say first. My eyes wander and scan the script, and I turn over the page to hide the text. I can't say that to my dad. It's still ringing. Where the hell is the answer service? Ah well, at least I can show H I—.

"Is that you, Cassandra?" He sounds shocked. "Are you okay? What's happened?"

"Yes, it's me, and no, no one has died. Only me when you left. I just..." I suddenly realise that I don't know if I have a stepmother or half siblings or anything, really. I only know what was, not what is. "Did you remarry? Have you had any other children?"

"Did you call me to ask me that? Why?" He sounds confused. Not surprising really.

"No, it's just occurred to me that I don't know what you've done since you abandoned us." There's an intake of breath, but he doesn't answer. "Do you not want to answer? Too much to confess?" Even I can hear the mocking teenager arrive, but there's no need, I'm an adult now. I backtrack. "Rude of me to ask. You don't need to tell me."

"Answers; no, and no. But how would it be rude? Cassandra, it's wonderful that you've called, but before we go any further, is there something you need?"

Okay, my back's up. "No, there's nothing I need. When have I ever asked for anything from you? I can't fucking believe you."

"Cassandra, don't hang up. You always hang up. I was trying to get to the point before you did."

"How can I hang up all the time if I never call you?" I demand.

"Calm down. When was the last time you called me?" he asks.

"When Mum died, which proves—"

"Which proves that the last time you called me, you needed me. I just wanted to establish that before you hung up."

Okay, that makes sense, but still. "But you thought I would hang up." Ha! I've got him now.

"That's the usual pattern. Let's start again. I'm well, busy as always, but happier for hearing from you. Much happier. How are you, Cassandra? What's going on in your life?"

"I'm well. Thank you. Busy, busy, here too," I lie, unless you count the sex. I'm pretty busy on that front, but I'm guessing he doesn't want to know that.

"How's the acting going? Anything exciting on the horizon?" he asks.

I glance at the script. "Depends what your take is on exciting. But I'm going to say no."

"Are you seeing someone? Is it serious?" He gives a sharp intake of breath and falls silent.

"Why did you ask that?"

He sighs. "Honestly? Because something has caused you to make this call. I don't care what it is, I'm grateful, but if you don't need anything, and you're not ill...I'm trying to work out what it could be. It occurred to me you might be getting married, or perhaps be...Tell me honestly, why did you call?"

"Because a friend said I hadn't been fair to you, and that I should talk to you. So, here I am." I feel like I've ripped open my chest and said take your best shot.

"Well, I hope I meet this friend, because I am in their debt. So do you want to talk now or shall we do it in person?"

It's my turn to stay silent. Do I want to do this over the phone? Will it be worse if it's in person? I mean, on the phone I can simply hang up, but if I'm with him I might punch him. H can testify to that.

"Cassandra, I don't care how we do it, what we talk about, or when. I'm guessing you're feeling undecided. I can be in Bristol next week, but if you want to do this before then, via the phone, please just call me. Don't disappear on me again. Deal?"

"I'm not sure what would be best. But I would like to hear your side of the story," I say, and suddenly I feel guilty.

"Do you want me to tell you now?"

He can't see me shaking my head. "No. When I see you next week, will do." My eyebrows rise as the words leave my mouth. Shit, I guess I'm going to see my dad again. H will be proud.

I can hear the joy in my dad's voice. "Thank you. Thank you. I'll call to make arrangements."

Like a couple of love-struck teenagers, we do the never ending you say goodbye first, until I hang up. I drop the phone onto the script and close my eyes. I'm asleep within minutes.

The smell of cooking wakes me. I stretch and see H jumping away from the hob. Something has splashed him, and all he's wearing are his shorts. He collects some cutlery and, as he walks to the table, he sees I'm watching him. And then he smiles. His dimple is in excellent form.

"Hello, beautiful. Dinner is almost ready. I hope you're hungry."

"We have to eat first?" I ask with a pout.

H laughs, drops the cutlery on the table and walks towards me. There's purpose in his movement. His eyes pin me to the sofa and my breath flutters in my chest.

"You sound disappointed. I thought I'd show off my skills," he says, and forcing my legs apart, he lies on top of me, a forearm on either side of my head as he rubs that nose against mine.

"Did you?" I ask, feigning surprise.

"I did." He runs his tongue across my lips as he thrusts his hips against me.

The tingles are gathering pace, and I draw in a breath. "In which case, why are you mucking about in the kitchen, and why have you still got your shorts on?"

He doesn't answer; he kisses me, and all the while, his hips maintain a slow rhythmic movement, until I'm gasping and the tingles explode into fireworks. As the last firework fizzles to a warm glow, I try to shift him. "Get your shorts off. That was cheating."

With a laugh, he jumps up, blowing me a kiss. He doesn't take off his shorts, but hurries back to the kitchen. "All in good time," he calls. "That was your starter. Your main course will be ready in two ticks. Lay the table."

The stir-fry he's created is good, and just like a normal couple, we tell each other about the ups and downs of our day. The warm, fuzzy, comfortable feeling settles in, and I let it.

"So, I started reading the script and called my dad. He's coming to Bristol next week, and I've agreed to meet him. Wish me luck."

H beams at me. "Well done. I'm proud of you, but I think it'll be him who needs the luck. Promise me two things," he says.

"Depends on what they are."

"First, you'll hear him out and let him finish."

"Already decided to do that. What else?"

"You won't hit him if he says anything you don't want to hear or agree with." H runs his fingers down his nose and along his lip. "You pack quite a punch, and your punches are not always deserved. Take it from one who knows."

I nod slowly. "I'll do my best. Good advice, H."

"Who taught you to punch? I'm guessing it wasn't your dad."

"It wasn't. Where's my pudding? I feel shortchanged." That's a story I don't feel like sharing, but I do feel like I should be delivering fireworks to H.

"Are you still hungry?" H asks, and I shake my head. He waggles his eyebrows. "Then what do you have in mind?"

Getting to my feet, I hold out my hand and lead him back to the couch. "Your turn. Sit down. But shorts off first."

I pull my T-shirt off, and as I drop it, several pages of the script flutter to the floor. H stoops to pick them up. He scans the first page and looks at me, a grin bringing his dimple back into play, before he returns to reading the few pages he's holding.

"H, you're getting distracted," I complain.

He clears his throat. "Not distracted from you." He hands me the pages from the script. His shorts hit the floor, and he lies down on the couch. "Read. Read in the sexy voice you'll be using and see where it takes us."

I giggle. "But you won't be able to see your lines." My leggings join his shorts.

"I'll improvise. Trust me, it'll work." H puts his hands behind his head and nods. That's my cue.

I run the flat of my hand down over my face. My smile disappears to reveal a pout as I look at him. I stroke his erection before straddling him and sitting on his thighs. My tongue wets my lips.

"Is this for me? I'm not sure it will fit," Husky Nigella tells him as she strokes him gently.

H grins at me. "I think we'll find a way." He's really not in character. I'll have a word later.

I glance at the script. That doesn't work, so now I have to improvise too. Just as well, I'm good at this.

"Are you sure? I don't think I'm ready." I place the script on the back of the couch and lower my free hand between my legs, slipping my fingers under my very un-granny like knickers, and gasp as I throw my head back and look at the ceiling. "Oh, that feels so good, so good," Nigella tells him. "Is it good for you, big boy?"

"Yess," H hisses and reaches for me.

"That isn't in the script, H," Nigella tells him with a shake of her head. "Now you should be—"

"Sod the script. Come here."

It turns out Nigella is good at improvising, too.

Afterwards, we lie pressed together in a sticky, hot mess. Neither of us wanting to break the spell. H strokes my back.

"Do you believe in fate, Cassie?"

"Not really. I hope not. Why?"

H forces his head on an angle to look at me. "Why do you hope not?" He looks disappointed.

"Because if fate is a thing, it's not been very good to me or...it's just not kind."

H drops his head back with a sigh.

"Go on, tell me why you do."

"Nope. The moment is lost." He slaps my arse.

"I don't agree, I'm here, you're here, nothing's changed. Tell me."

"I'm lying here thinking I'm the luckiest bastard who ever walked and wondering how I got to be so lucky. Answer? Fate. But you don't believe in it, so not fate. Not so romantic. You've burst my bubble."

"Go on, tell me about fate," I encourage.

"Just think about all the things that have brought us to this moment. If I hadn't chosen that hotel to stay in, I wouldn't have met you. If I hadn't forced myself to go down to the bar and try to socially interact with other humans, I wouldn't have met you. And if you and Joel had decided on another bar, no meeting. When your handbag caught on the door, I was there to pick you up because my boss called at the right time. We connected that night and I know you felt it too. Then you took a job dressed up as a bee. A bee. I bet you said no to that job at first, didn't you?"

I lift my head and grin at him. "I did. Carry on."

"So, dressed as a bee, you needed water. You came to my building. Mine. What were the chances? I have to save you, and that sex, that cementing connection. It was on another level, Cassie, another level. But you get hold of the wrong end of the stick and punch me. I hadn't given up on you, but it was touch and go. I was going to phone you, to explain. But all ends well because the number Joel gave me led me to take a house share with you. And here we are, naked on the couch, and I'm the happiest man in the world. Fate. Not bloody coincidence. Fate."

"I'm glad I make you happy, I—"

H is on a roll. "And it's not just that. My mother came down here to make me go home to Ana. Nothing needs to happen for her to realise that this," he waves his finger between us, "this was meant to be. Fate. She knew not to fight it."

I sigh against his chest. "And where does fate take us next?" I ask.

"Who knows? That's why it's so bloody exciting. Doesn't this make your blood pump a little faster? Make you smile all the time? It does for me."

H is getting quite animated now, and the warm, fuzzy, comfortable and safe feeling is kicking in. Safe. I can't remember the last time I felt safe.

He's still going. "And you're meeting your dad. I don't know how that will pan out. There are three ways it could go, but it doesn't matter. You'll know that you tried. And whatever the outcome, you can get on with your life without regrets. Do you see?"

"I think so, H. It's certainly making you happy."

"Happy? That doesn't come close." H sits up and pulls me onto his lap so he can look at me. "I'm fucking ecstatic, Cass. Why are you looking like that? What's wrong?" His hands are cupping my face. He doesn't look happy now.

"I am happy. Too happy. I don't know...I mean, it's so hard..." I feel the first tear tickle out, and his thumb brushes it away.

"What? Keep talking, you'll get there."

"I'm frightened, H. Fucking terrified. Every time I allow myself to be happy, it all goes wrong. Everyone moves on, everyone leaves me. I don't think I'd cope with losing you." My tears are now falling Niagara-like. It's been so long. I'm so close. But I can't do it. I can't expose myself to that again, so I push myself off him before he can stop me. "You won't mean to, I'm sure, but I can't let you hurt me. I don't want to end up like my mum." I tell him as I head for the door. "You're married, you'll move on, move away. I'll be left behind, again, and I simply won't cope. Not this time."

I hear his feet thundering towards me, and he grabs my hand just as I reach the stairs.

"No, I won't," He tells me as he pulls me to him.

"You don't know that. H, you can't promise that."

"Yes, I can."

"How? How do you know?"

"About something that might happen in the future, is that what you're asking?" H demands.

"Exactly that."

H throws his arms into the air. "That's the most ridiculous thing I've ever heard. Sit down." He points to the stair, and I comply. "Are you telling me you will never take a chance on love in case it goes wrong?"

"Pretty much." Here we go, the L word is in play.

"That's crazy. Cassie, I can't believe you're prepared to deny yourself. Why?"

"Is it, H? You married a girl you claimed not to love and stayed with her for ten years. If she hadn't taken a lover, you'd still be with her. You survived."

"But—"

"No buts. What if you'd loved her properly? What if you were planning on babies, and happy ever afters, and she told you she'd found someone else? Would we be in this hall naked? Or would you be punching the lover on the nose and demanding her back? Who knows?"

"What's your point, Cassie?"

"The point is that according to you, you survived without love." I make speech marks around the L word. "And look at the fun you're having now. This was fun, wasn't it?" I flip my finger back and forth.

"No past tense. Is fun. Is spectacular. Why are you running away from me?"

I clench my hands to stop them shaking. "Because I'm getting in too deep. You're too nice, too good, and too fucking convincing."

H kneels before me and rubs his hands along my thighs. "I know it's not been long, but I've fallen for you, Cassie Henderson, Actor and Entertainer. I love you. Let me in."

"You're on the rebound, H. It's lust, not love. Time doesn't come into it. You sneaked in, and you shouldn't have made me feel safe."

"Safe?" H frowns.

"Yes, bloody safe. I can deal with the tingles, and the fireworks, and you being here walking around looking like that, making me laugh, you even make me talk to you about serious stuff. I don't do that often. But not the making me feel safe." I swipe away my tears and hold up my chin.

"I still don't understand. You're saying that me talking to you, giving you tingles and fireworks and amusing you when I walk around naked is all good. But me loving you is bad. How? Why?"

"Because when it all falls apart, you won't be around to catch me." I stand up, suddenly embarrassed by my nakedness. "I'm going to bed. Don't follow me, H."

I hurry to my room and lock my bedroom door.

He didn't follow me, but I heard him try the door later, then I listened to his footsteps as they went up to his room. So I carried on weeping, and I know I must have slept, but it doesn't feel like it, and now I look like some bloated, bug-eyed fish. I never cry, and yet since meeting H I seem to do nothing but. I need to get a grip on that.

Okay, it's gone eight. H will have left for work by now. I'm going to shower, grab what's left of that cucumber, and then enter wallowing mode and try to work out how to share a house with him. I can't move, and before long he's going to be moving on, but I need to avoid him and those eyes and that dimple in the meantime. Shit!

The shower is waking me up and I'm questioning my actions. Did I overreact? Am I wrong? Did I panic and miss my chance? Will I live to regret this? So many bloody questions, and what do I know? I can't even decide whether or not to ignore the eucalyptus and mint body wash. Do I want to have that reminder of H all day? Fuck it, I'll think about him all day, anyway. I snatch up the bottle.

"Room for one more in there? Here, let me." H takes the oversized bottle out of my hands.

My scream might have been loud, but now I've developed the inability to speak. So I hand it to him. He squeezes some into his hands.

"Head," he commands.

I step out of the flow of water, and hands on knees, I lean forward. And there it is. I never think these things through, and I definitely didn't think about the view. I close my eyes.

H massages the soap into my hair. Then he washes me. Simply washes my body. He does nothing sexual, well, other than being H, and it being necessary to use his hands. When he's satisfied that I'm done, he wraps me in a towel and just holds me.

I have no tears left to cry, no words that will make any sense, so I just sigh, a lot of big juddery sighs.

We've both drip dried by the time he walks me to my bedroom, sits on the bed and pulls me onto his lap.

"I don't want you to speak. Just listen to me. I will never, ever, knowingly hurt you, and I will always try to be there when you fall. I want to catch you, Cassie. Think about that. I doubt you slept much more than me, so get back into bed and think about what I'm saying. If you still don't want me when I get back from work, then I'll move back into a hotel. But I will be heartbroken, and I will never give up." His lips brush mine, and he pulls back the duvet. "I'll be home as soon as I can."

H tucks the duvet around me and blows a kiss before closing the door. He looks so bloody sad. I did that.

It seems I have some thinking to do.

Chapter 19

Christos

TALK ABOUT A ROLLER coaster. I realise now that life before Cassie Henderson, Actor and Entertainer, was easy. So easy. But I'm strapped in and ready for the ride. I think. I'm not sure anyone can truly be ready for Cassie.

In the middle of last week, I thought that I'd lost her. That she was walking away from me. Why? Because I was honest. I told that beautiful, funny woman the truth about how I felt. That should have been a good thing. But oh no, not when Cassie is involved. Feeling safe, which in Cassie's book means being loved, is the exact opposite of what she wants. She told me it was over and locked her bedroom door. I washed her in the shower the next morning, and tried to reassure her, but when I left the house, I thought I'd be packing my bags that night. She couldn't even speak to me.

I didn't move out because when I got home, Cassie explained the new rules to me. She was sitting on the stairs waiting for me to walk in. I was much later than usual, and I don't know how long she'd been there. A while judging be the look on her face.

"Hello, you. What are you doing there?" I pull off my tie, wondering if I should just kiss her. Life seems to be easier if I don't speak.

"You're late. New rules, H."

"I couldn't get away, I—"

"Hush. Just listen. This is important. New rule number one: No more slushy talk. Although you may compliment me, because I have an ego that needs a stroke now and then, but no more L words. Rule number two: I will continue to be your pretend wife if it's absolutely necessary, but don't make it so. Plus one invites should be accepted with, 'Oh no.

Cassie is away.' Or similar. Rule number three: I will continue to assist in your efforts to improve your sexual technique. I feel that's only fair." She allows herself a smirk. "But no more spending the night together. No more waking up together. I haven't decided about the shower yet. I like you washing my hair. Other than that, we can do meals, films, even the odd outing. If you think you can obey those rules, I don't think there's any need for you to move out. What do you think?"

I showed her with my actions rather than with words, which I might get wrong.

From then on in, I think it's fair to say I'm in heaven. Work is going so well I'm waiting for the bomb to drop to disrupt it. Mark Bowman is doing his flying visit this week, and despite what's going on with the building, which is taking shape, we're still hitting targets. When I say we, I mean me and two of the new recruits, who were happy to come and work on a building site and are smashing it. I chose well. And at home, well, at home I have Cassie. Nothing more needs to be said. Especially L words. So I just think them. I can handle that. I've also discovered that I'm good at feigning sleep, so other than the first morning when I was too scared to cock up, I've woken up with Cassie beside me every day.

Life is pretty perfect.

It's Monday, and I'm walking around with the project manager, George, taking photographs of the lighting. We have Bristol Bees coming today to check out the suitability of our roof. That makes me think of Cassie, so I'm smiling. When I get any spare money, I must make a donation.

"You're smiling again," George tells me.

"I'm a smiley sort of bloke."

"Granted, you're not a miserable bastard, but your smiles just appear from nowhere. I won't ask what goes on in your mind," George says, as he lays flat on a desk and takes a shot of the ceiling.

"Best not. Good shout," I tell him as I pull him upright.

"What's the boss man like? I've only ever exchanged emails. He's in here on Wednesday. Shift to the left." George flaps his hand and snaps several more photographs.

"How do you know that? I didn't know that. But in answer to your question, I don't know him. Not really. I've only spoken to him for probably twenty minutes in all. He's sharp, he knows what he's doing, has a shit hot memory, and doesn't need to be buttered up. Working with him on a day-to-day basis...who knows?"

"A straight talker then?" George asks.

"Yes, I think so. I hope so. So much easier when nothing's left to interpretation. So tell me again how you know before me that he's coming?"

"Had a text from him asking me to make sure I'm around. I'm guessing he knows you'll be here."

I leave George to it and go to my office. It's huge. Not decorated yet, no flooring down, and I'm using an old desk that was abandoned here by the previous occupants, but it's mine, and it's too big. I flip open my laptop. There's the email.

Chris,

I'm in the UK. I should arrive in Bristol either tomorrow night or Wednesday morning. Looking forward to meeting you. Well done on the Cartwright deal. Impressed.

See you then. Mark.

I'm halfway through the response when Cassie texts.

Guess who I'm having dinner with this week? Only my father. Dad, Daddykins? I don't know what to call him. It's been so long since it's not been a swearword. Oh, and I'm filming for Gemini next week. Yikes!

I grin as I tap out a response.

Ditch the swearwords. Dad will be adequate. Congrats on the filming – make sure you take the right script though. This is a family-friendly company.

The dots are dancing across the screen.

H. You made me laugh. Can you imagine? Still need to come up with my audio porn narrator name. Ideas?

George steps into my office, so the opportunity to be creative is lost.

Busy, but thinking about it! H x

The rest of the day passes in a blur. If Cassie wasn't at home waiting for me, I'd probably be here until midnight. But she is.

It's still nearly eight by the time I arrive home. A familiar aroma reaches me as I pull off my tie.

"Hello?" I walk into the kitchen and take a peep at what's in the oven. If I'm not mistaken, that's a stifado in there. My mother is back. I groan inwardly, wondering what's happened now. There's no sign of either Cassie or my mother, so I go upstairs to change.

Cassie screams as she opens the bathroom door.

"H! Don't creep about. You're usually thumping around like an elephant," Cassie says as she walks past. That towel needs to go. She's used the eucalyptus and mint again.

"Where's my mother?" I ask, keeping my voice down.

"Why are you whispering? Is Mrs B coming? She didn't say." Cassie heads for her bedroom.

"Not that I knew. But there's a beef stifado in the oven."

Cassie bounces up and down, clapping. The towel falls away. "You knew what it was just from the smell? I did it right? I can't wait to tell Mrs B."

"You cooked it? Wow! I can't wait to taste it, but there's some other tasting I need to do first."

Cassie dodges me as I step towards her. "Oh, no you don't. I'm not letting that ruin because you're feeling horny."

"It's a perpetual state when I'm near you and especially when you're naked. Can we agree I'm on a promise?" I ask, still stalking towards her.

"We can, but with conditions," she tells me as she dashes into her room and grabs her robe.

I follow her in. "More rules?" I finish unbuttoning my shirt and let it hang open as I loosen my belt.

Cassie holds up the flat of her hand. "Oh, no you don't. You can take all of that upstairs now. Dinner will be in twenty minutes."

"I can make it quick." I wink and she raises a doubtful eyebrow.

"But you don't, do you? Get changed. If you behave, I'll be the dessert. Don't you take those...H! Get out of my way."

Cassie pushes past me and flies down the stairs. I pick up my trousers and head upstairs. She didn't tell me the new rules.

The stifado is good and she messages my mother from the table to show her I'm eating it.

"Since when have you had my mother's telephone number?" I ask.

"Since she gave it to me. I think it was an additional way to monitor your wellbeing. She messages me almost daily to ask."

"Oh, you poor innocent child. That's checking up on me. Nothing to do with my health. She's such a sneaky—"

"Don't knock it, H. Someone cares. And do you know what, I don't mind. She's funny, I enjoy it. How things change. A few weeks ago, all I had was Joel. Now, I've got a pretend husband and a surrogate mother, all this and a real father about to put in an appearance. I feel I'm almost normal."

"Cass, you are normal...ish." I wink and lift my glass. "Cassie Henderson. Actor and Entertainer. Talented, beautiful, witty, dramatic, exaggerator, charmer of mothers, perfect pretend wife, and normalish. What's that look for?"

Cassie's shoulders have drooped. She looks sad, and I'm hoping I haven't put my foot in it again, however innocently. She blows out a breath causing her lips to vibrate.

"I'm nervous about seeing my dad, H. More nervous than when I played Snow White at the Hippodrome after the lead fell ill. More nervous than knowing next week I'm going to be recording an audio porno with people watching. Don't laugh, it's difficult, even for someone with my talents. You couldn't even stick to the script. Your performance was way off, too." She laughs and my hands find my hips. "Okay, it was passable. Like I say, there's work to do, but back to my dad. I don't know what to say to him."

"Just be you, but without the punching. Ask the question. The why question and let him answer you. Don't interrupt, just listen. Then you might have more questions. Ask them."

"But what if he tries to change the subject? You men are sneaky. You start one conversation and before I know it, I'm talking about something else, and it's difficult to go back."

"Make a list. Like you did with me, so if you get distracted, you can go back to the list," I suggest as I pull her up from the table and take her to sit on the couch.

"Good plan, H, only one flaw. I only have one question."

"Why did you leave?" I guess, and Cassie nods. "Then how can you get distracted?"

"Because whatever the short answer is, there's going to be a more complicated explanation. And that's the bit where it will all go wrong, and I'll get stroppy, and as hanging up isn't an option, I'll probably storm out."

I lie flat on the couch and pull her down so she's tucked under my arm, her hand splayed on my chest.

"So, you already know the potential outcome, so you have to avoid it. However mad you are, think: I'm bigger than this. I won't storm away. Do you want to practise?" I ask.

"How can we practise something like that? H, you're losing the plot." She pats my chest.

"Easily, I'm your dad, ask me the question. You think about your response, then tone it down. That way you've got half a chance of not punching him on the nose and or storming off before you've had the conversation."

"Like improvisation? Can you act, H?"

"Cassie, do it. It's got to be worth a try." I squeeze her hand.

"Okay, this won't work, though." She wrinkles her nose.

"Ask and give honest responses. It won't help otherwise."

"Why did you leave us?" she barely whispers.

"Because things were just too tough at home. Our marriage was over. We were rowing all the time. It couldn't be repaired, and I thought it was for the best."

Cassie sits up. I've seen that look on her face before, and I'm glad we're only playacting.

"And what about me? I was thirteen!"

Yep, she's mad. She wipes the spittle from her bottom lip.

I grab her hand. "So, this would be the part where you channel your inner calm and wait for him to answer. You already know you won't like that answer, so prepare for it. Ask me again."

Cassie is frowning, but she asks again. Her voice is louder and there's a determination there. "Why did you leave us?"

"Because our marriage was over, I was only staying for you, but then I met someone. Someone who made me happy." For a moment, I wonder what I would have done in that situation. Would I have stayed with Ana? I think I probably would have, not that I regretted Ana's decision. But if it had been Cassie I'd met...I'd have been out the door like a shot, and despite my feelings towards Yorgos, I hope Ana is happy.

Cassie's taking her time with this one, and I watch the changing expressions on her face. Eventually, her nose wrinkles.

"And your happiness was more important than ours?" Her voice is calm, but she clenches her fist.

"Not yours, never. You need to understand that I tried. For years I tried—" Just when I think I've got this improvisation down, she interrupts me.

"Not very bloody hard. Mum wasn't a difficult woman. Not before she started drinking."

I watch her chest rise as she draws in a breath, her fists clench and release. She's controlling herself.

"She wasn't difficult for you, because she loved you. Your mother didn't love me."

"Yes, she did. She told you that, she asked you to...Okay, H. Let's leave it there. I see what you're saying, and whatever he says, I'm going to get angry." Cassie collapses back onto my chest. "I need to prepare myself for failure."

"No, you don't. You need to prepare yourself to listen. Take it from someone on the wrong end of you storming off before you've listened. You can't ask a question and storm off. Even if you don't like the answer. Ask another question. If you don't like the answer to that one, be dignified and leave calmly, throwing no punches. A simple: this won't work, or thanks for trying, but no thanks. That's not failing. That's proving your point to yourself that you were right." I give her a squeeze. "But what if one of those answers rings true? What if, even if you don't really agree with him, you can see it from his point of view now you're an adult? You might get your dad back, Cassie. Maybe not the version of him you remember, but from what you say, he wants to be back in your life, and you want him back in yours."

I can feel the movement of her head as she gives brief nods, and I don't know why I'm surprised by her response, but I am.

"I've managed this long without him, I don't want him back, and I don't need him back, but for you, H, I'll do my best to be civil, and not to hit him."

And there she goes again, protecting herself from feeling 'safe'. I hope her dad's a good bloke, with a tonne of patience and quick reactions. Her right hook is lethal. I decide to change the subject.

"So, who taught you to punch?" I ask.

She lifts a shoulder. "A friend's brother."

"Any reason? Were you going to take up boxing, or was it a self-defence thing?"

"Oh, I did a self-defence class, too. I could disarm you in so many ways, but I wanted to learn to punch properly. You know, controlled, and on target. Anger but precision." She bops her fist softly on my nose.

"Why?"

"Because a girl should be able to protect herself. Shouldn't have to, but it's a sad reality of life." She jerks her shoulders. "You can be very naïve, H."

"You're talking about no meaning no?" I ask, wondering how far I should push this. Wondering if someone ignored her when she has said no, and I feel sick at the thought of it.

"Well done, H. Yes, that and pride."

"Other than me, how many blokes have become acquainted with your self-defence skills?" I ask, because I was no threat to Cassie, yet she still felt it necessary to whack me.

"I don't want to talk about it." She puts a finger on my lips to end the conversation.

"No problem. Let's change the subject. I need to protect this nose. I know someone who likes it."

She flies up to a sitting position again. "I have some self-control, you know. I wouldn't hit you because I didn't like the conversation. But I will never let someone...let's just say I needed to learn. Self-preservation."

My heart lurches at the sadness in her eyes. Someone hurt her! "Who hurt you, Cassie?" The question's out before I can stop it.

Her hands come up to her face, and she rubs it slowly. "You don't want to know."

"I do if you want to tell me. If not, lie back down. I miss you." I try to pull her down on me.

"There's a list. It could take a while."

Now I'm sitting up too. I pull her on to my lap and hug her. "A list?"

"Yes, H, a list. I didn't become a fucked-up mess all by myself, you know. I had help." She holds up her hands as though that should have been obvious.

And now I definitely want to know. Just the thought of someone hurting her makes my heart ache, and I want to punch them too. And I'm not a violent man. "Will talking about it help?"

"Nope. Tried that, I just get angry. It's exhausting being angry."

"Okay. Let's move on." I decide to let it drop. I'll probably come back to it, because I'd like to know. But now is not the time. Not with the meeting with her dad on the cards. She needs to be calm for that, not angry. I wrap my arms around her, and we fall silent, just sit there on the couch.

"I learned to punch because my mum's boyfriend felt me up. Put his arms around me from behind and grabbed me." Cassie places her hands over her boobs. "He said he was joking around, and it was an accident. I didn't know, wasn't sure, because he was a man and I was this spotty teenager with lank hair, who couldn't get a boyfriend let alone a man friend. I obviously didn't want the latter, but you know what I mean.

There were mirrors. He couldn't fancy me, I knew that, so I let it go. I'd heard about men liking kids, I wasn't totally innocent, but not me, never me. I was revolting."

I close my eyes and kiss the top of her head. "I'm sorry. You don't have to talk about it."

"I know." She falls silent for a while before she continues. "A couple of days later, he was in the kitchen with my mum. We'd been shopping for a dress for a party I was going to. I went up and tried it on but wasn't sure. I thought it was too childish. Too flouncy. I wanted to be grown up. My mum said I looked lovely, but if I wasn't sure we could change it at the end of the week, then she went into the garden to get the washing in. As I went to leave the kitchen, he stopped me. Told me to do a twirl, so I did. When I was facing him again, he pulled up the skirt of the dress and told me it looked okay to him, and he was going to touch me. He put his hand...I slapped him and he just laughed. When I threatened to tell my mum, he grabbed my wrist and pulled me to him, he was strong, and I couldn't push him off. I can't remember the exact words, but basically it was a guilt trip about lying to my mum, making her sad, especially as it was all my fault. He rubbed his chin up and down my boob as he asked me why I'd do that, and who did I think she'd believe? Then Mum opened the back door, and he let me go."

"Jesus. I'm so sorry, Cassie. What did you do?"

"Went to my best friend's house. Swore her to secrecy and asked what I should do. We went round in circles for ages, then her brother came in. He was a year older and had been listening. He told me I had to learn to defend myself, that adults always believed other adults, and offered to teach me how to fight. Their granddad had been a boxer, so that's what I did. We went to his bedroom, and he had this punch bag there, and I learned how to throw my arm, how to put my weight behind it, how to target my punches, and how to control my energy." Cassie smiles. "And we had a hate campaign against his car. William, that was her brother, slashed a tyre that first night, then he put an apple in the exhaust, and the best one was when I sneaked the car keys out and unlocked the petrol cap. We filled the tank with sugar. Alan had to ride a bike then, so William and his mates stole a wheel. He didn't know I had anything to do with it. Anyway, the next time

Alan touched me, I punched him. I think it hurt me more than it hurt him, but it shocked him. He told me I was a tease. Then he shit himself when I said I was going to call the police. He left and never came back. I didn't tell the police because my mum was devastated, and I couldn't tell her it was my fault. I felt too guilty for making her so upset. I didn't want to make it worse by confessing."

"You did nothing wrong."

"I know that now, but back then. . .it didn't feel like that."

"And I assume you blamed your dad for leaving you. If he hadn't gone, none of it would have happened?" I ask, gently.

"Not at first. That was when he refused to come home. But I'd made her ask him, because I thought if he came home, I'd feel safe again. He said no, and I thought that was my fault too. She didn't want to do it."

"I can see how you'd think that, and I'm sorry, Cassie, I shouldn't have asked."

"It's okay. You might as well know why I'm almost a basket case. Do you want to hear about Ollie? That's how I became friends with Joel," she asks.

I can tell by her tone that this story isn't going to hurt so much. "Only if you want to tell me."

"When I went to uni I met Ollie. The first month there, a bunch of us became friends, and we went out partying together. He was funny and handsome in a pretty boy sort of way, and we became mates. One night we went to a club, and I danced with him. It was a laugh. Then the slow songs came on and he dragged me onto the dance floor, after which he offered to walk me home. That was a bit weird because we all lived in halls, so we were all going the same way, so I said yes. There were about ten of us but by the time we reached halls it was down to four, me, Ollie, Joel, who I didn't know well then and another girl. Joel went off to her room, leaving me with Ollie."

"Hang on a minute. I thought Joel was gay?" I lift her face to look at me.

"He is. He was borrowing a book. Do you want to hear the end of this story, or are you still worried about Joel and me?" She kisses my nose. "You really are jealous."

"No, just establishing the facts," I tell her, with a wink, and she carries on.

"Ollie told me he liked me, and we kissed. It got passionate, and I stopped him and reminded him we were outside. Ollie asked me to go to his room, but I wasn't sure. So, I said no, and I'd see him tomorrow and headed back to mine. I didn't know he'd followed me. He caught up as I was unlocking the door. We kissed some more, and he told me how much he liked me and all that bull, and I told him I didn't know him well enough to let him in, and I'd see him tomorrow. The door was now unlocked, and he opened it and pushed me in. Told me he knew I wanted it really, and not to tease him. Up to that point, I thought he was just a horny boy, same as most of the boys were. I wasn't scared, and I wasn't angry. But saying that to me reminded me of Alan. So I hit him. He asked me if I liked it rough, and ripped my blouse, and I was so fucking mad as it was new. So I flew at him, I punched and scratched and kicked. He didn't like it, got very angry, and grabbed my throat. Just as I thought I was in trouble I couldn't get out of, Joel appeared. Joel pulled him off me, and seemingly effortlessly, had Ollie pinned up against the wall with his arm up his back."

"Joel kicked his arse! Good old Joel." I was warming to Cassie's tall, dark, and handsome friend.

"Nope, just held him there." Cassie was grinning.

"Why is that making you smile?"

"Because Joel turned the tables on him. He told me to undo Ollie's belt and pull his trousers down, because he felt like having some fun with Ollie. Ollie went berserk, called Joel all sorts of names, but couldn't shake him off, because every time he tried, the pain got worse. Joel licked his face and told him he knew he wanted it really and to stop struggling and that it wouldn't hurt. Ollie started crying. Proper shaking and sobbing. Joel stroked his hair and told him it would be alright. That he wouldn't take him this time, but he had to stop teasing and leading him on. He let him go and told Ollie if he ever heard that Ollie had tried anything similar with anyone else, he'd start rumours about him, and he didn't totally rule out coming after him, because he had a cute arse. Ollie left and never came out with us again. Joel was my hero. He stayed with me that night because I was scared Ollie would come back. When our year in halls was up, me, Joel and two other girls shared a flat together, and Joel taught us how to look after ourselves, we all went to self-defence classes together, I even went to kickboxing with Joel, but that didn't last long, it hurts. Even when you're only training." Cassie sighs.

"I'm now Joel's number one fan. Why are you sighing?"

"Because I think Joel taught himself how to fight, how to protect himself for a reason. He's never said that, and I never asked because that first night he stayed with me, he cried. He didn't know I knew, but I think what happened brought back memories for him. So I've never asked because I don't want to make him sad."

And we're silent again. Lost in our own thoughts. After a while, Cassie nudges me.

"So, shall I tell you about the next one? You know, full disclosure."

"Bloody hell, Cassie, there's more?"

"There are."

I'm guessing she needs to get it off her chest, and while the thought of these slimeballs hurting her makes my stomach churn, I agree. "You don't have to, but if it helps, of course."

"I think it will help you understand me." It's barely a whisper.

"Then you'd better tell me." My kiss is soft, undemanding. I want her to feel safe.

"Don't distract me, H. I'm on a roll. After my encounter with Ollie, I decided boys were off the menu. First Alan and then Ollie, was it me, was I leading them on, albeit unintentionally? My reasoning was, if I kept myself at arm's length, I couldn't give anyone the wrong impression. I wasn't a virgin. I'd had a couple of unfulfilling encounters, and as far as I was concerned sex wasn't all it was cracked up to be. So, I knew I wasn't missing much. And that worked for a year or so, and then I met Rich. He was gorgeous, and I had hormones, so when he asked me out, I went. We had a few dates, and on the fourth or fifth I went home with him. It was nice. He was nice. Not spectacular like with you, H, but nice."

"Glad to hear it," I mumble into her hair.

"But the next day he gives me the cold shoulder. He wasn't horrible as such, just not nice. Polite. That's what he was. I was miffed. He'd done all the chasing, been nice, but when he finally got what he wanted, he moved on. By the end of the week, he was taking someone else out. And, yet again,

I was asking myself if it was my fault. Was I that boring? Would Ollie have dumped me anyway if I'd have given in? So I set myself a challenge."

"A challenge? What sort of challenge?"

"I'd only sleep with men I found attractive, but not ones I liked. That way, I got to have a normalish life, and I didn't have to question myself every time it went wrong. Don't misunderstand me, I didn't walk into a pub and think you're not bad looking: do you want to get your leg over? For the best part, I remained celibate. Then Matthew happened. I went to a club, he asked me if I wanted a drink, we danced, I liked him, I took him home. Then he sent flowers, and the card told me to meet him at a restaurant the next day. I did. Then he came to see me in a little production I was in. It was a tiny part, you know, girl three, third act, half a dozen words, but when I did my bow at the end he was on his feet whistling, whooping, the whole bit. So I took him home again. He was so fucking refreshing after what had gone before. Kind, thoughtful, not pushy, talked to me, listened to me and we became a couple. He didn't mind that I couldn't see him when I was in a production, and he'd turn up and take me to breakfast instead. I was smitten."

"You loved him?" I already don't like Matthew, and I don't even know what he's done yet.

"Maybe. Suppose I thought so. He made me feel all the things I wanted to feel." Cassie's shoulders twitch, and she lifts her head to look at me when I nudge her.

"Safe. He made you feel safe. What happened?"

"His wife called while he was in the shower. She called twice, and I ignored it at first. The third time I thought whoever this Karen is, she's desperate to get hold of him. It might be important, so I lifted the phone to take it to him and answered it by mistake. I didn't realise I'd done it. So I walk into the bathroom and said I don't know who Karen is, but she's desperate to get hold of you. Turns out one of his kids was in hospital. But I heard enough of their row to know he was still very much married. I didn't have a clue. No wedding ring."

She huffs out a breath. "I wasn't safe, and I wasn't loved. Simply a bit of excitement on the side. I never saw him again. Not that I wanted to, but he didn't even try. I wasn't important enough. Conclusion? All men are bastards and only good for one thing. Except Joel. Joel has never let me down. Do you see?"

Fuck me. No wonder she went ballistic. I press my lips to her temple and whisper.

"You are safe, you are loved, and yes, you are fucking exciting, because I might need meds for my blood pressure soon. But you're not my piece on the side, Cassie. No kids, no wife to run back to. I'm sorry I'm doing the sloppy stuff. I know the rules and I will try not to break them again, although I can't promise."

Cassie nods. "Apology accepted on this occasion."

"You are a generous woman. But you've broken a promise too."

"I don't think so. I've been very clear. What promise?"

"You told me you'd be dessert."

Cassie grins. "I did. Come on." Taking my hand, she leads me upstairs.

Mark Bowman arrives at lunchtime the next day. I show him where we are with the business and the building and he asks so many questions, jumping from one topic to the other, in the blink of an eye, and I'm glad I almost had an early night yesterday. But I manage them, and he accepts my answers, rarely questioning them. He's a pleasant bloke, but so sharp. He doesn't say much apart from what's necessary, but he misses nothing. We go for a drink when he eventually calls it a day. And it's like he's become a different bloke, or someone has flipped a switch, one that says work's done, now chill.

Cassie texted to say she was going to go to bed as we agreed to part company and meet at eight the next morning.

"Is the wife after you? I'm sorry I kept you. I have something on tomorrow, but hopefully I can extend my stay. If I can, and if you and your wife are available, we'll do dinner on Thursday," he says as we leave the bar.

Suddenly I feel guilty, so I stop walking. "I have a confession to make. I've lied, and I need to tell you the truth." As I say the words, I watch the switch flip back the other way and his smile is gone. His face expressionless.

"Keep talking." No emotion at all. He gestures to the wall around the carpark. "We're blocking the path. Take a seat."

I perch on the edge of the wall and scuff the dirt about with my heel, wondering where I should start.

"Spit it out, Chris. I'm knackered. I've barely stopped for the last two weeks, and I was looking forward to an early night. Looks like I might need to be firefighting this evening now. Will I?"

"No. It's nothing like that. It's just, I'm not married. Not really." I grimace but look him in the eye.

"How can you not really be married?" MB perches next to me.

"On the day you emailed to say I had the job, I went home to tell my wife, but before I could, she told me she was leaving me. She was in a relationship with someone else, and then she left. I even carried her bags to the car. I was shocked, mainly because of the who, but if I'm honest, it was a long time coming."

MB nods. "I'm sorry to hear that. It stinks. So, where does the lying come into it?"

"When we spoke, you said you'd chosen me because I was married, settled. I was anything but, but I didn't tell you. But worse than that, when Jackson was here, he saw me kissing a young lady in the street. He thought I was married, and Gemini doesn't do scandal, so I said she was my wife. I'm sorry. Pathetic, I know, but this girl is something else. I have never felt this way about anyone, and I won't ask her to pretend for me again. It's not fair, and it's not honest."

"This is the girl who had dinner with Jackson?" he asks.

I nod confirmation.

He purses his lips. "You love her?"

What? What sort of question is that? Is it relevant? Not sure where this is going, so I answer honestly.

"Yep, I think so. Barely been two weeks, but when I'm not thinking about work, I'm thinking about her. She's remarkable. Amazing. Shit, I sound like a teenager. But she's special. Anyway, I'm sorry, I should have been up front. There is no scandal, and if I'm very lucky, it won't be too long before I'm married again. Or engaged at least."

MB gets to his feet and holds out a hand. "Good luck. I hope it works out. Jackson said you were the perfect couple. He's rarely wrong in his judgement. I'll look forward to meeting her. Now I can relax again, there's a bed with my name on it around the corner. I'll see you in the morning."

When I get home, Cassie is in bed. I shower quickly and climb in with her.

"Good day, H?"

"The best. Not one complaint from MB, and I took your advice and told him about you. If he's still around on Thursday evening, he wants dinner with us. No more pretending to be my wife, little bee. You can relax."

"Good news. So, if I'm not still your wife, why are you in my bed?"

"Because it's where I belong. Are we talking all night? I've got to be up early." I slide my hand down her thigh and groan as she rolls away.

"Oh dear. 'Night, H. I'll let you get your beauty sleep."

She screams as I flip her back over.

The next morning, the spring is back in my step, because I'm going to meet the boss and there will be no pretence involved. I'm in by seven thirty, much to Cassie's annoyance. I'll have to learn how to creep out of the bathroom and apparently singing in the shower is banned until after the normal world gets up.

MB arrives just before eight, and we spend the morning going through the investments Gemini inherited from Brad and those that were currently favoured by Gemini. He's like a dog with a bone, and we go through about seventy percent of the clients with money in those investments to make sure it's the best ones for them. Lunch is a sandwich from the corner shop, and once eaten, the pressure is off me, just a little, because this afternoon we are going through the same exercise but with the new staff. It's an interesting, if a little nerve-racking, process, but Andi and Charlie are good. They did well. The only irritation is the repeated calls from my mother. She knows I'm at work. On the fourth call, I wave my phone at MB.

"Sorry, it's my mother. Something must be wrong because she's not giving up. I'll step outside and be back as quick as I can."

"Don't rush. Mothers are important." MB's switch flips and he's back to work.

I pace the corridor outside as I answer the call. "Mama, what's the problem?"

"You must come home, because..." I can't hear her, because the workmen start doing something that sounds like the building is collapsing around me.

"I can't hear you. It's crackers here today and my boss is here. Can I call you later?" I'm trying not to shout.

"Christos. Christos. Where are you? I need you."

And suddenly everything goes quiet. MB has stopped the workmen. He must have heard me.

"Okay, there's no noise. Can I call you later, Mama? I'm at work."

She's still shouting. "You think I don't know that! Would I call you if it wasn't important? Come home. Come home as soon as you can."

"Why? I can't drop everything, you know that. Tell me what's wrong."

MB taps my shoulder. "Where's home?"

"York. It's okay, she's shouting at me, it can—"

"About four hours? If you leave now, you'll be there at a decent hour. I'm good here. I'll be around until the end of the week. Call me later. Let me know what's happening. Your mother needs you."

Oh god. What do I do now? She's probably being dramatic over something Stella has told her, but if I don't go, MB will think I'm a total bastard. I nod and return my attention to my mother.

"Okay, but you're sure you need me?"

"Christos, was that your boss?" she demands.

"Yes, but—"

"Then listen to him. Come home." And then she hangs up on me.

I turn to MB. "Are you sure? It's probably just her being dramatic."

"Then go and find out. Stay the night, come back tomorrow. If it needs more than that, call me."

I thank him and head home to tell Cassie and pack an overnight bag.

Chapter 20

Cassie

JOEL JUST CALLED ME contrary, and I'm seriously considering finding a new best friend. All I said was that I was disappointed not to be the pretend wife anymore. That's not contrary. But who cares? He was pleased I was meeting my father tonight, and so am I, I think. I'll apply H's advice and hopefully we won't have a major showdown.

Miss Allison called to me earlier, asking if I'd received a parcel for them. I told her no and had to listen to twenty minutes on why one used to be able to rely on the postal service, and who she'd be complaining to. In the end, I had to tell her I was having dinner with my estranged father and had to get ready. She asked if H was going, and for some reason, which I'll never work out, I explained how complicated our relationship was, and that it wouldn't be fair to drag H into that drama. Now armed with the knowledge that H would be catering for himself, she offered...no wrong word, insisted he join them for dinner. So, I had to get him out of it by saying he was working all hours as his boss was in the country for a short while. We compromised, so I'm now writing him a note.

Hello H,

Hope you've had a fabulously successful day. Wish me the same for this evening, I'm getting nervous. Anyway, Miss Allison is cooking you dinner. She knows you won't be around to dine with them, but says as long as it's before 9.30, you can collect it. Bet you can't wait! I'd tell you to wait up for me, but I might get home before you do! Just kidding...I think.

Lust you, (which is an allowable L word)

Cassie xxxxxxxxxxxxxxxxxxxxxxxx (Yes, I went mad with the kisses. Think you've earned them.)

I prop it up against the fruit bowl and go to collect my laundry. I've never changed a bed so frequently in my life. Think I'm going to suggest we use H's room in the future and let him take the strain. I'm halfway through the fight with rolling the fitted sheet into a flattish ball when I hear his voice. What's he doing at home?

"Mama, it's me. I'm at home. No more interruptions. Now tell me what was so urgent?"

Oh dear, this doesn't sound good. It's clear he's not impressed. I'll keep out of the way and resume the fight with the sheet.

"Christos, it's Ana. She's here. She needs you."

His phone is on loudspeaker. Oh, that's interesting. I step closer to the door; the sheet clamped to my chest.

"Here where?"

"At the house. My home. Do the video thing."

There's a pause and I place the sheet on the pile and pick up a pillowcase.

"There, can you see me?" H asks.

"Yes. Look home."

"Okay, Mama, I can see the television. Why is Ana there? And what's it got to do with me?"

"Christos, how could you ask that?"

"Because I...where are you going? Keep still."

"No. She will tell you. Here, Ana, come here and talk to him."

"Hello, Chris, I'm sorry about this but..."

Her voice breaks. She's crying. The pillowcase also gets screwed into a ball.

"Ana, what the hell is going on?" H demands.

Okay, I relax a little. He's not happy with Ana either.

"I need you to come home, I need—"

"What the hell? Jesus, Ana, what the...I'll leave now. I'll be there as soon as I can."

What did she say? What did I miss? I step closer to the door.

"Thank you, Chris. I knew—"

"Ana, don't thank me. Who else would you call? Shit! Are you okay? I'm so sorry, lovely girl. Get off the phone, so I can get going. Put me back on to Mama."

"You see, Christos, was I right or was I right?"

"You were right. Keep her there, Mama. Tell her I'm coming and do not let her leave. Can you do that?"

"Of course. You're a good boy, Christos."

"I'm something. 'Bye, Mama. See you later."

I'm guessing he hung up, but I hear him curse a few times more, run upstairs, back down and the front door slams. I pick up the laundry. That was one conversation I didn't want to hear, and I seem to have missed a crucial bit. Although perhaps I needed to hear it. I can't decide. At least now I know he'd run back at the drop of a hat. Not impressed with Mrs B, though. I don't know the whys and the wherefores, but I thought she was on my side. Just goes to show, you let your guard down and bam. Right between the eyes. I feel like...I don't know what I feel like. Shit scared comes top of the list. Fucking hell, all this and my father tonight. That's H's fault too.

As I cross the kitchen, I see the note. Bloody hell. As if I haven't got enough on my plate. I don't want Miss Allison on at me later for not letting him know. My phone pings and it's a message from my father.

Cassandra, hope you are well. I'm really looking forward to seeing you tonight. I'm going to be free earlier than expected. Can we bring our meeting forward to 6.30? That way I'll get more time with you.

Oh God. Why me? Why today? Well, if nothing else, I'll be able to get home to sulk earlier than expected.

Yes, sure. Why not? See you there.

I check the time and groan because I should get ready. At least H's dress will get another wearing before I decide if I have to shred it. Shit, now I'm going to cry. I will not cry. He'll call and explain, and I'll let him. I won't hang up but hear him out. Blinking, I head for the shower.

Good news, half an hour to go and I'm ready. Bad news, I'm pacing the kitchen, because I'm nervous about seeing my father, and I'm worried about whether H will come back, and if he comes back, how long he'll stay, and if he comes back to stay, if he'll be able to convince me he really doesn't love her. I mean, who runs out on the new boss and drives for hours to get to an ex-wife? Shit, I'm driving myself mad. I knew I shouldn't have put mascara on.

He's not called me.

Spotting my note for Miss Allison, I screw it up and throw it across the room. I'd better let her know, because if I don't she'll be round here. If I go now, I can waste a few more minutes on the way to the hotel.

I fix a smile on my face as she opens the door.

"Cassie, my goodness, you look wonderful. I once had a dress just like that, although probably not so pretty."

Elizabeth calls from her makeshift bedroom and Miss Allison beckons me in. "Let her see you or I'll never hear the end of it."

I like Elizabeth, and it will keep my mind occupied, so I go in.

Elizabeth oohs and coos, and it cheers me up. I promise that once she's fit enough, we'll put her glad rags on and go and have a cocktail in a swish hotel. She's still clapping when Miss Allison brings me back down to earth.

"Your father will be so proud to have a daughter like you on his arm. Daddy loved going out with us. Did you let Mr B...I still can't get that right. Did you let Christos know I've done dinner for him?"

"No. I couldn't H has gone..." I clear my throat. "That is, he's..."

My chin quivers, my bottom lip is doing the samba, and the tears I've been holding back all afternoon arrive. Elizabeth joins in, and Miss Allison flaps about with a box of tissues. She doesn't do public shows of emotion, and she doesn't do them in her living room either.

"Don't cry, Cassie. It makes one's eyes puffy. I would ask what the matter is, but I'm sure you don't want to tell me. I'm guessing it's got something to do with Mr Baros, but...well, I don't know. But tears will not do. You are meeting your father. He won't expect you to be in a state. Now blow."

I'm pleased H has been demoted to Mr Baros again. She might not know why, but Mr Baros is clearly out of favour.

"His wife called him. Said she wanted him to go home, and he has." I sniff. I sound like a sixteen-year-old.

Miss Allison stills and shoulders back, hands the box of tissues to Elizabeth. "Why?"

"I don't know. I was eavesdropping, which I know is wrong. He did a FaceTime call with her. I missed some of it. He swore, she said come home I need you and he said I'm on my way."

"I have no idea what you're talking about with regard to the call, but what did he say to you?"

"He didn't." I sniff again. "Bloody hell. Has my mascara run?"

Miss Allison takes my chin and turns me to face her. "No need for language, and only a little. Tissue!" She holds out her hand and a still snivelling Elizabeth pulls out a tissue and places it there. "Hold still."

First, she dabs the tissue to my cheeks and then screws the tissue into a point and tells me to suck it. I obey, because I'm past caring. Satisfied with her work on removing rogue mascara, she asks if I have my compact with me.

"My what?" I ask.

"Your powder dear," she explains.

I shake my head. "No, just my lippy."

And she's gone. She comes back with a tiny gold *compact* and dabs the sponge first on the rather pale powder and then on my face. She asks if I want rouge. Now I know what that is, because my nan used it. I walk to the mirror above the fire and find the damage isn't too bad for what was nearly a disaster zone. I take my lipstick from my bag, put a small dot on each cheekbone, and blend it in, before putting a little more on my lips. I turn back to face them.

"How do I look?"

"Beautiful," gasps Elizabeth.

"Exquisite. I don't know what Mr Baros is up to, but you'll always have somewhere to escape to, should you feel the urge to get out of the house. Now chin up, shoulders back, go and see your father. I know men can be overbearing and opinionated, but he is your father. Whatever has gone before, he loves you. Remember that. Come on."

Elizabeth calls goodbye as I am led to the door by my elbow.

"Thank you, Miss Allison. If H has done nothing else, he's shown me I have wonderful neighbours."

Miss Allison smiles and gives a brief nod. "Have a lovely evening, Cassie. I shall expect a full report tomorrow. Oh, and it's probably best not to mention Mr Baros's current whereabouts. Fathers are very protective of daughters, as I myself can attest. It wouldn't get them off to a good start, should a start be necessary."

I thank her and head for the hotel. As directed, I keep my shoulders back and chin up. I check my phone before I go in. H has not called or left a message. Fuck him.

I spot my father straight away. He's not as tall as I remember and his hair is speckled with grey, and lines crease his forehead and the corners of his eyes. But the overwhelming image is that he's much younger than I thought he'd be. Unless he's one of the lucky ones who age well. If I'm twenty-seven, that would make him...Oh, he's not fifty yet.

When he spots me, I try for a smile. Don't cry, don't cry, don't cry. I chant silently as I walk across the bar to him. When he opens his arms, I walk straight in. He hugs me tight. And now my eyes are leaking again. I blink away the tears. When he eventually releases me, he holds me at arm's length and looks me up and down.

"You were always a pretty girl, Cassandra, but now you are beautiful. Let's sit." He takes hold of my hand, leads me to a table, and sitting next to me he doesn't let go of my hand.

A waiter appears. "Would you like a drink?"

"Yes. A strong one," I announce, still looking at him. He's here. My dad is here, and he's holding my hand.

He laughs and the waiter smiles. "We need a bit more of a clue."

"Oh yes. What's your most popular cocktail?" I ask the waiter.

"At the moment? Dirty martini, espresso martini, or negroni."

"A negroni, please."

My father orders a scotch and squeezes my hand, and when I look at him, his eyes are glassy. He pulls a hankie from his pocket and holds it scrunched up on his knee.

"Cassandra, thank you for coming. I can't tell you what it means to see you, to be with you. Are you well? Are you happy?"

Awful questions, and I don't think we'll go there, so I just nod. It's easier. "I have questions," I tell him.

"I'm sure you do, but before you ask them, can I ask why the change of heart? Why did you decide to meet me?"

Another awful question, but I do my best. I remember Miss Allison's advice, which was basically don't drop H in it, just in case. In case of what I don't know, but I consider my words before responding. "A friend, my housemate, H, told me I should hear you out. That whatever your answer, and however this evening ends, I can move forward with no regrets. So I called."

"Well, I'm glad your housemate did that. I am forever in her debt." He blinks again and the hankie remains on his knee.

"His debt. H is a he," I tell him.

My father nods. "Okay. Well, I owe *him* a drink, a handshake, and a very big favour."

"I wouldn't jump the gun, Dad. We've not started yet. Not really."

Another blink and a tear escapes. The hankie is brought into play. "Are you kidding me? You're here. I've hugged you, and look, I'm holding your hand." He holds up our hands. "And you called me Dad. Do you know how long it's been since you've done that?" He rubs the hankie across his nose and shoves it back in his pocket.

"Eight years?" I hazard a guess.

"Pretty much. Now the questions. Before or after we eat?"

I purse my lips and tip my head to one side as I consider this. "That's a tough one. If we talk first, there's a chance I won't eat, but if we eat and talk, probably indigestion and or a loss of appetite. Maybe we should eat first, then at least I'll have a full stomach? What were you thinking?"

He's laughing. "I'm thinking that's the longest sentence I've had out of you, since you got a detention for setting fire to the biology lab. Do you remember that? You know, Cassandra, you are such a beautiful, funny girl, I regret even more missing out on your evolution into the woman sitting here holding my hand."

I'm suddenly embarrassed. The heat rushes to my cheeks, but I think it would be childish to remove my hand. So I go with, "Don't change the subject. If we're eating first, then let's get on with it. There are a lot of questions, and if we're not, are you avoiding the first one?"

My father nods solemnly, but I can see the twinkle in his eye. "Fair point. Let's eat." He beckons the waiter, asks for menus and a table as soon as possible. The waiter escorts us to the dining room, seats us and leaves us with the menus.

My father watches me as I open the menu and scan the list. Now I'm here, I have little appetite. Aware my father hasn't moved, I look up at him. "Are you not hungry?"

He gives a little shrug. "Right at the moment, I'm just happy. You choose for me."

"You might not like it."

"I promise to eat whatever you choose."

"That's ridiculous. Stop looking at me. Choose your food." I tap my menu.

His menu flips open, and he scans it for all of thirty seconds. "Prawns to start, then the chicken. Can I look again now?"

My lips twitch and I hold back the smile. "If you must." I slam my menu shut. "Garlic mushrooms, and tagliatelle."

He smiles and catches the waiter's eye. "Wine?" he asks.

"Oh yes. You choose I'm too poor to be proud." I instantly regret saying it, because I don't want a conversation about money. Anything but.

He doesn't bite but places the order for both food and wine.

"So we've established that I'm single and only have one beautiful daughter. What about you?" he asks.

"Same. Not married, no kids. A reasonably handsome father."

He seems to know that I don't want to speak about me, and he tries another question that shouldn't be contentious. "How's work?"

I groan. "Ask me another."

"No work?" he pushes.

"Not the sort I'd like. Oh, here's a question that's not on the list. What—"

"There's a list? Where's the wine? I feel I'm going to need a drink."

Questioning the list reminds me of H, and I'm glad that the waiter arrives and makes a fuss about removing the cork. I take advantage and sneak a look at my phone.

Nothing. Fuck him, fuck him, fuck him!

When I look up, my father is watching me.

"Everything okay?" he asks.

"Brilliant." End of conversation, move on, my eyes tell him.

"You were going to ask me a question?"

Okay, it's mean, but I'm not feeling very compassionate. "I need a porn name. I don't want to use my own. What do you think would suit?"

He barely misses a beat, not even his nose wrinkles, but he releases the stem of his wineglass and presses his hand flat on the table. The veins on the back of his hands rise. He's applying pressure. Interesting technique. Let's see if it works. "You're making pornography? That surprises me."

"Why? You know nothing about me," I accuse, but know that's my fault, not his.

"Correct. Why don't you tell me about it? Not the details, the why and how." His voice is low and calm. The pressure remains on the table, and I can tell by his eyes that he's processing this rapidly. Weighing up what to say, what to save.

"The why is money. But we're not talking about that. The how is my best friend Joel talked me into it because he's fed up with me talking about the lack of money."

Another sage nod. "And you thought doing that was preferable to accessing the money you already have? I have to confess I don't understand that. But I'm not you. Tell me about Joel. You say he's your best friend."

"He is and always will be. Joel saved me from being raped in my first year of uni. He's clever, funny, talented, and very loyal. I wouldn't be half of who I am without him. He's an actor, too."

"He looks out for you. Another man I need to shake the hand of. I'm sorry to hear about what happened. You should have called. Were you hurt?"

"Only emotionally. But what doesn't kill you makes you stronger and all that. I learned that most men were not to be trusted, however nice their words. Joel is one of the exceptions that proves the rule. Listen to me and all my clichés. Next question. Blimey, Dad, you're good. It's supposed to be me grilling you."

"If Joel is such a good friend who looks after you, why is he encouraging you to do pornography and not access the money?"

I laugh. "Oh, he did. He told me he refused to listen to my moaning about being broke if I was cutting off my nose to spite my face. Another cliché for you. I'm full of 'em tonight. Bottom line, he convinced me to do the porno with him." I shrug. "It's good money. That's if I don't get sacked for giggling. Took a while to get the audition done."

My father's face remains impassive, but I see the tightening of his jaw. "Oh, Joel is doing it too?"

"Yep, he's my leading man. As you would expect, the storyline is absolute crap, the hero is superhuman sexually, and the leading lady is a slapper. But money is money."

"I don't want you to do it." It's not a demand, just a statement of fact.

"You sound like H. Not telling me what to do, but still saying what you'd rather I did. Sorry, Dad, I've already signed the contract."

"I'll buy you out of it. Pay you whatever you're losing in income." He holds up a finger as I open my mouth. "I sort of understand all your resentment towards me. I don't agree with it but I understand it. Whether you will regret this meeting remains to be seen, but I know absolutely you will regret doing pornography."

"Hence my need for a suitably slutty name. I was thinking something along the lines of James Bond's favourite, Pussy Galore, if it helps."

"Are you wearing a mask? What difference will your name make?"

It was my turn to hold up a finger. "Two seconds." I run back over our conversation and giggle. "Sorry, Dad. Oops. It's an audio book. I am not baring all for camera, dear god, I can barely speak the words let alone do the actions. It helps that I'm doing it with Joel, but still." And I'm giggling again.

My father smiles and his hand leaves the table and reclaims his glass. "Well, that's a bloody relief. If I were a betting man, I'd say you knew exactly what I would believe. Audio is better, but the offer remains on the table."

"Thank you, but no thanks. I won't push you for a name."

"Okay, but the offer remains. The same goes for Joel if that helps ease the situation." He glances up as our starters arrive. "Thank goodness. Eat and don't talk. I'm concerned about what you're going to say next."

We exchange a smile, and I realise I'm not feeling edgy, the situation with H aside, I'm feeling comfortable, I wasn't expecting that. We make quick work of the food, and our plates are cleared away. My father leans forward as though he's about to share a secret.

"Tell me a subject I can ask you about that won't cause heart failure when you answer me."

I suck air in through my teeth and give my head a shake, like a plumber looking at a boiler. "Tough question, Daddy." I drum my fingers on the table. "No, nope. Nothing coming through."

He laughs. "No wonder you ended up on the stage."

"I'm not kidding," I answer dead pan. "Oh, look, the main event. I can start my interrogation soon."

"That's how you think about your list of questions? An interrogation?" His eyebrows rise, but I can see the twinkle in his eye.

We eat the main course in virtual silence, our only comments being about the food. My phone vibrates in my handbag halfway through, and it takes all my willpower not to look at it. I'm going to need to dash to the loo as soon as we're done. The tension is building in my brain, wondering what H might have to say for himself.

Meal over, my father carries our wine glasses back into the bar while I excuse myself. Once in the ladies, I lock the cubicle, take a seat, and look at the screen of my phone.

It's not H, it's Joel.

Hi Cass, sorry if I'm a little late, but good luck tonight. Keep your temper. Must dash, on in ten. Love to H, and even more to you. J x.

I bang out a quick response.

All good so far, barely irritated, but about to ask THE question. H has run back to his wife without a word to me. Don't want to talk about it. C x.

I get up to go back to my father when my phone vibrates again. I whip it out.

WTF!?!? No time for details, but I'll call you as soon as this is over. J x.
PS DO NOT TAKE IT OUT ON YOUR DAD

I didn't need the warning because I've been very well behaved so far. Reapplying my lippy, I stare at my reflection. I like this dress, I'll have another reason to hate H if I have to get rid of it. But now it's question time. Lifting my chin, I head back out to my dad. He watches me as I approach and lifts himself out of his chair. A gentleman. Unlike H, who ran off without a word.

"You really do look stunning. Would you like a drink, or are you happy with the wine?" He pulls out a chair for me before returning to his.

"Thank you. Flattery will not avoid the questions, and the wine will do nicely." I place my bag on the table and rest my elbows on either side of it. "Ready?"

My father takes a swig of his drink, places his glass carefully on a coaster, before linking his fingers and resting his hands on his stomach.

"As I'll ever be, fire away."

I won't mess around. I'm going to be blunt. Calm but blunt.

"Why did you leave us?"

"I didn't leave you. I left your mother."

"Same difference."

"No, it's not. I tried to keep in touch with you. With my work commitments, you were better with your mother...initially."

"No, I wasn't. I needed both of you."

"You could have had me. You chose not to."

"I don't agree, but if that's what you believed, why didn't you come back for me?"

"It wasn't possible. You could have come to me. I offered. You could have split your time as you wanted."

"I was thirteen!"

"You were. All hormones and sassy, as I remember. I didn't put pressure on you because I didn't want you to feel guilty."

"I had no reason to feel guilty, because I hadn't abandoned my family!"

"Nor had I. I left my wife. I wanted my daughter. She rejected me."

"And that surprised you?"

"No. It was a risk I had no option but to take. I would never give up on you, have never given up on you."

"So you were willing to risk losing me to get rid of mum. And even when you knew how horrible it was, you chose, chose, Dad, not to come home."

"Coming home wasn't an option. I looked after you as best I could from a distance."

"Giving money isn't looking after someone."

"Agreed, but it helps. I had no other choice."

"There's always a choice."

"Not in this case."

I drum my fingers on the table. He's good. He's not shown one iota of irritation. Back to the beginning, I'll ask the same question, but phrase it differently to make him tell me.

"Why did you leave mum?"

He nods. First movement from him since I began my interrogation. "Because she cheated on me with a man I knew. A man she thought was my friend."

"Alan Carter?"

His nose wrinkles. Now I'm on the right track. "Yes."

"She was seeing Alan before you left?"

"Yes."

"I didn't know that. He didn't appear in the house for a couple of months."

It's not a question, but he gives a weary sigh. "That doesn't surprise me. Your mother didn't want to lose you, either. She begged me not to tell you. I thought she might end it with him when he told me."

"He told you, not mum?"

"Yes. Your mother would never have told me. She was devastated that he had."

"Why did he tell you?"

"I realised afterwards it was to get rid of me. He knew I had very strong views, Cassie. I believe in love and loyalty, and I had many opportunities to cheat on your mother, but I never took them, even when she made her dissatisfaction with our relationship very clear. I would never have abandoned my family and Carter knew that. He knew that once her infidelity was revealed, I would leave her."

"And you did." This is tough. Much harder than I thought it would be. It's all sort of making sense, and I almost feel sorry for him.

"Not initially, I didn't ask for the details from him. I wouldn't lower myself. Pride. So I asked her. She told me she hadn't meant for it to happen, but she loved him. She went on to say that she would have told me, but she was frightened she'd lose you. She said she would end it with him if I never told you." He presses his fingers into his brow and rubs his forehead. "To get to the bit that's least damaging, I promised never to tell you if she allowed my unrestricted access to you. She agreed. I also asked that she didn't allow him to move in. If he moved in, the house was to be sold. I would support you financially, but he would support her."

"Why?"

"For many reasons, not least I wanted that house to come to you, not be split with him in any way when their relationship failed. I didn't like the man, didn't trust him, and I wouldn't line his pockets."

"How did you know it would fail?"

I watch his chest rise as he sighs. "Because he had a track record. He always got involved with young married women. Took advantage of their situation, be that boredom or husbands who worked away. The relationships never lasted long, so I doubted this one would either. But irrespective of that, there was no going back for me. He knew that, she knew that."

He leans forward and reaches for my hand, and I allow him to take it. "Look, you were thirteen. Even without her asking, I wouldn't have badmouthed her to you. It would serve no purpose other than to hurt everyone involved. When I told you my leaving was for the best, I meant it, because it was. I would rather have taken you with me, but then you'd lose your mother, your home, your school friends, and what did I have to offer? A new everything that was strange, long working hours and a substitute mother in the form of a nanny. I knew that wouldn't work, so I had to settle on high days and holidays. Only you wouldn't agree to that. I was hoping once you were old enough, your mother would tell you the truth. If she didn't, then I was prepared to. Only she died, and I couldn't bring myself to do it. To ruin the memory of her for you."

I swipe away my tears. "You should have told me. You should have told me! Perhaps not when I was thirteen, but later, when she started drinking too much."

"When, Cassie? You wouldn't speak to me. I called every four weeks. If you weren't there, she told me she'd leave a message for you. If you were, you told me to fuck off before I could get a word out. When was I supposed to tell you? When you went to university, you rejected my calls. I wouldn't do it via text. You deserved more than that. Please don't cry. We're here now. It's done."

I hold out my hand. "Hankie." His smile is gentle as he hands it over. I wipe my face, blow my nose, and hand it back. "I'm sorry, Daddy, but I've been hurt so many times that I thought if I didn't listen to the lies, I wouldn't get hurt. H told me that if I took the chance and listened to you I might get you back. Can I get you back?"

He stands and holds out his arms, and I jump up and bury myself in his hug. It's warm, and comfortable, and safe. I'm such an idiot. I weep for all the wasted years.

Pulling me to his side, he walks me towards the door. "Let's get you home."

We leave the hotel, and he walks me slowly back to the house. Every time I try to speak, he hushes me and says we can talk more tomorrow. We don't need to say anything else tonight. And I agree.

As we pass next door, I see Miss Allison looking out of the window. She smiles at me and gives a little nod and waves before drawing the curtains.

"I'm glad to see you have friendly neighbours," my father says as he gives me a squeeze.

"She's a witch. But it turns out a very nice one, even if she is as mad as a...how do you know where I live?" I pull away and turn to face him. "Have you been following me?"

He purses his lips and gives a low hum. "Which answer will not have you telling me to fuck off?"

My brows rise. "It's your house, isn't it? You and Sarah set me up. Is that why I only pay half as much as the others? I thought it was a big discount for just making sure everything ran okay."

"No, it's not mine. It's yours."

"Mine? Mine? You mean I've been breaking my neck, dressing up as bees and doing porno books to pay rent to me? Fucking hell, Dad. That falls into the category of self-harm. You could have told me."

"How? When? Shall we go inside? We have a lot to talk about. One of them being your language. You swear too much."

"It's good for the soul. Have you got a key, or shall I use mine?" Sarcastic, but necessary, I think.

"No key. It's not my house."

"Was the correct answer. Don't get too comfortable, I don't know how much alcohol is in here, you might be sent back out on a mission. I need a drink."

Chapter 21

Christos

FIVE HOURS. FIVE LONG frustrating hours stuck in a car with no phone. The battery ran out before I'd even reached Birmingham. I haven't told Cassie I won't be home, wished her luck with her dad, or made sure my mother has kept Ana at hers. I'm busting for a pee, and I'm ready to kill someone.

At last! My mother's house is in sight. A narrow street, her house sits almost at the bottom of the hill. There are no garages or driveways, and I sigh with relief when I manage to park almost outside. If she nags me, I won't be responsible for the words that leave my mouth. Ana's car is here. That's something.

I snatch my phone off the passenger seat and rush up to the house. The door opens before I'm halfway up the path, and I shove it into my mother's hands. "Put that on charge," I shout as I head upstairs to the bathroom.

Never has a pee felt so good. The emptier my bladder becomes, the calmer I feel. Perhaps I might control the words now. I wash my hands and stare at my reflection. I'm knackered and I look it. My overnight bag is still in the car, and I think I'll leave it there. I'll sleep better in my own bed than here. Who am I kidding? I'll sleep better with Cassie than anywhere else. But I mustn't get sidetracked, because there are people to see and things to be sorted.

Mama's voice comes from the kitchen, so I head that way.

"Chris, thank you for—"

"What the fuck, Ana? Look at you. Come here." Ana steps into my arms, and I know she's crying. My heart breaks. I jumped in the car because her lip looked like someone had gone mad with filler. Not that she'd ever do that. But now I can see the bruise running the length of her cheekbone.

Her eyes are puffy from crying, well it had better be from crying. I push her back and look at her again. She looks like shit. "Who did this?" I demand.

"Yorgos told—"

"That's it. Fucking hell! Come with me." Grabbing her arm, I pull her out of the house, ignoring my mother's calls. The lights flash on the car as I release the locks, and I yank open the passenger door. "Get in. Is he at the flat?" I ask.

"Chris, calm down, let me—"

"Get in the fucking car. You can talk later. Is he at the flat?"

"I don't know. But—"

"No buts. Let's find out." My tyres screech a protest as I pull away, and I wonder what Stella will have to say about that?

I won't let Ana speak on the short drive, because I'm so mad. I don't want to tell her how stupid she was to leave me. Mainly because it's not true, not for me, because I've got Cassie. Ana has a thick lip, and a bruised face because someone has used her like a punchbag. I'm glad she had the sense to go to my mother's, though. That would have taken some courage, what with Stella's curtain twitching across the street.

I park outside the restaurant, and grabbing her arm, I drag her inside. Ignoring the looks from the diners, I raise a hand of greeting at Kostos, the chef, as I push her through the door leading to the flat.

I don't knock but barge straight through to the living room. Yorgos jumps to his feet. Jumps off my sofa!

"Chris, mate, I—"

I've never been a violent man, had a few punch ups here and there, but only as a teenager. It's not who I am. Not until he calls me mate. I let go of Ana's hand and rush forward, grabbing him by the throat, and I push him backwards until he hits the wall.

"Don't call me fucking mate. Mate? Mate? What sort of mate shags his mate's wife? Aye? Tell me Yorgos. What right do you have to call me mate?" I'm spitting each time I say mate.

Yorgos tries to loosen my fingers, and I tighten them until he croaks a plea. I ignore him.

"Tell me what *mate* would do this to a woman, any woman, let alone the woman he has shamed and made fodder for the gossips? Let alone the woman still married to a mate. Don't answer me. I don't want to hear your excuses. But get on your knees and apologise to her now, or so help me, I'm going to kick the shit out of you."

Ana grabs my arm. "Chris, let him go. Listen to me, please, he—"

She's still trying to fucking defend him. "Ana don't, I'm mad enough already. I might kill him if I get any more wound up. On. Your. Knees." I apply a downward pressure. Yorgos is not resisting, and he drops to his knees. I stand over him. Not that I think the woman-beating coward will run. "Apologise."

"I'm sorry."

It's almost a whisper and I kick him in the leg. "Properly. And once you've done that, I'm taking her home to my mother's and you will never, never, go near her again. Do you understand?"

"No!" He tries to get up, but I grab a fistful of hair and hold him down, and Ana bites my arm. "Ow! What the...Have you lost your mind?" I release Yorgos and rub my arm.

"He didn't hit me, Christos. He didn't do it. Why won't you ever listen?"

"You said he did!" I look at Yorgos, who gets to his feet and massages his neck. That's going to bruise. "Is someone going to tell me what's going on?"

Ana jabs me in the chest. "Are you going to listen?"

"Yes. If someone is going to talk some sense. Stop biting and jabbing me. You asked me to come." I point a finger at Ana. I have no idea what's going on. It's like I've entered the twilight zone.

"Not to beat Yorgos up, Christos. To talk to my father." Ana rolls her eyes as though that should be obvious, her hand now clamped to her hip. A familiar pose when she's pissed off with me.

"What's he got to do with it? Why? He doesn't even like me."

Yorgos snorts a laugh. "No, he just thinks you walk on fucking water. Won't even let me in the house, he's sacked me and told me to get out of the flat."

"You made your bed, *mate*," I spit a final one for good measure and turn my back on him. "Ana, why did he do this? He's an old bastard, but I can't believe this."

"Because I refused to come to you. To follow you to Bristol and take my shame with me. He said I'd paid him back, and now I had to do the right thing. I told him about me and you and what listening to him before had done for us, and he hit me. So I told him a few more home truths. He said if I didn't come back to you, he'd disown me. I told him to do his worst, and he was no father of mine, that no father of mine would ruin my life twice. So he hit me again. Then he sacked Yorgos and told him to get out of the flat. He won't listen to anyone. Not even your mother, and she takes some getting rid of. I'm sorry, I didn't realise how you felt, how this has hurt you. I can't come back." She flips her finger back and forth between her and Yorgos and blinks rapidly.

I run my hands through my hair. "Fucking hell, don't start crying again. I didn't mean what I said. Not all of it, anyway. I wanted to put him in his place." My nose wrinkles as I look Yorgos up and down. "You did nothing? You let her call me after what you did?"

Yorgos looks confused and waves the flat of his hands in front of his face. "Stop talking. Everyone stop talking. I have questions."

I poke him in the chest. "YOU have questions. You have no right to questions, because you didn't just drive for five fucking hours because of this." I point at Ana's face, and she rolls her eyes. Nice to have backup from the wife.

"Which was one question. Why did you come?"

Yorgos's hands are clenched into fists now. My anger has abated, and I don't want a fight. I want to go home. Home to Bristol, home to Cassie, so I answer him.

"Because she asked me to." I shrug.

"And that's enough. She calls and you run back like a lapdog?"

Okay, now he's winding me up again. "Yes, when she looks like that." I jab a finger towards Ana. "I shouldn't have had to. You should have manned up and dealt with it."

"How?" Yorgos demands. "Beat up an old man? Is that what you're saying?"

"Of course not. You sit, you explain, and if he doesn't want to give way, you leave. With her." Another jab towards Ana. "The best fucking prize you're ever likely to get. Did you even try?"

"You still love her."

I don't know if it's a question or a statement, but I'm knackered and I'm really pissed off, so I stand square to him. "What does that matter? Are you worried, Yorgos? Worried I'll take her back because you can't face down an old man?"

"So that's a yes?"

He steps a little closer. We're now nose to nose. And I know Cassie likes my nose, but I think it might get a little damaged the way this is going. I can't back down now. "It is. I will always love her. But not in the way I should, not in the way she deserves to be loved. Do you?"

He shoves me in the shoulder. "Yes, I fucking love her, but I could do without having you as this little ghostly fucking gargoyle on my shoulder day in and day out." He holds a hand next to his shoulder and flaps his fingers against his thumb. "Christos this, Christos that. It's fucking unbearable. I told her you wouldn't come, and yet here you are, Christos to the rescue."

I don't know who's been giving him grief about me. In one way I'm glad, but only if it's not Ana. No, it wouldn't be good if it was Ana, so I turn to face her. "Why did you call me?"

"I didn't. It was your mother's idea. She—"

I throw my arms into the air. "You listened to my mother? Since when? What the hell did she think I could do?"

"Tell him you would never take me back. Tell him you were divorcing me, and that he should let me be happy with Yorgos."

I look at my feet while I consider this. Not a bad shout. "What's the time?"

"What's that got to do with anything?" Ana asks.

"Will he be up? I'm not dragging him out of his bed," I tell her.

"Oh. You'll do it?" Ana gives a small smile, at least I think she does, but her lip is going nowhere.

"What's the time? I don't want to stay the night." I was sure about that earlier, but it seems I've made up my mind. I'm going back to Cassie tonight.

"I don't know. He sleeps a lot these days."

"What, when he's not beating the crap out of people? Only one way to find out. Come on." Heading for the door, I look over my shoulder at Yorgos. "You too."

"But—"

I spin back around. "Don't even start with the buts. You really don't want to wind me up any more than I already am. Move it." I'm so relieved when he does, I haven't got the energy for a fight.

Ana's dad lives on the outskirts of town. It's gone ten by the time we get there. The house is in darkness. Ana lets herself in to check but is back in minutes.

"He's in bed," she whispers as she climbs back in the car.

"Fucking marvellous." I drive them back to the flat and head to my mother's.

My mother is still up, the lights are on. Every one of them by the look of it. I see Stella's curtain twitch as I grab my bag from the car, so first I wave, then I give her the finger. Childish, but necessary. My mother opens the door.

"Where have you been? What happened?"

"I need to sleep, but because you've asked so nicely, I've been to see Yorgos, and then Ana's dad, but he was in bed, so I'll be going back tomorrow. Now before I go to sleep on my feet, where's my phone? I need to call Cassie. Why are you looking at me like that?"

"I forgot about it. I was so worried. It's only been on for five minutes. It's in the kitchen. Was I wrong, Christos?"

"Do you want a list? But if you meant about not charging my phone, I can call while it's plugged in." I know I shouldn't speak to my mother like that, but I have no patience left. I'm worried about Cassie.

"Christos! You have a list against me now?" Her hands are clamped to her face and her eyes fill. "I thought it was for the best."

Pulling her into a hug, I kiss her forehead. "It probably will be. We'll know tomorrow. It will all work out in the end, I'm sure. But for it to work out for me, I must phone Cassie. Two minutes and we will talk."

I go straight to my phone to find there's only three percent battery. My mother probably remembered when I pulled up outside. Shower. I'll have a shower and by that time I should be able to call Cassie from bed. A little privacy. I walk past my mother, collect my bag, and head upstairs. "The phone isn't ready. I'll shower first."

"Have you eaten? Shall I get you something to eat?"

"Just a sandwich. Don't make a fuss. I don't want to upset you by falling asleep at the table."

Needless to say when I come down there's enough food on the table for four people. I tut and shake my head. "Are you trying to fatten me up? I'll never eat this lot."

The phone is now at twenty percent. If I eat first, I can escape to the bedroom. I pull out a chair and sigh as I drop on to it.

"Don't sigh, Christos. You are doing the right thing. You are a good man." My mother pushes a plate closer to me and pats my shoulder.

"I don't know about that, I—" My phone rings, and I jump to answer it. It's probably Cassie wondering if I'm still alive. I haven't spoken to her all day. "Oh." I stare at my phone.

"Christos, who is it? You look worried."

"It's my boss. It's almost midnight. Something must have happened." I release the phone from the charger. "Hello, Mark. Is everything okay?"

Chapter 22

Cassie

MY FATHER FOLLOWS ME into the house. A house I apparently own, and I don't know what to say. I've just let my father, my dad, follow me into my house willingly. Would have put money on that never happening. We've had a nice evening. I've got a lot of thoughts to process. Perhaps I shouldn't have let him in. I wish H was here to talk to. I wonder what he's doing, if he's with Ana? And now I'm mad again.

"It's nicer than I remember." My father brings my thoughts back to him.

"You've been here? When?" I demand.

"When I bought it. It was a little unloved. I wanted to make sure it had worked out as planned. But it's better now, probably because it's lived in. A home. You do think of it as home, don't you? I lived in a house for four years once. It was never home. Just the place that I slept in."

"Four years! Why didn't you move? And yes, I think of it as home most of the time. I get lonely sometimes, even if the others are around, but Joel usually sorts me out."

Still thinking about H. I'm going to have to get rid of my dad and call him. If I'm going to be miserable all night, I might as well have good reason to be. But will he be with Ana? Will he sleep with Ana? I realise my dad said something and I look at him. "Sorry, what?"

"I said, I think your phone is ringing." He points to my handbag.

"Shit. I might need to get this. Help yourself to a drink. There must be some somewhere." I snatch my phone from my bag. Bugger. It's Joel. "Hi, Joel, how was the show?"

"Alright is about the best I can manage. I really am going to kill that woman, but I didn't phone about that. I mainly called to see how it went with your dad," Joel tells me.

"That was kind. It went well. Great. He's here now. I've abandoned him to speak to you." I catch the smile on my dad's face. He knows I've just been positive about our meeting. I'm glad I can still make him smile. "Oh, and guess what, he's not so keen on the porno audio work, said he would pay us both not to do it."

"What? You mean I haven't got to pretend to like doing naughty things to you? Wow! What did you say?"

"I told him I'd signed the contract." I smile and nod at my dad, who is waving a teabag at me.

"We can get out of that. That's just to cover off what happens with delays and payments and stuff. Cass, I'll be your best friend if you take him up on his very generous offer."

"Joel, you are already my best friend. You'll have to come up with a better bribe. Oh, and that's not the big news. You'll never guess what that is." I wait for him to guess. He doesn't. "Go on then, guess."

"Really? Just tell me, Cass."

"Guess."

"He's moving in with you?"

"Nope."

"You've got fifteen siblings."

"No!"

"Cass, tell me."

"Guess who owns the house I've been breaking my neck to pay the rent for?"

"Your dad? That's why you get it half price? Well, that's good news. Bet you were mad, though."

"Nope, because it's not his. It's mine apparently. I've been paying rent to me."

"Fuck off!" Joel shouts. "Do you know how much that house is worth? Am I still your best friend? Please."

I'm laughing with him. "You'd still be my best friend if I found out I owned Buck House."

"Glad to hear it. But if you owned Buckingham Palace, I'd be demanding my own suite after what I've put up with from you. Talking of which, have you heard from H?"

My mood plummets. “Nope, don’t want to. Don’t want to talk about it either.”

“Why not? Because you’ve gone all knee-jerk again, or because you know something factual about his visit t’up North.” Joel puts on his best Yorkshire accent. It’s pretty good.

“No, because one, you can’t know the facts unless they are presented to you, and two, because my dad’s here and has already told me I swear too much, and three, because it takes seconds to pick up the phone or send a fucking text and he hasn’t.” I glance at my dad, who’s sitting at the table with a steaming mug in front of him. Better bring this conversation to an end. “And four, my dad is still here, and I’m ignoring him. I’ll call you tomorrow. ’Bye Joel, love you.”

Joel makes me promise to call him again and hangs up. I join my dad at the table and he points to the mug of tea.

“Wasn’t sure if you still took sugar, so I didn’t put any in.”

“You remember I took sugar?” I’m shocked.

“I remember most things about you, Cassandra. I’ve had no new memories to replace or compete with the old ones,” he tells me,

And although I don’t hear it, I see his chest rise with the sigh, and I feel so guilty. That’s my fault, not his.

“That’s true, I’m so sorry, Dad. I should have listened to you, but I’m not good at that when I’m emotional. I’m sorry.” Tears threaten, and I pinch the bridge of my nose, because I don’t want to cry.

“We can make some new ones now, I hope. We can, can’t we?”

There’s doubt in his voice, so I smile at him.

“Yes. Yes, we can. I’ve got a list. The zoo comes top, although it’s not in Clifton anymore. Do you know that? Do you remember the penguins?” I ask, with a smile as I sit down opposite him.

“I do. How could I forget? No one throws a fish like you do. And a list, Cassandra? Another one?” He grins at me, and I think if only H was here, my life would be complete. Warm, comfortable, and safe. But he’s not. He’s with his wife. “What made you look sad, then? It was only a zookeeper. I’m sure he was used to being hit in the face with a dead fish.”

My hand flaps the question away. I don’t want to talk about H with my dad. What I want to do is find out what’s going on. “Been an eventful day.

I was pondering. So, the zoo project. What else? Think there should be a fair or a circus in there too?"

"Disneyland? We never did Disney."

I clap my hands. "Yes! That's a must."

When he smiles at my excitement, he looks so kind, so handsome, that I hope what happened with mum, with me, didn't ruin his life.

"Why aren't you married?" Well, that came out more bluntly than I'd intended.

"Never met the right woman." He opens his mouth to say more but changes his mind.

"But you've been looking, right?" I push.

"I've been on dates, if that's what you're asking. I'm not dead yet. Although I'm not sure this is an appropriate conversation to be having with my daughter."

"Let me rephrase. Have you been happy? I know what Mum did, and what a total bitch I've been, but I want to know that didn't stop you having a happy life." He's pursing his lips as I speak. I know he's going to lie. That's what I do to avoid awkward questions. In the end, he settles for an insincere laugh.

"I've been fine, Cassandra, really. Apart from being married to my work, life has been kind."

He's lying, and my heart is breaking. I want to ask him the last time he had a girlfriend, but he's changing the subject.

"I'm not here to talk about me. What about you? Do you have a current boyfriend?"

I waggle the flat of my hand. "Don't want to talk about him. The jury is out," I reply, quite proud that I saw that question off without drama.

"Okay, what about the last one? I'm not being ultra nosey, just trying to work out what makes you tick."

"Don't want to talk about him, either. He was a liar and a total waste of my time. Next question." It's like being on Mastermind. Specialist subject: How to choose totally inappropriate men.

"Tell me about your housemates, then. Who are they? Do you get on with them?" His smile is kind, because he doesn't realise he hasn't actually changed the subject.

"You mean you don't know?"

He shakes his head. "No. Nothing. My brief to Sarah was to let you have free rein. If you couldn't find someone to share with you, she would find someone nice. How's that going?"

"Yes, good. Steve is a cameraman for the BBC. He's always in and out because he's filming on location. Nice bloke, good sense of humour. Jerry moved out a few weeks ago. He was so funny, his girlfriend was too. We had a laugh. They've both moved to Cornwall. He inherited a house from his grandmother. He'll have us down to stay once he's renovated. Apparently, the decorations haven't been changed since the eighties." Not going to bother to mention H. Too messy, and too complicated.

"So, H took his room, did he?"

Bloody hell! What's a girl got to do?

"Yes. Appears to be a nice guy."

"A very nice guy. I wouldn't be sitting here if it wasn't for him, would I? You also said he wasn't keen on the porn thing, so why has he been relegated to just appearing to be nice?"

Bugger, I forgot I mentioned H earlier.

"Is that what I said? I meant, nice. He's a nice guy." I glance at the clock and it's almost midnight. What if he wasn't in bed with Ana? What if he'd been in some horrific accident and couldn't call me? Shit. I'd better try to get rid of my dad. I raise my hands above my head and yawn. "Blimey, that was rude. Sorry, it's been a long day."

"I'd better let you get to bed. Are you okay being here on your own?" he asks.

"Yes, Dad, I've spent most of my adult life on my own. I'll be fine." This time it's me who offers the hug. "When do you go back to wherever you came from?"

He wraps his arms around me and kisses the top of my head. "New York. It was going to be tomorrow, but I think I'll extend my stay. If I do that, are you around to cross some of those things off your list?"

"I am, and if I wasn't, I'd make arrangements."

"Then I'll stay until the weekend and get back for Monday. Let me just make one call."

"Okay, I need the loo."

He puts the call on speaker and starts to load the dishwasher as I head for the toilet.

"Hello, Mark, is everything okay?"

"Yes, absolutely perfect. I want to change my plans for the rest of the week. I have family stuff I want to take care of but wanted to check when you're around. Andi is good, but I'd like at least one of us to be around for the call with Barratt on Friday."

I smile as I head out of the room. He said family stuff. There might only be two of us, but I like that. I could do with having a family again.

When I come back, Dad is being boss-like and listing off a load of names, which mean nothing to me. Whoever he's talking to is agreeing by interspersing yep, aha, and okay throughout the conversation. I hope whoever it is had a pen handy. This is a heavy conversation for this time of night. I'm impressed with my dad though, he's got some memory.

I rearrange the fruit bowl while I wait. If I sit down, he might stay, and nice as that might be, I must speak to H. Or try to at least.

Dad holds up a finger and mouths sorry before winding it down.

"Okay, looks like we're set up. Good work. Glad I didn't wake you up...What am I like? I'm sorry, how was your mother? All sorted? Was it a panic over nothing? I bet she was glad to see you."

H chuckles. "Yes and no, not really my problem, but I should be away by lunchtime tomorrow, and..."

Wait a minute. H? H chuckles? Oh, no. Oh no, no, no, no. I look at my dad, clicking my fingers to get his attention. "Who's that?" I mouth. He frowns and shrugs, as he doesn't understand me.

"Hang on, just one minute. Sorry, what did you want, Cassandra?"

I roll my eyes. "Who's that?" I ask quietly.

"Chris Baros," he responds at normal volume. "Sorry, Chris, I should—"

"You should tell me what the fuck is going on! That's what you should do," I say. "H, want to explain why you disappeared off the face of the earth, and are now having midnight conversations with someone other than me?"

"Cassie? What are you doing with Mark?" H sounds confused.

"No, no, no. Not the question in answer to a question game. What are you doing in York?"

"Cassandra—"

I hold up my hand to stop my dad speaking. "Not yet. You'll get your turn. H, I asked you a question."

"Cass, calm down. I'm speaking to my boss. What I don't understand is why you're also on this call? Why are you with Mark? Can he still hear me?"

"What the hell difference does that make?"

"Because if I'm right and you're going to be your usual self, I need to warn him to keep his distance, I think. But it depends on why you're with him. Mark, why are you—"

I'm not having this. "Let's take a vote. Who the hell cares what you need? Nope. No one. Have you two set this up behind my back? You take a room in the house, talk me into seeing him. Is that what happened?"

"No, don't be so ridiculous, Cass. Why would I want you to see another man? Tell me th...Oh no, is Mark your dad? You've got to be kidding me! Cassie, stay calm. Mark, can you hear me?"

"I can. So you're H? The H she looks all gooey-eyed over when she talks about you?" Dad's lips twitch a smile.

They're trying to hoodwink me. Make me think this hasn't all been part of the plan to reunite us. It's elaborate, and it nearly worked. Can't believe me jumping into bed with H was part of the plan...or was it?

"H, honest answer required. Think you can manage that?"

"Cass, I've had a bitch of a day. Ask the question and cut the sarcasm."

H sounds pissed off. Well, tough, he's not as pissed off as I am.

"I don't think you're the injured party here, H. You'll forgive me for not caring how your day has been, because I don't know where you've been and why. And I probably should, don't you think? So, back to the question. I want you to answer honestly, because my dad clearly thinks you've been to see your mother."

H doesn't answer.

"H, can you manage an honest answer?"

"Fuck me, you are the most infuriating...ask the question. Honest...Mama! Stop hitting me."

I can hear Mrs B in the background now. "Put your phone on speaker," I tell him.

My father is pacing the length of the table and back. It's irritating. "Oi. Keep still. This is probably your fault. Hush." I wag my finger as he starts to question me. "H, am I on speaker?"

"No. Why do you want to be on speaker?"

"Because I want your mother in on this conversation."

"No."

"Okay, hang on a minute." I get my phone and ring Mrs B and hit the speaker when she answers.

"Hello, Cassie, I thought you were speaking to Christos. He's very angry tonight, says he has a list about me."

"Ignore him, Mrs B. You're almost perfect. Can you tell me why H came back to York today?" I look at my dad and point to the phone. "You want to listen to this."

"He didn't tell you?" Mrs B asks, tutting.

"Cassie, my phone was dead. I couldn't call then I had things—" I cut H off.

"H, will you shut up? Mrs B has the floor."

"What floor. Why are we on two phones? Why didn't you tell her Ana needed you?" Mrs B demands.

"Don't say—" H attempts to hush his mother.

"Shut up, H! His wife needed him, and he ran back to York. Is that what happened, Mrs B?"

"Yes. But I called him. Ana came to me and—"

"That's okay, Mrs B. That's all we needed to know. Thank you. Have a lovely life. Your boy is home."

"I am not fucking home! Cassie, I can't believe this! Mark, I'll call you later. You don't need to listen to this."

"Oh, but he does. Didn't you tell him you were going home for your mother? You did. Lying bastard! Did you tell him you were screwing his daughter? No. Deceptive lying bastard!"

"Cassie, if that man is your father, you shouldn't be saying—" Mrs B tries.

"It's okay, Mrs B, he's only a part-time dad."

"Cassandra, that's not fair," my dad pipes in.

"Probably not. But like H says, it's been a bitch of a day, and I'm not in the mood for any more of it. So...actually were you telling the truth about the house?"

"Yes. I don't lie."

"You want to teach H some of that."

"Cassie, I didn't and haven't fucking lied to you. Sorry, Mark, but she's driving me crazy, absolutely fucking crazy. Glad I'm up here at the moment or she might punch me...Mama, do not hit me with...Ow!"

"Cassie, why has he lied to you? I'm sorry he keeps swearing, Cassie and Cassie's dad." Mrs B is a sweetie, even though she encouraged him to go back to the wife.

"H, stop swearing. Mrs B doesn't like it. I'm not going to punch you. But I am kicking you out. If you come back to Bristol, with or without the wife, you won't have a room here. This is my house, and I get to choose who lives here. I don't choose you."

"You can't do that," H says. "I'll be back tomorrow, and I'll be taking that room. You can punch me all you like, but you will listen to me."

"Yes, I can, and no, I won't. Did you not hear? It's. My. House."

"Ha! I've paid a month's rent. I've still got two weeks to go."

"I'll refund you. You promised me, and..." My voice croaks, and I clear my throat. "I'll pack your stuff up."

"Make sure all my shirts go in! I don't mean that, Cassie, I—"

"And that's enough. End of everything. 'Bye, Mrs B. It was lovely to meet you. I'll think of you every time I see dolmades. Fuck off, H." I hang up on both phones and hand my father his.

"I'm guessing you didn't know, so I'm sorry you had to listen to that. Now I think you should go. I'd like some time on my own."

He slides the phone into his pocket. "I won't interfere because I don't know what went before, but I think you should—"

"No, no, no. Enough. Your concern is appreciated but not needed. I'll call you in the morning. Come on, I'll show you out."

I lock the door behind my dad and go up to bed. Bloody hell, the bedroom smells like H. I lift his shirt from the linen basket and put it on.

What a bastard. I hope Mrs B hit him again.

Chapter 23

Christos

I THROW MY PHONE down next to the kettle and point at my mother.

"Don't say a word. Not a word. I'm going to eat something and go to bed. Ana and Yorgos will be here at nine, so I want to get some sleep."

"But you—"

I slam my hand down on the table and everything shakes. "Enough!"

My mother lifts her chin, tuts and shakes her head at me. She says nothing as she makes a meal of tidying other areas of the kitchen. When she's done, she leaves the room.

"And he tells Cassie to calm down," she mumbles, and I hear her climb the stairs. "Clean that kitchen up after you," she shouts and her bedroom door slams.

Collecting my phone, I start and delete numerous messages to Cassie, settling on:

Once upon a time, there was a beautiful princess who was sparkly and tingly, but she never listened.

It wasn't her fault because evil, poisonous toads had tricked her in the past. One day a handsome frog jumped into her world, and she named the frog H because he was Handsome, and Hot.

The princess was confused because she liked him, but decided if she didn't listen to him, he couldn't hurt her like the toads had.

So, the frog was banished from the kingdom. The princess left him broken-hearted, without a home and probably a job, because the King would always take his daughter's side. But the frog didn't care about the job. All he wanted was to make the princess happy. To make her safe. But how would he do that? How could he make her tingle again if he wasn't allowed to enter her kingdom?

To be continued.

I won't sleep either. Call me xxx

I clear the table, wipe it down, and pull the charger from the wall. When I get to my childhood bedroom, I find the bedside lamp on, the bed turned down, and a pair of PJs I'd not worn since I was fifteen sitting on the pillow. I'll apologise tomorrow. Plugging in the charger, I set the phone on the bedside cabinet, strip naked and lie on the bed. I wait half an hour before turning off the lamp.

My phone wakes me at five thirty, and I wonder if she's been up all night composing, or if it's another knee jerk response.

She's been composing.

Once upon a time, an ugly frog hopped into the kingdom of a very lonely princess. The frog was kind, and he shared all the tingles, and he made such wonderful promises, so the princess let him stay. One day, the princess kissed him and allowed him to become a handsome prince so he could catch her if she fell.

But the frog was naughty, or weak, or simply a liar, probably all three. He'd even fooled the witches who lived next door to the palace. The princess didn't know that, and just when she thought she was safe, the handsome prince ran away to a different kingdom and a different princess without a single word to the tingly princess. So now she will live alone wondering why she didn't realise he was a poisonous toad.

THE END

Fuck it.

An hour later, I hear my mother get up and bang around in the kitchen. I'm in no mood to talk, so I stay in bed. I know I should call Mark and try some damage limitation, although was it worth it? Did I want to be in Bristol with Cassie so close and yet so far? I could find another job. I'll call after I've sorted the Ana fiasco out. At half past eight, I throw the duvet back and get up.

"Christos, I was going to call you but I didn't want to make you angry again."

"Come here." I hold out my arms and pull her into a hug. "I'm not angry with you, not really. Just angry with the world. But I don't want to talk about it. I'll have a cup of coffee and nothing to eat. Ana and Yorgos will be here soon. I don't want a row before they get here."

"I won't row with you." She pushes me away. "Why would you say that? You must eat."

"I'm not hungry." I can feel the argument brewing.

"Did you speak to Cassie?"

"No." I drum my fingers before snatching a mug from the rack.

"Why?"

"Mama, enough." I bang the mug down.

"Did you speak to her father? He's your boss."

"Yes. I know who he is now. That was an unwelcome surprise. I don't want to talk about that either." I lift the pot and pour my coffee.

"But you spoke to him, unwelcome or not? Although it is a good thing. Not unwelcome, Christos." She steps closer and peers up at my face.

"Am I going to sit in the car and wait for them? Because I will if you don't stop."

"You go and sit in the car and phone her father. That's what you should do. Tell him about you and Cassie. Tell him."

"Jesus. Will you just leave it?" Luckily for my mother, I'm not as tired and grouchy as I was last night, but I reckon she's got about another five minutes before I blow.

"And watch you ruin your life, is that what you're asking of me?"

"No. I'm asking you to stop talking to me. I have a headache, and nothing you say or suggest will help it go away. I have to deal with Yorgos and Ana's dad this morning, and I'm not looking forward to it, but I will do it, and then I will come back here, and I will talk to whoever needs talking to."

"Okay. Good. I thought you might not be going back today." Finally, she turns away and starts pulling food out of the fridge.

"No food. I mean it. And I might not be going back today. Cassie says she's kicking me out. Her father might not want me back at work. But finding out later will be soon enough. If I have a job, I'll need to find a hotel."

My mother bangs a plate down on the table with force, and I hear the crack as it splits in two. I shake my head at her.

"Why did you do that?"

"Because it's what I want to do to your head. Phone her father. Now."

"That's it. Do not follow me." Taking my coffee, I walk to the top of the garden and perch on the wall. I would have gone to sit in the car, but I won't give Stella the satisfaction. The stones are uneven and it's uncomfortable, but I stay there watching my mother watch me through the window. I sip my coffee slowly. Ana and Yorgos had better be on time. My mother is not wrong. I need to speak to Cassie and Mark, but which one first, and do I want to hear what they have to say?

"Christos. They are here," my mother calls, and jumping down from the wall, I hurry inside.

My mother is arranging cups on the dresser.

"No. You're not entertaining. We're going out," I tell her and look at Ana. The bruise on her cheek has darkened, making her look pale. "Are you okay? Are you ready for this?"

"I'm not coming." Ana knows this won't impress me and she lifts her chin in challenge.

"What do you mean, you're not coming? What the fuck did I drive all the way up here for if you're not coming?" I demand.

My mother swats me with a towel. "Christos. The cursing."

I ignore her and keep my eyes on Ana, who shrugs.

"He won't have me in the house, Christos, and even if he listens to you which is fifty-fifty, I don't want to see him, not at the moment." Ana blinks back tears. "I won't beg for his love."

And yet she wants it. Bam, she's taken me back to Cassie. Two beautiful women who deserve to be happy. I hold out my hand, and she takes it. From the corner of my eye, I see Yorgos stiffen.

"Ana, don't be too proud. He will need your forgiveness, and you need his love, but you know he won't chase you because he will never admit such a weakness." I turn to Yorgos. "Are you ready?"

He steps forward. "Of course."

"Then let's get this done. I also have my own life to sort out. Mama, look after Ca...Ana."

I snatch my keys from the table and leave before my mother can say too much. Her gasp was enough.

Stella's curtain twitches as we reach my car, and I turn to Yorgos.

"What?" he asks. "Why are you looking at me like that?"

"I want you to smile at me, then walk forward, shake my hand, and pat my back. No, you're frowning. Bloody smile, man."

It makes him look a little constipated, but he does his best. "Why?"

"Because Stella is watching. If we put on a show, everyone will know there are no hard feelings."

His smile becomes more genuine, and holding out his hand, he steps forward with his hand held out. I take his hand, pull him to me, and we slap each other on the back.

"That's enough. Get in the car. Let's get this over with," I snap and resist the urge to wave at Stella.

"Thanks for that. Don't know if it will help, but I appreciate the gesture," Yorgos says as he fastens his seatbelt.

"I just want my mother off my back, Ana to be happy, and to get back to my life, so you're welcome."

"Ana tells me you've met someone. Is it serious? It seems very quick. A little too convenient." He glances at me, and I jerk my head to look at him.

"My mother is getting as bad as Stella. And what do you mean, convenient? It's a fucking nightmare, is what it is."

"So, there is someone?" Yorgos pushes.

"Yes, I hope so." I let the sigh out. "I've probably fucked it up by coming here. Too long a story."

"Ana said you were in love. I thought that was a story your mother made up." Yorgos holds up his hands. "Hear me out, don't jump in. I wasn't joking yesterday about everyone doing the 'such a good man, poor Christos' thing. You became a saint in your absence. So when your mother comes back from her visit and tells Stella you're in love, I got to hear about it. I thought that was intentional. You know, you might have taken my wife but look at me now. I wanted it to be true because that way I knew I'd keep Ana. She was being told by everyone to go back to you. When she didn't, I thought your mother was face-saving on your behalf. If she wasn't, I hope you work things out. I mean that."

I'm not sure what to say. I'm pissed off because my mother is gossiping about me, but it's obvious Yorgos thinks I might still have feelings or some claim on Ana. Me driving all the way back here, and my show of temper yesterday, will have done nothing to ease his worry. I throw my hands into the air before returning them to the steering wheel.

"I've met someone. She's funny, sharp, beautiful, and all sorts of other things I can't even explain. But she was hurt in the past and is terrified she'll be hurt again. So she makes poor decisions in an effort to protect herself. She doesn't understand how I can love Ana and not want her."

I glance at Yorgos and grin. "Much like you. So, I should have explained why I was coming here, probably should have brought her with me, but I just saw red when I saw Ana, because like Cassie, I didn't wait and get the full story. I saw Ana's face and assumed you'd done it. Sorry about that, by the way. Anyway, I didn't explain. Then my phone died and...it doesn't matter, it's too messy and too distracting. Let's just get the old man sorted, and then we can both try to sort our lives out."

Yorgos is nodding as he considers this. He falls silent for a while before asking, "Do you think this will work? That he'll listen?"

"I don't know. But if he doesn't, you have to do the right thing. You'll have to start again. Find a job, find somewhere to live, and make Ana happy."

"That's all I want to do. But I'm not a rich man, even poorer now I don't have a job. I can't give her what you did."

I bark out a laugh. "You're talking about the big house, with the empty rooms, and a fuck off huge mortgage? She wanted all that because she didn't have what she really wanted, what she needs. Maybe you're it." I shake my head. "God knows why or how, but who knows what goes on in women's heads?" I laugh. "Shit, I'm the last person who should give advice on that front."

"Tell me what she wants, or what you think she needs." Yorgos thumps the dashboard. "I can't fucking believe I'm having this conversation."

"Me neither. But in answer to your question, she needs a man who loves her like his life depends on having her. Loves her enough to have a family with her. I'm not that man, and to be honest, I'm surprised you are. Are you that man?"

When I glance at him, he's grinning. "I am." He nudges me with his elbow. "You really think she wants my babies?"

"I think you should ask Ana that. But she walked away from me. Me!" I joke, thumping my chest, and he laughs. "And away from the big house, and the secure future, for a bloke who lives in a flat above a restaurant. So yes, I think it's a possibility."

"Thank you." Yorgos stares out of the windscreen, a soppy smile on his face, before he taps away on his phone. When he's done, he slips it into his breast pocket and slaps it. "I asked her."

"Asked her what?"

"I've already asked her to marry me, once you two are divorced, so I asked her if we could start trying for a baby now."

His grin is infectious, and I smile and nod approval. At least Ana might get her happily ever after. I hope she does. If she doesn't want babies with Yorgos, I hope she doesn't tell him via text while he's in the car with me. That might be awkward.

We park outside Ana's dad's house, and I turn to Yorgos. "Whatever the provocation, try to keep your temper, although, to be honest, sod him. He's not averse to a display of passion. Be honest with him. Tell him what you feel."

"Can we just get it done?" Yorgos is climbing out of the car. He's nervous.

I nod and lead the way up to the house and knock on the door. No one comes, so I knock again. "The old bastard better not have died on us," I mutter, and I'm about to peer through the front window when his neighbour appears.

"He's not in. It's his day for therapy at the hospital," she tells us. "He usually gets back at midday, unless he goes out for lunch, then it depends on who takes him."

She seems very well informed of his movements. Bet her middle name is Stella.

"Who took him today?" I ask.

"Lucas. So he'll probably be back by two." It's not worth asking why she didn't just say that. "Aren't you..."

"I think you know perfectly well who I am, and who my friend here is. So the answer is, yes." I slap Yorgos on the shoulder. "Let's go."

Back in the car, my control slips. "Fuck, fuck, FUCK! I'm never going to get back to Bristol at this rate."

Yorgos shifts in his seat to face me. "I'll come with you."

"Come where with me?"

"To Bristol. It's the least I can do. I'll come and see your woman and tell her why you were here. That I'm going to marry Ana and have loads of kids with her."

"Thanks for the offer, but she'd never believe you. Cassie would think you were a cousin or a mate I'd bribed to say it." I check the time. "Oh god, it's not even ten yet. I can't face going back to my mother's. Do you fancy some breakfast?"

"Already eaten, but I'm sure I'll manage something. What are we going to do, just waste time until two o'clock?"

"Probably." It's a lovely day, and rather than drive into town, I head for the layby on the bypass, and park behind a lorry. "They do a great bacon bap here."

We order our food and sit at a dirty plastic table on cracked chairs and watch the traffic thunder past.

"I think I misjudged you," I tell Yorgos as I wipe away the grease with an ineffective tissue.

"How? What did you think about me?" Yorgos asks.

"Nothing originally. Bit jealous actually, heard tales and saw you out and about with a different girl on your arm each time. But I didn't think you were right for Ana and when I found out it was you she'd left me for, I thought she'd lost the plot. You weren't the settling down type. You wouldn't make her happy."

"Jealous of me?" Yorgos rests his elbows on his knees and stares at his feet, shaking his head. "That would be funny if it wasn't so sad."

"What do you mean?"

"When I started work in the restaurant, Ana captivated me. She was kind, funny, so bloody beautiful inside and out, and married. The longer I worked there, the more I wanted her. Only I couldn't do anything about it. I'd see you come in. Peck her on the cheek, pat her hand, and think, what is wrong with that man? I wouldn't be able to keep my hands off her. Even in public. But I had to, because she was yours. So I went out with other women. None more than once or twice. I didn't use anyone. I often ended up telling them that I loved someone else."

"How did you get her?" I ask. I'm not jealous, just genuinely curious, and I lean back against the dirty plastic chair and cross my legs at the ankle.

Yorgos grimaces. "Are you sure you want to hear this?"

"I wouldn't have asked. Tell me."

"Ana arrived early one day, and I was seeing a lady friend out, and she rolled her eyes when I joined her in laying the tables. She wasn't her usual self, so I asked her what was wrong, and she told me I was. That I was a man-whore who should find a decent girl to love and settle down with. I told her I had, but she belonged to someone else. Her eyes widened, her cheeks flushed. I'd never seen her blush before. It was so cute. So I told her I thought she knew that, and she shouldn't judge me because it was her fault. I won't go into detail, but how we never ended up across one of those tables is a miracle. And, for the record, as soon as I realised she felt the same way, I wanted to come and tell you. But I think she...I don't know, either didn't want to hurt you, or was afraid of her father's reaction. Maybe both. We sneaked around for a couple of months, and then I put my foot down. Told her it wasn't fair to anyone, and so she told you. You know, I didn't really believe her when she said you didn't mind."

I smile at him. "I'm glad she's found someone to love her properly, but I'll still come and kick your arse if you hurt her. Your round, I'll have tea, the coffee tastes like shit."

And we sit there for a couple of hours wasting time, talking about anything and everything except women, and drinking treacle-like tea.

At one o'clock, I get to my feet and stretch. "Come on. We'll sit outside his house. Can't miss him then." I've just started the engine when my phone pings. Cassie?

Christos, come home. I've told Theo to come here. He says he will.

"Bloody hell, my mother is interfering again. She's told him to go to her house," I tell Yorgos. "The not knowing what is going on is probably killing her. Still, if he turns up, Stella might have a coronary."

"Perhaps it's for the best. Home turf and all that. Watch my back. Lucas doesn't like me either. Thinks I've ruined his sister."

"Lucas is alright. He's just looking out for her. I'll have a word. So the question now is, do we wait until he's there, or go home and listen to my mother's advice for however long it takes?"

"Good point. She's not a fan either. Another cup of tea?"

So we sit for another twenty minutes, then drive back to my mother's, slowly. Whatever happens, I'm driving back to Bristol today. I'll sleep in the car outside the house if Cassie has locked me out.

I have to park at the bottom of the hill, and we walk up slowly.

"That's Lucas's car." Yorgos swings his hand towards the Audi estate parked near my mother's car.

"Yep. I spotted it. Brace yourself, it's nearly over, bar the shouting, of course."

"I'm so braced I can barely move my shoulders. Uh oh. Stella's on the move." He nods across the road.

"Bloody woman. Ignore her. Whatever happens, you'll be leaving here with...bloody hell, I wasn't expecting a welcoming party."

We stop walking as my mother, Lucas, and Ana step out of the house. My mother leans on the gate and beckons me forward. Lucas turns and holds out his hand. I'm guessing to help Ana's dad.

"It looks like they're leaving. Stella's going to have enough to keep her going until Christmas if we have to do this in the street." A car drives past and toots its horn. Everyone looks at it, but no one waves. "Come on." I give Yorgos a slap on the back.

We're fifty yards from my mother, who looks worried and worn out. I glance at Ana's dad. He's gesturing towards Lucas's car, and I call to him.

"Theo. Wait up. I need a word." I start towards him. "With me, Yorgos."

I don't catch his answer as someone calls from further up the hill. Jesus, how many more people want to watch this? I bet Stella's been on the phone. I glance up and stop walking.

"Who's that?" Yorgos asks.

I ignore him.

Chapter 24

Cassie

H SENDS ME A sweet story about a princess and a frog, but it's too much. I have to stop wishing, because I know better than most that wishes don't come true. I don't reply, but I do worry about him not having a home and I must ask my dad about his job. But not now, tomorrow will be soon enough.

Sleep comes fitfully and at five thirty, I give in and I tell him how the story ends. H doesn't reply. Not a lot he can say to that, I suppose. While I'm on a roll, I message my dad.

Hi Dad, sorry about yesterday. I don't know what happened with H, but he doesn't deserve to lose his job. I'll call you later. C x

He replies almost immediately.

I know. Fancy some breakfast? I make very good scrambled eggs.

What does he mean he knows? How can he know? Has he spoken to H?

Yes. Think we need to talk. Give me an hour to make myself awake and presentable.

I go into the bathroom and run a bath. Then lie there trying to work out why my dad has taken H's side. What a coincidence my dad being his boss. H would call it fate. I nod off and am awoken by my dad banging on the door. I grab my robe and let him in.

"Sorry, I fell asleep," I tell him.

"Thought that might be the case. I take it you didn't get much sleep?"

"I got some. You go and make a start. Everything should be in an obvious place. I'll get dressed.

While Dad makes a start on breakfast, I go back upstairs and dress in baggy jeans and a paint-stained sweatshirt. It looks awful, but it's clean and it's comfortable. Dad glances at me when I return.

"You might regret that. It's a glorious morning already. Sit. Nearly there."

I wait until he's dished up and is seated opposite me before I begin questioning him.

"So, did you speak to H after you left here last night?"

"No, I was expecting to, but then I thought it better to leave it until today to speak to him."

I nod. "And what will you be saying to him?"

"I have several questions. Making lists must run in the family."

"You're avoiding my question."

"No, I'm not. What do you want to know, Cassandra? Ask and I'll answer you honestly." Dad forks some egg into his mouth.

"Did you know H and I had a...thing going?"

"I knew he had a thing going with someone, but I didn't know it was with you." More egg goes in. "Eat and talk, Cassandra. I promise not to scold you for talking with your mouth full."

"Yeah, H told me that was rude. So what did he say about me?" I know, I know. I'm after a confidence boost.

"Eat something and I will tell you."

Dad points at my plate with his fork, and I shovel some egg in.

"Oo. That's good. I'm eating. Talk."

"He told me he'd lied about his marital status, and I had visions of a scandal, or at the very least, a bumpy ride while he sorted himself out. I relaxed when he said his wife had left him for someone else and was glad when he told me he'd met a very special girl. He seems to be a decent bloke. From memory, he said you were amazing, special, something else. Shall I go on?"

I purse my lips and nod.

"He said he'd never met anyone like you, he'd never felt about anyone like he does about you, and he thought he loved you. I was glad that he'd been given a second chance. His excitement made me feel happy. Call me soft, but I like happily ever afters."

"You're soft. You, of all people, should know that they don't happen. So his job is safe?"

"Watertight."

"Good. You think I'm a total idiot, don't you?"

My dad smirks. "Not total, no. I think you are headstrong and impetuous. I think that sometimes you need to apply some logic before you open your mouth. But there's nothing that can't be fixed if you want to fix it." He holds out his arms. "I'm sitting in your house having cooked you breakfast. Things can change if you want them to. And going back to your happily ever after comment. This is my happily ever after. It's what I've prayed for since the first time you told me to fuck off. Which has to stop, by the way."

"Noted. I'll do my best. Should I call him, Dad? I basically told him it was over. The end. Look."

I grab my phone and open the princess and frog text. I watch him read it. He smiles and shakes his head before tapping the phone. I snatch it back. "Best not to look at any of the others," I say and feel the heat hit my face.

"He says poisonous toads have hurt you. Want to tell me about them?"

"Not now. Maybe one day. They're history. What if he has gone back to her, Dad? I can't...that is..." And the tears are back. I've never cried so much in my life, not even when Dad left.

"Oh, Cassandra, I don't think you mean that. He said you were more important than his job. Despite your rejection, he said he hadn't given up. Come here." Dad walks around and pulls me into a hug, dabbing my tears away with a tea towel. "Calm yourself down and work out what you want to say to him. Then call him. I'll make myself scarce. Then—" The doorbell rings. "I'll get it. You sort yourself out."

It's Miss Allison, who hustles past my dad and hurries to me holding a cake tin.

"Cassie, sorry to interrupt. Elizabeth thought you might still be sad, and I can see you are. She insisted we bake you a cake, because cake always cheers one up. By the look of it, it will take more than cake, but here it is." She taps the biscuit tin and turns to my father. "I'm assuming you're the father. How do you do? Jennifer Allison. I hope Cassie has been careful in her comments." She places the tin on the table and holds out her hand.

"I am the father, yes. Mark Bowman. Nice to meet you too. I take it you live next door?"

"I do. How did you know that? Has Cassie mentioned me?" Miss Allison looks at me suspiciously.

"Only to say that H, or Chris as I know him, has charmed you." My dad smiles. "It was all good."

"Charmed? Oh no, although he is charming. He impressed us. He's a good man, and there aren't many of those around these days. But talking of Mr Baros, any news?"

I flip the tea towel at her. "I did it again, Miss Allison. Told him to f...go away without listening to him. He called last night. I made Mrs B listen to it too, but my dad was here, so I thought let everyone know and then it will be done."

"But why did he run back to his wife? What did he say?" Miss Allison's hands are clamped to her chest.

"She didn't let him tell her," my father pipes in.

Miss Allison tuts. "You really should let people finish what they are saying, Cassie. I told Christos the day I showed him around that you never let me finish a sentence." She turns to my father. "I'm hoping you'll talk some sense into her. Make her listen to him and then meet him and form your own opinion. Cassie can be a little dramatic."

My dad is grinning and gives her a thumbs up. "Will do."

"He's met him. H has charmed him as well. My dad is H's boss." I throw the tea towel on the table and slump into the chair.

"Are you? Well, I hope you don't let this business tarnish your opinion of him. He loves that job and I'm guessing he's very good at it, too." She looks over her shoulder as the doorbell rings again. "Are you expecting someone?"

Dad holds up a hand. "I'll go."

I hear Jan's voice. "Cassie, I was passing and...Oh, hello. Who are you? No, don't answer, that was rude. I'm Jan. Is Cassie around? I was surprised someone answered because...Cassie."

I've gone into the hall followed by Miss Allison. My dad looks amused. "Hello, Jan. This is a surprise."

"Isn't it? I'm doing this couch to five K nonsense and forgot my phone. Can't buy a drink and I need a drink." She runs her hands over her figure-hugging outfit, and glances at my dad. "No pockets. I don't usually wander the streets dressed like this. I was running." She flips her hand down her body again, still looking at my dad. She's wearing a fluorescent pink and blue cycling suit, which is very snug, and her ample boobs are trying to escape the V where she's pulled the zip down a little too far.

I roll my eyes as my dad smirks.

"Come on through. It's like Piccadilly Circus here." I'll never get to ring H at this rate.

"I'll catch you up," my dad says and disappears into the loo.

"Who the hell is that? What did you do with the other one?" Jan asks, lowering her voice only a little. "Bloody hell, Cassie, you know how to choose them. Can I be your proper friend and come out with you? I don't know where you find them, but I want one."

I smile for the first time in hours. "That one is my dad."

"Your father? But he's gorgeous. He doesn't look old enough. I need a proper drink, but water will do." Jan pushes past me, takes a used glass from the table, and rinses it under that tap, before filling it and drinking it down in one. "I don't suppose he's single, is he? Oops." My father has reappeared, and she slaps her forehead. "You didn't hear that, did you?"

Miss Allison tilts her head. "I don't think he's deaf. What colour would you say your hair is? No, don't answer. You clearly are quite mad. I'd better get back to Elizabeth. Oh, Mr Bowman. I shall leave Cassie under your supervision. Do not let her do anything silly."

Jan grins at my father. "Are you a disciplinarian?" Then she winks at him and goes bright red. "I said that aloud too, didn't I?"

My phone rings and everyone watches as I dash to pick it up. I wave it in the air.

"It's Mrs B. Should I answer it?"

"Yes," snaps Miss Allison.

"Of course," encourages my father.

"Who's Mrs B?" Jan asks, pulling out a chair. She points at the phone, and snaps, "Answer it."

"Oh shit, it's FaceTime. How do I look?"

Jan flips her hand. "Awful. It'll be fine. Answer it."

I hit the button and Mrs B's chin appears.

"Cassie, thank God. Do not hang up on me again."

"It wasn't you, Mrs B, it was H I hung up on. Is he with you?" I know I'm blushing, so I turn my back on my audience.

"No, he's gone with Yorgos." Mrs B's cheek tells me.

"Mrs B, lift the phone. I can only see your cheek. When you say Yorgos, do you mean the man Ana ran off with?"

"Yes. Of course, how many Yorgos' do you know, Cassie?" Mrs B tuts. "I need you to speak to someone."

"Speak to someone? Who H?"

There's a rustling and I see the ceiling light, part of a table, and then a dark-haired woman with big brown eyes, perfect eyebrows, and a badly damaged face. I close my eyes and draw in a breath. I don't need two guesses. "Ana?"

Ana nods and clears her throat. "Hello Cassie, I've heard a lot about you. I'm sorry I've caused so much trouble between you and Chris, but I needed his help."

"What happened to your face?" I ask.

Jan gets up and peers over my shoulder, then sits back down with a gasp. Miss Allison walks closer to her and I can hear them whispering as Ana answers.

"My father. It's why I'm calling. My father wants me to go back to Chris, who doesn't want me, as you well know, but Chris is the only one who can convince him of that. My dad thinks Chris left York because I'd shamed him. I didn't. He's happy for me."

"Okay. How did that go?" I ask.

"It hasn't as yet. My dad was in bed by the time we got there last night. And Chris didn't want to wake him because he's an old man. Now Yorgos has messaged to say my dad is out this morning and he and Chris are waiting for him to come home." Ana gives a shrug. "But Chris is angry. So mad. He thinks he's lost everything because he came here, and I wanted to tell you that—"

"Cassie. He needs you. He won't listen to anyone, and gets mad, and then madder. Do you know he has a list of things against me? You must come and calm him down. You have no work. Can you come? If you come, all will be well. He's happy when he's with you. Calm. I don't like this version of him. Now. Ana has told you she doesn't want him, and he doesn't want her. But he wants you, Cassie. Can he have you? Will you come for him?"

I open my mouth to speak, but before I get that far, both Jan and Miss Allison shout yes, and I grin at Mrs B. "I guess that will be a yes. I don't know how or when, I haven't got a car. Let me—"

"I have. I'll drive you." Jan stands up. "Give me half an hour to get changed and I'll be back."

"Oh Cassie, such good news. Let me know when you're almost here. My address is..."

Less than half an hour later, Miss Allison waves us off. Jan doesn't mess about. She's convinced my father that he must come too, because she needs someone to navigate, and I'll be useless because I'm all loved up. He looks too shocked to argue. I think he's rather enjoying himself.

As we drive away, my father taps the large square screen on the dash. "You have satnav built in," he says.

Jan flashes him a smile. "I know, but she lies sometimes, says left when it should be right, and the map keeps going upside down."

"That's because you've changed direction."

Jan laughs and slaps his knee. "You see. I need you. You know things."

Oh my god, she's flirting with my dad again. This is going to be a long journey.

And it was. After what seems like a week, the satnav instructs her to turn left, and our destination will be on the left.

"There he is," screams Jan and toots the horn.

I spot Mrs B standing by a gate as Jan looks for somewhere to park, and Mrs B smiles at me and turns to Ana. I don't know who the two men were. There are no spaces, so Jan stops at the top of the hill.

"Get out here. We'll find a parking space and walk back. Go and get your man. Me and your dad will be fine."

When I get out, H is walking towards his mother and looking at his feet. It looks like Mrs B has a welcoming party.

"H, I'm here." I wave at him.

"What are you doing here?" He's grinning, I can't see it, but I know that dimple's there.

"That's the best you can do, H? I come all this way, and that's all you have to say? I'm looking for a frog." I'm laughing and hold up empty hands.

H holds out his arms, and I run towards him. Shit, this hill is deceptively steep. I'm gathering momentum, and I'm not at all sure I'm going to be able to stop. "Catch me, H," I shout.

And he does. I fly into his arms, and he staggers backwards as he scoops me up. I lock my legs around his waist.

"You found your frog," he tells me as he plants little kisses over my face.

"You caught me. H. You caught me."

"I told you I would."

Chapter 25

Epilogue

One year later

Yorgos kisses Ana and everyone cheers. She looks beautiful. Her dress clings to all her curves. She's made no attempt to hide her pregnancy and looks totally and perfectly radiant. I see my mother dab her eyes. Cassie pats her hand as she catches my eye.

"I love you," she mouths, and I grab my heart and stagger backwards, making her giggle.

Ana's dad shakes my hand before he leads the rest of the guests out behind the bride and groom. "Thank you, Christos. I will see you at the christening."

"You will, Theo."

"When are you going to marry your girl? You're dragging your feet."

"Not me. She's happy as we are. I'm happy as long as she's happy. You need to move. Everyone is waiting."

As I follow him out, I grab Cassie on my way, leaving my mother with Jan. Ana and Yorgos had insisted Jan came after driving Cassie all the way up here to confront Theo.

"That was lovely," Cassie says. "I even shed a tear myself."

"It was. Shame your dad couldn't make it. I think Jan was disappointed."

"I know. She's got a real thing about him. Will Ana throw the bouquet?"

"I suppose so. Why? Do you want to catch it?" She doesn't answer, but she's blushing. "Cassie, look at me."

"I might," she whispers, then screams as I lift her off her feet and twirl her around.

"You don't need to catch the bouquet, you know that."

"I do. But you're such a stickler for fate, and I've said no so many times, I've decided that if I catch it, it's a sign. Your weird beliefs must be rubbing off on me."

My nod is solemn. Understanding. "So, you'll only marry me if you catch a bunch of flowers."

"Not any bunch of flowers, that pretty one."

"Well, I'll keep my fingers crossed."

We arrive at the reception, and I deliver what I hope is an amusing and heartfelt best man's speech. The others seem to like it. Before the festivities begin properly, Ana's cousin takes the microphone and calls for silence.

"Attention all single ladies. Ana is going to throw her bouquet. If you are single and want to be in with a chance, take your position." Cassie joins a group of about ten women all jostling for prime position, and she waves to me. I hold up my crossed fingers.

Ana smiles as she walks past me and takes her place in front of them and then turns her back. "Ready?" she calls. They all shout agreement, and Ana counts down as her guests clap in time. "Five, four, three, two...one!"

The bouquet flies into the air and Cassie dashes forward, bends her knees, jumps into the air, and snatches the bouquet.

"Yes!" She grins at me, and I'm laughing and clapping. Cassie turns to apologise to the other ladies and finds they haven't moved. She turns back and looks at Ana.

"Sorry, Cassie, he deserves you. Go get your man. I'll sort the girls out."

Cassie walks towards me, shaking her fist. "You set me up," she accuses as Ana starts another countdown.

"I did. Because I had to be sure, because I will have you as my wife, Cassie Henderson. I'm glad you didn't change back to your dad's name now." I kiss her, and when I look up, my mother is coming towards us. No doubt to ask for a date.

Cassie pats my chest. "You're right. It wouldn't have been worth it, because I think I'd prefer my baby to have their daddy's name."

I squeeze her tight. "You'll have my babies? I'm the happiest man alive."

"Present tense, H. Having."

I frown. "What do you mean? That's what I said."

My mother reaches us. "Have you told him? Does he know? Why isn't he crying?" she asks.

"I'm trying, Mrs B, but he's so slow, it's hard work," Cassie replies.

"Told me what...Are you saying what I think you are? Not that you will, but that you are. Are you? Fucking hell. Just tell me, Cassie." My heart is beating a little too quickly, and a heat I've not experienced before has taken over my body. I pull my tie loose.

My mother hits me with her bag. "That language will have to stop. You can't teach an innocent child that sort of cursing. By the time that baby comes, you'll be black and blue if you don't sort it out."

I'm blinking to hold back the tears my mother knew would come as I lower myself to my knees.

"Not here, H. People are looking. Wait until we're alone," Cassie jokes.

My mother chortles and hits Cassie with her bag. "That goes for you, too. Now, where's Stella? Now he knows, I can spread the news."

As she wanders off, I pull Cassie closer and place a kiss on her belly and look up at her as she ruffles my hair.

"How long have you known?"

"This morning. Your mother insisted and got a test from the chemist for me. I reckon we're about three months gone."

"But I didn't even know we were trying. Practising but not trying."

"I didn't want to tell you and keep disappointing you. Thought it would be more of a surprise." Cassie gives one of her shrugs. "Now get up, H. You're being dramatic and I'm the actor in this family." She holds the back of her hand to her forehead.

I laugh and get to my feet. "This is true, and for the record, you could never disappoint me, and it's the best surprise ever." Taking her hand, I lead her towards the exit. "It's been a long day. We've done our bit, so I don't think we'll be missed if we pop up to the room for a rest."

"You've got no intention of resting, have you?" she asks as we step into the lift.

"None whatsoever."

"I love you, H. Have I told you that?"

"You have, but do you know what's better than that?" I ask, and her brow furrows.

"No. What could be more important?"
"You're going to let me keep you safe."
She smiles and snuggles against my chest. "I am and you do."

From the Author

Thank you for reading Fighting Fate. It's far removed from the murder mysteries I usually write, so if it raised a smile or an 'ahh', I accomplished my goal! If you did enjoy it, I'd be grateful if you would be kind enough to leave a review on Amazon when you have a moment. Constructive reviews are invaluable to authors. If you would rather contact me personally, the details are below. If you want to read more of my work, published as M K Turner, you can grab a free ebook copy of The Making of Meredith, the prequel to the Meredith & Hodge series, if you sign up for my mailing list at https://www.mkturnerbooks.co.uk/about

ABOUT ME

I escaped the corporate treadmill in 2010. I began writing quite by chance when a friend commented, "They wouldn't believe it if you wrote it down!" So I did. I enjoyed the plotting and scheming, creating the characters, and watching them develop with the story. I kept on writing, and Meredith and Hodge arrived. Then, in 2017, the Bearing women took hold of my imagination, and the Bearing Witness series was created. In 2023, it was The Little Compton Mysteries, and 2024 saw the arrival of the JJ Jenson series. Romcom/Romance is a departure from what I usually write, but I thoroughly enjoyed writing Fighting Fate.

In between all the new ideas, I do, of course, keep going back to Meredith & Hodge.

I am married with two children, two grandchildren, and a German Shepherd. We live in Bristol, UK.

I would love to hear from you and can be contacted here:

Website: https://www.mkturnerbooks.co.uk

Printed in Dunstable, United Kingdom

68946384R00147